you belong
with me

Center Point
Large Print

**This Large Print Book carries the
Seal of Approval of N.A.V.H.**

you belong with me

RESTORING HERITAGE
BOOK 1

TARI FARIS

CENTER POINT LARGE PRINT
THORNDIKE, MAINE

This Center Point Large Print edition
is published in the year 2019 by arrangement with
Revell, a division of Baker Publishing Group.

The text of this Large Print edition is unabridged.
In other aspects, this book may vary
from the original edition.
Printed in the United States of America
on permanent paper.
Set in 16-point Times New Roman type.

ISBN: 978-1-64358-396-9

The Library of Congress has cataloged this record
under Library of Congress Control Number: 2019946804

you belong
with me

To my husband,
Scott Faris.
You are my true hero.

one

Was she really the only one left who cared about this town?

Hannah Thornton shivered as a chill traveled over her skin. Her '76 Volkswagen Bug might be a classic, but it didn't offer much protection from the icy cold of February in Michigan. The street-light highlighted a few scattered snowflakes that drifted down from the dark sky. Cold or not, she loved winter and all its beauty.

Hannah popped open the car door and paused. Gray slush merged with a murky pothole just outside her door. Ugh. Winter was also this.

Stretching one of her long legs out, Hannah attempted to hurdle the mess, but the icy stream that filled her new pink pumps testified to her failure and stole her breath. With a slam of her door, Hannah turned toward the sidewalk and then hobbled over to Otis, the town's brass hippo. She dusted off his wide, brown back and sat. "Thanks, Otis. You have a knack for being right where we need you."

"Hannah—wait. I need to talk to you." Her brother, Thomas, slammed his front door a few yards away, then hurried down the porch toward her. "I thought you had a house showing tonight."

"I did. Or tried to. But only Dale Kensington showed up."

"Sorry."

"I don't want to talk about it." She shook the slush from her shoe. "Why wouldn't someone want to live in Heritage? We are halfway between Ludington and Muskegon and a stone's throw from Lake Michigan. It's a summer vacation dream."

"You have to admit, it's seen better days."

"Heritage is full of history—ours and other people's. Maybe the sidewalks are cracked and the roads need repaired, but they're the same sidewalks we played hopscotch on as kids and the same roads we learned to ride our bikes on." It was home—an anchor no matter what life threw at you. Hannah pushed back her emotions as she tapped the side of the brass animal. "And we have our likable quirks—like our wandering hippo."

"Why are you sitting on Otis when it's thirty degrees out?" His breath created white puffs with every word.

"Fixing my shoe." She waved the pink pump at him. "And I came to vent to Luke." Hannah motioned to the old Victorian in front of her. The windows were dark but Luke was home. He was always home. Her constant.

One of Thomas's eyebrows lifted.

"Stop it. He's my best friend."

"Friend?"

10

Her focus snapped to his piercing blue eyes, so much like Dad's. Totally unfair—while she had to see Mom's dark hair and murky hazel eyes in the mirror.

Hannah slid her shoe back on and stood. "Yes. Luke is my *friend.*"

"Whatever. There's something I need to tell you." Thomas shifted from one stocking foot to the other on the freezing cement. Where were his shoes?

"Thomas?" The door of his house slammed again as his girlfriend, Madison Westmore, emerged, hugging her too-tan-for-February bare arms. "What are you doing out here? I have to go home soon."

His shoulders stiffened. "I'll be right—"

"Hannah?" Her sweet tone—no doubt for Thomas's benefit—fell flat. No love lost on either side. What did he see in her?

Madison closed the distance to Thomas, gripping his arm as if to claim his warmth. "Did you tell her?"

A look of panic crossed Thomas's face. "I was about—"

"We're engaged." Madison thrust her hand forward.

Hannah blinked several times then darted a glance at her older brother. "Wow. That's . . . wow."

How could he be marrying her? He should be

marrying Janie. Kind, wonderful Janie, who was coming home from Europe in a few days. This was going to devastate her.

Hannah clenched her teeth and forced her face into what she hoped looked like a smile. "Congratulations. When's the big day?"

Madison tossed her bottle-blonde hair over her shoulder. "It depends on how long it takes to sell this dump."

Hannah's mouth dropped open as a sudden coldness far more intense than the icy bite of Michigan winter spread through her core. Madison did not just call the house her great-grandfather had designed and built a dump.

"Hannah." Thomas's voice held a desperate edge. His arm dropped on her shoulder before he faced Madison. "You look cold. Why don't you go back in? I'll be just a minute."

Madison eyed him a moment and then kissed his cheek. "Fine."

Hannah swallowed the avalanche of words that sprung to mind as Madison and her miniskirt disappeared into his house.

Thomas squeezed her around the shoulders, sharing a bit of warmth as he rested his chin on her head. "I was trying to tell you. I hadn't even planned on proposing so soon. It just . . ."

Her hands flew into the air and she stepped away. "Not planned? She has the ring. Wait, why didn't you use Grandma Hazel's ring?"

He stared up at the stars before focusing back on her. "I'll tell you everything, but not tonight. Tonight I need you to be happy for me, bug."

Hannah inhaled a lungful of frigid air and let it out, slow and controlled. Pulling out the childhood nicknames? So unfair. "I will be. I . . . am. Just don't sell the house."

Thomas rubbed his arms as he glanced back at his place—the place she'd grown up in. "Madison wants you to list it this week."

She bit her cheek until the coppery taste of blood filled her mouth. "I'll buy it."

"I'd love for you to have it, but after buying your half last year I can't afford to give it to you." He shook his head and crossed his arms in front of him, shifting his feet again. "From what I remember, you put all that money into paying off student loans and your Realtor business. So what happened tonight? I thought Kensington wanted that property."

"He wants to tear that sweet little house down." She shifted her gaze from her brother to Otis when her voice wavered. "I'll convince the Fergusons to wait for another buyer."

"You think that's wise?"

"No." Why had she ever thought she could be a Realtor? Why had she let Thomas buy her half of the house? Because she thought he'd planned on marrying Janie and raising a family there—not selling it and marrying *Madison*.

Looked like she'd been wrong. Maybe she'd been wrong about a lot.

"I've got to go." Her breath fogged in the cold air.

"Think about it. We're selling it—like it or not." He shrugged as he stepped toward the house. "At least this way you'd get the commission."

The wind nipped at her cheeks as she hurried to Luke's side door as fast as her heels would let her. She banged on the screen door and waited as the kitchen light flicked on. The door stuck, then creaked open. Luke leaned against the door-jamb in jeans and a white T-shirt, backlit by the kitchen.

A scattering of drywall dust highlighted his short brown curls as they escaped in a reckless mess around his head. The five-o'clock shadow and the tool belt that hung low on his hips confirmed that he didn't have any big plans. She couldn't see his brown eyes in the shadows, but they were as familiar as her morning cup of coffee. He crossed his arms over his broad chest, pulling his shirt snug across his shoulders.

"Hannah, Hannah, Hannah." That endearing dimple formed in his left cheek. If she hadn't wanted to slap the smug expression off his face, she might have been tempted to kiss it. Best friends really shouldn't be allowed to be that good-looking. Besides, she knew better than to kiss Luke. Again.

14

She pushed past him into the house. "Don't say it!"

No way did she want to hear whatever was behind that grin right now. She needed comfort. She needed an escape. She needed ice cream.

Hannah claimed her regular spot at the kitchen table, the same table where she'd been finding comfort since elementary school. Only then, the house had smelled of coffee and homemade chocolate chip cookies. The aroma of coffee remained, but now it mingled with the lingering scent of leftover pizza.

Luke pulled a half gallon of chocolate ice cream from the freezer and set it before her.

She stared at the offered gift. "How did you . . . ?"

A smile tilted his lips. No, a smirk. After setting a spoon and a bowl on the table next to the carton, he crossed his arms again and lifted one eyebrow. "Everyone knows Kensington wants that land— not the house. I don't know why you thought you could talk him into anything else. Did anyone else show?"

"No." Hannah peeled the lid off the ice cream with a sigh. "I have to convince them not to sell to him."

"You're the only Realtor I know who actually tries to talk people out of selling and buying. Might be time for a different job."

Hannah jabbed her spoon into the ice cream and started to carve out a ball. "I help them

15

understand the history they're throwing away. Or in this case, wanting to destroy in the name of progress." She dropped the scoop in the dish and lifted her chin. "But I *can* be a Realtor."

"Really? You could sell a house to Kensington, or any other developer, if that's what the owner chose?"

"It's possible."

"Were you even able to finish the meeting tonight without losing your temper?"

Hannah worked at forming another ball with her spoon. "I may have emphasized my position with volume at one point."

"I'm guessing it was more like . . ." Luke made the sound of an explosion as he lifted his hands in the air.

Ugh! She whipped her spoon at him.

He ducked and laughed as it clanged against the stove. "What was that for? Honesty?"

She bit back the smile that tugged at the corner of her mouth. She may have overreacted a bit in the meeting. "Yes. Sometimes I'd rather you lie to me. As one of my best friends, your job is simply to feed me ice cream and tell me I'm pretty."

"You're pretty."

Did he have to sound so sarcastic when he said it? She focused back on the ice cream. Shoot. Now she didn't have a spoon.

"I'm simply passionate about preserving history." She stood, grabbed another utensil, and then bumped the drawer closed with a smack of her hip. "My great-great-great-grandfather—"

"—helped found the town. I've heard. But this town is full of houses with history, and from what I can tell, the Kensington family has plans."

"Yeah, well, I hate their plans. More than that, I think George Kensington would hate their plans. *He* loved this town. If he was here to see what his brother was doing with his company, it'd break his heart." Hannah dropped a final scoop in her bowl, then returned the lid to the carton.

This subject was going to give her a migraine. Then there was her brother.

She returned the ice cream to the freezer and slammed the door. "Here's a news flash. Thomas proposed to Madison."

"What? They've been dating—"

"A few months. *Only* a few months." She squeezed her spoon, the metal pressing into her palm. "What does he see in her, anyway?"

"Well . . ." Luke leaned against the counter, lips twisted as he wrinkled his forehead.

"Do guys only think of one thing?" She tapped him on the forehead with her fingers. "They've got nothing in common."

He pulled a Coke from the fridge and cracked it open without looking back. "I seem to remember a day you thought differences didn't matter."

She paused with the spoon halfway to her

17

mouth as warmth washed over her face. Oh no he didn't. She popped the spoonful of ice cream into her mouth, letting the sweet cream cool her from the inside.

She'd never let on how much he'd hurt her that day, and she wasn't about to change that. She forced a smile and hoped it looked casual. "Good thing you were there to set me straight."

He took a sip and studied her. "Maybe things are different now. People change, you know?"

She squirmed under his gaze, the intensity of it burning a dangerous path into memories better forgotten. No. She had to be reading too much into it. After seven years of radio silence on the subject, he wouldn't bring it up now. "You mean Madison?"

His Adam's apple bobbed before he looked away and cleared his throat. "Maybe she's different. A lot of people make mistakes in high school."

"Maybe." Were they talking about Madison? Or her? Or him? The boy could give lessons to the military on being cryptic. Didn't matter. Having her heart stomped on once in a lifetime was quite enough. She had the unworn prom dress to prove it.

She scraped the last of her ice cream out of her bowl. Empty already?

Luke tossed his pop can in the bottle-return bin. "Whether she's changed or not, it's not your choice who your brother marries. What's really bugging you?"

"It *is* my business. Who he marries impacts the family. She's already—" Her fingers massaged at the pain building in her temple. "Thomas wants to put our—I mean his house on the market."

"Ah." Luke paused and stared at her.

She blinked faster to keep the tears back. No crying. Luke opened his mouth as if to say something but shut it again. He pulled the carton of ice cream back out of the freezer, peeled off the lid, and slid the whole thing to her.

He was too good to her. Hannah dipped out a spoonful. "First Caroline and Leah left me—"

"They didn't leave *you*. They closed the WIFI." Luke slid into the chair across from her. "Caroline got married and Leah became a missionary in Costa Rica. Even you can't complain about that."

"Fine. They had good reasons to leave, but the fact remains that two of my best friends are no longer here. And now Thomas. You don't know how glad I was when you bought this house, even if you're making more changes than I'd like. At least you're sticking around."

Nothing.

Hannah's focus snapped to his unreadable expression. "You are staying in Heritage, right?"

Luke rubbed the back of his neck as he picked at the wood grain of the table. "I better get back to pulling that bathroom sink out."

"Luke?"

He didn't look at her as he stood. "Is it getting cold in here? I better check that fire first."

"Luke."

He disappeared into the living room without looking back. He had to be joking. If Luke left it would be worse than losing Caroline and Leah. Worse than Thomas.

Hannah gripped the edge of the table to steady herself. Heritage without Luke wasn't something she was willing to consider.

Could he settle in Heritage? That was the million-dollar question. Or at least the one that plagued him on sleepless nights. Luke stalked to the fireplace, grabbed another log, and pitched it on the flames. The air shifted and smoke filled his throat. He coughed but didn't turn away. Warmth flooded his face, either from the fire or from the rise in his blood pressure.

What would it take for this place to feel like home—like he belonged?

The faded flowery wallpaper and pink shag carpet weren't much to look at now, but this place was his. He was no longer a kid who had nothing to his name. He was a person of property.

But a home? How would a person who grew up in foster care know about that? A home took more than two-by-fours and drywall. But what exactly it took, he wasn't sure.

In the kitchen, the freezer door clicked shut.

Luke forced a whistle through his lips and returned to where he'd been working in the downstairs bathroom. Renovations were one thing he could figure out. He'd already torn down one of the plaster walls, but the sink needed to be pulled out before he could get to the next one. He released the buckle on his tool belt, dropped it in a five-gallon pail, and knelt down to inspect the bottom of the molded porcelain.

Hannah stepped up behind him. "Wow, you're... making a mess."

"Yup." He glanced at her over his shoulder. Her long dark hair framed her face, highlighting her hazel eyes. Only Hannah could pull off the carefree appearance of a fifteen-year-old and yet still look twenty-five.

"Please tell me you aren't destroying history, worry-whistle man."

Luke twisted his neck to get a better look at how the old fixture attached to the wall. "What did you call me?"

"You whistle that obscure tune when you're upset. You don't even realize it, do you?" She sighed and sat on an overturned bucket in the doorway. "You didn't answer me. Are you destroying history?"

"I don't have a worry-whistle, and some history needs to be destroyed—replaced, anyway. These plaster walls for starters. Not to mention

21

this knob-and-tube wiring, which stopped being standard in the thirties."

"You do have a worry-whistle, and history needs to be restored, not destroyed. Plaster is classic and I love the thirties."

He'd let the whistle argument go. "It's a bathroom. The walls need greenboard to handle the moisture. And I'm not keeping the wiring even if you love the history of it. If the crazy splice job some electrician did years back wasn't enough of a reason, the rubber insulation is degrading to the point that it's a fire hazard. But thanks for the suggestion." He worked the bolt to see if it was loose. Nope. "Can you hand me the Crescent wrench?"

A cool metal tool dropped in his hand. He glanced down to adjust it. "This is an open-end wrench."

She sighed, snatched back the tool, and returned it with a clang back in the toolbox. She lifted another. "This one?"

"Pipe wrench."

"There are pipes under there." Hannah dropped the tool but didn't offer another.

"Yes. But right now I'm trying to disconnect the water." Luke sat up, grabbed the tool he needed, and returned to his place under the sink, the chipped tile floor cooling his heated skin.

"That doesn't even look like a crescent."

"It's the brand name of the original maker."

Luke loosened the compression fittings from the hot and cold water, then inspected the sink brackets. With any luck, they weren't as rusted as they appeared.

"Maybe I should invent something and name it a Thornton. That'd do a lot to restore the family name in town."

Luke adjusted the tool to one of the rusted bolts. "Thornton is a respected name, and in Heritage any connection is better than no connection. Trust me."

"So, are you staying or fixing this place to sell? I mean, this is the house you grew up in. It's like your family home."

The wrench stilled as a torrent of unwelcome emotions from his past surfaced. He gripped the tool tighter. "Family homes are inherited. I bought this—am buying it. I may have grown up here, but it wasn't my home . . . not really."

"How can you say that? Mrs. Shoemaker was your—"

"Foster mom." He sat up in a quick motion and narrowly missed hitting his head on the sink. "She cared for me in her own way. But I wasn't her son, nor did she want me to be."

"She cared for you, Luke. A lot of people care about you. You just can't see it." Her voice wavered at the end.

People cared about him? Not likely. He leaned back under the sink, found the next bolt, and offered a fair amount of pressure. Nothing.

He had no real roots, no connection to this town. He could disappear and no one would notice. He wasn't even sure God would notice. "A lot of people move out of Heritage, Hannah. Does it really matter if I do?"

"Yes. Because I love . . . this town. And you're an important part." She cleared her throat but her words still came out rough.

"The lumberyard pays the bills, and you know Chet gave me a bargain with this rent-to-own contract. But who knows what'll happen after I finish my degree—if I ever finish."

"You will. This fall will be your final semester, right?"

"Yup." Assuming his last semester grades were good enough. Web design had nearly done him in. "And when I'm done, it might be nice to have a newer place." Luke worked on the nut again. *Snap.* Rusted crumbs dropped in his face. He winced. "One with less baggage."

"Not baggage—nostalgia."

He sat up, brushed away the grit, and tossed her the busted nut. "Well, here's a bit of nostalgia for you."

She rubbed her thumb over the rough metal. "What about volunteering at the fire department? If Thomas leaves, they'll already be one man down. You can't just walk away. Don't you want to raise your family here?"

She did know how to go to the heart of a matter.

Family. The one thing that had been just out of reach his whole life. Well, as much as he could remember. He'd had a family once, but only a few ghostly memories remained. He pushed away that train of thought and forced a smile. "I believe you're out of questions, but thanks for playing."

Hannah pulled a hand towel off a hook and whipped it at him. "I hate it when you push me away. You push everyone away. The only reason we're friends is because I won't let you shut me out."

"No kidding." A snicker escaped.

"Do you want me to leave?"

Words from their friend Caroline, spoken a few months back, echoed in his head. *If you keep pushing Hannah away, eventually she might actually leave.*

"No." Luke dropped the wrench back in the toolbox with a clang and stood up, brushing his palms against his jeans. "I don't want you to leave."

Hannah stood, putting her hands on her hips. "Good. Then I'll help. But I'm going to get some water first. Need anything?"

"Water would be great," Luke called as she disappeared around the corner.

If he was going to be working in close proximity to Hannah, he should probably smell a bit fresher. He tugged off his dirt-smudged T-shirt, tossed it toward the laundry room, and reached for a gray one from a basket of clean laundry that he'd left in the hall. Pretty wrinkled but at least it smelled better.

Hannah rounded the corner and stopped, eyes wide, mouth half open.

He pulled the shirt over his head in one quick motion and tugged it down.

Her gaze snapped to his face and then away. Red crawled up her neck. "Did . . . you want ice?"

"Sure." He leaned down, grabbed another shirt, and tossed it toward her. "Wouldn't want you to ruin that sweater."

Hannah snatched the shirt out of the air and disappeared back the way she'd come, never making eye contact with him. No witty comeback?

Interesting.

Maybe he should have stepped into the laundry room to change his shirt, but they'd been friends for almost twenty years. Perhaps she was modest. Or perhaps—

Luke swallowed and shook away the thought. No good going there. Not yet anyway. Because until he had something to offer, they might as well be back in high school.

Hannah reappeared in record time with two glasses of ice water and wearing his shirt hanging down to her thighs, her long brown hair pulled back in a loose knot/bun thing. Man, she looked cute. He'd managed to keep his feelings for her in a neat little box over the years, but lately that didn't seem enough.

"Are we going to do this sink thing or what?"

"Right." He followed Hannah into the bathroom. She plopped onto the wooden stool and dug through his toolbox.

"What do you need next? How about this baby?" She lifted up a large monkey wrench and waved it back and forth. The top-heavy wrench crashed into the wall, a chunk of plaster chipping away.

"Don't break my house."

"I'm sorry." Hannah tried to fit the pieces back over the hole.

"Relax. I'm tearing that wall down tomorrow." He lifted his eyebrows at her. "Go ahead, destroy a little more history. I dare you."

Her knuckles whitened on the wrench before she crashed it onto the wall again, sending more plaster crumbs flying.

"Fun, isn't it?"

A smile tugged at her tight lips as she offered one more solid swing. A strange clang echoed from the wall.

His focus darted from Hannah to the crater she'd created. "What was that?"

Hannah dropped the wrench. "I was just

swinging at these wooden boards. I swear."

"They're called laths, and they're for the plaster to hold on to, but they shouldn't sound like that." Luke grabbed a small crowbar from his toolbox and wedged it between two of the wooden strips. The sound of splintering wood split the air as he leaned his weight against the tool. Pushing the pieces aside, he squinted into the dark hole. A black metal box rested in the gap between the studs.

"Now that's history." Hannah's gaze traveled from the box to him then back to the box. "We have to see what's in it."

Luke jabbed the crowbar in another gap to widen the hole, pulled the box free, and examined the lock. It needed an eight-digit code. So much for that. He set the box aside and reached for the wrench.

"You're giving up?"

"Do you know all the junk I've found in these walls? The wall in the upstairs bathroom had hundreds of old razor blades from a slot in the medicine cabinet that was designed to just drop them into the wall. Weird, if you ask me."

"You don't lock trash." Hannah picked up the box and shook it.

"One man's treasure is another man's trash." He pointed to a large bucket that had a growing pile of debris.

"You even want to shut the box out." The words

carried a teasing tone, but the frustrated glint in her eye told him this was about a lot more than the box.

Luke dropped the wrench to his toolbox. "Fine, let's try to get it open."

Hannah squeezed his arm. "You won't be sorry."

She was probably right. What trouble could the box cause?

two

Surely six days would be long enough for Thomas to see his engagement and moving plans for what they were—huge mistakes. Hannah approached the three-way stop and flipped on her right turn signal. Just ahead, a couple entered Donny's diner. She ate most dinners there, but Thursday night was—and always had been—family dinner night. Even if family dinner was just her and Thomas now, they never missed it.

Hannah turned down Teft Road and avoided looking toward the WIFI as she passed. When would the darkened windows and "Closed" sign stop being a sore spot?

Leah and Caroline were gone and Heritage had lost one more business. She didn't fault them, but the old general store had been an icon of Heritage for over fifty years. Everyone seemed to be moving on. Why couldn't she? Between the failed businesses and the run-down, abandoned row of houses, her little town of Heritage was quickly becoming downright depressing. But it could be more—much more.

Hannah took a left at Henderson Road and parked in front of her childhood home, which stood a hop, skip, and a jump from Luke's front door. Could she really be the one to sell this place to the highest bidder? She might be sick.

She grabbed the grocery sacks from the passenger seat and slid out of the car. The old Manor across the street appeared so sad, forgotten by the world. The main floor had been rented out for grand events until fifteen years ago. She would sit up at night watching the lights, listening to the music, and dreaming about someday dancing in those very rooms. But time hadn't been kind. The windows looked out over the town like a friendless old man who'd once known a good life but now waited for the end to come.

"Are you coming in or what?" Thomas's voice reached her from the porch.

She trudged up the steps, letting the familiar creaks in the boards settle into her heart. "Our town has so much potential. Why can't anyone else see that?"

"Potential?" Thomas met her halfway up the steps and lifted one of the bags from her arms.

She pointed across the street. "They don't make houses like the Manor anymore. Wraparound porch. Complicated roof structures. A turret."

"It's condemned." Thomas lifted the second bag from her arms before she could stop him.

"Not officially." Hannah rubbed her hands together to warm them. "But if the town had the money to restore it to its former glory, it could be amazing again."

"And whose fault is it that they don't?" Thomas's words sliced through her.

"I don't want to talk about Mom." Her words puffed out in icy white clouds.

"You never do." He pushed through the front door, leaving her on the porch.

Hannah rushed up the remaining steps to follow, but Thomas had already disappeared into the kitchen. He always had to have the last word.

She slammed the door harder than she'd planned, rattling the cobalt-blue Depression-glass plates that sat on a shelf above the door. Her mother had insisted on placing them there both for their beauty and as a reminder not to slam the door. That they'd survived after all this time seemed more of a testimony to luck than their good manners.

The blue plates served as one of the few tangible memories of her mother. The plates, the kiln in the basement, and a strand of pearls were all that were left. Her father had left the kiln because it had been too much work to remove, but Hannah never knew why he left the plates and she hadn't been about to ask. He'd left the pearls on Hannah's bed one day in a red velvet box. He'd never said a word, but Hannah had recognized them from her parents' wedding photo that used to hang in the hall. She'd never worn the pearls and never would, but like with the plates, she just couldn't seem to let them go.

Hannah slid out of her coat and hung it on the hook next to her father's ever-present jacket and hat. The fact that they still hung here two years after his death and the plates remained above the door hinted that history and family meant more to Thomas than he let on. It was time to remind him of that.

Hannah pushed through the swinging door that led to the kitchen. The sweet scent of home intermingling with Italian seasonings and ground beef surrounded her. Lasagna night. The guy should own a restaurant.

Thomas stood next to the stove with their dad's old apron around his waist. "It's almost ready. The rolls didn't rise. I'm really *not* a baker."

Hannah stepped over to where he'd set her bags on the counter and pulled out a head of lettuce and a few tomatoes. "At least you can cook. All I can do is make a salad."

"But it is one mean salad." Thomas clicked off the oven and pulled out a couple hot pads. "Have you come to your senses about listing the house?"

Hannah shoved the lettuce under the cold tap and switched the spout to spray. "Have you?"

Thomas shook his head, his back still to her. "It's going to happen, Hannah. You're stuck in the past. Just like Dad was."

Dropping the lettuce in the salad spinner, she snatched up the tomatoes and started rinsing them. "Yeah, well, at least I'm not like Mom."

He spun to face her. "And I am?"

She paused her scrubbing and stared at him. "Marrying someone all wrong for you? Skipping town?"

Thomas's fingers tightened on the wooden spoon in his hand as he worked the muscle in his jaw. "I'm not skipping town like Mom did. How could you even compare the two?"

"Just tell me. Why her?" Her fingers ran over the tomatoes in double time. "You have nothing in common with her. I thought . . ."

"What?" he said. When Hannah didn't answer, he reached over her and shut off the water. "Tell me."

She stepped to the cutting board and set the tomatoes down before turning her back to the counter. "I thought you'd always stay here. I thought you and Janie would eventually—"

"Never mind." He turned back to the stove. "Unless, of course, you want to also talk about you and Luke."

"Luke? What does Luke have to do with anything? We never dated—not technically."

Thomas lifted one eyebrow in her direction as he stared her down.

"What? It's not the same. You and Janie dated for five years. You should've never broken up."

Aunt Lucy peeked through the doorway as she held up a plate covered in aluminum foil. Her silver-gray hair dusted her shoulders as she turned

35

her head to look between them. "We had some extra pie tonight at the diner and thought you might like it. I knocked but you couldn't hear me over the yelling. What's the hot topic tonight?"

Thomas took the pie from their aunt and offered her a hug, his large frame dwarfing her petite build. "Luke."

"Janie." Hannah poured herself a glass of lemonade and took a long sip, letting the sour sweetness linger on her tongue.

"Janie sure is a sweetie. Her mom said she should be back from Paris this weekend." Her aunt fanned her cheeks. "But Luke—oooh. I do like that boy. Quite the hottie."

Hannah choked on the lemonade and set down her cup. Did her aunt just say "hottie"?

"What?" Her aunt blinked at her. "You can't tell me you haven't noticed. I don't know why you haven't snatched that one up, dear."

Hannah coughed again, trying to dislodge the burning in her lungs. Luke? Hot? Yes, she'd noticed. Like when she'd walked in on him changing his shirt in the hall. When had his shoulders gotten that wide? And abs—the guy had abs.

It must be the workouts he did with the volunteer firemen. And with his jeans hanging low on his hips . . . Oh, she'd noticed. In fact, that image had been imprinted on her brain and had found a way into her dreams almost every night since. She shook off the memory.

"Thanks for the pie." Hannah barely recognized the squeak of her own voice.

Aunt Lucy and Thomas stared at her. Guess that redirect proved a little obvious.

Thomas rolled his eyes at Hannah. "Yes, thank you. Smells delicious."

"I guess Luke is a subject for another day." Aunt Lucy winked at Hannah and turned to the door. "Uncle Donny is waiting for me, so I'll show myself out." She disappeared as quickly as she'd come with a click of the front door.

Hannah spun back to face Thomas. "I can't believe you brought up Luke in front of Aunt Lucy."

Thomas carried rocklike rolls to the table. "And I can't believe you brought up Janie at all. I like Madison. In fact, I love her. I need you to accept that, accept her."

When they took a seat at the table Thomas cleared his throat, a pleading for a truce in his eyes. If she couldn't convince him to stay, who knew how many more of these family dinners she'd have left. They might only have a few months before she couldn't even eke out a once-a-week date with him.

They both needed tonight to be a good night. She cut off a small piece of lasagna and took a bite. The perfect blend of Italian flavors melted on her tongue.

"Is Janie really coming back this weekend?" Thomas's voice came out even—too even.

She'd pay good money to know what was going on in his head. "Yes."

Thomas opened his mouth to say something when a chime split the air. He reached for his phone. "Hey, love, what's up?" He closed his eyes and leaned back in the chair. "I'm sorry, babe. But now? You know Hannah and—"

Hannah couldn't make out the reply even when a wincing Thomas pulled the phone an inch from his ear.

He glanced at his watch before he looked up at Hannah. "I'll be there in ten minutes."

The lasagna turned to tasteless mush in her mouth as she reached for her lemonade.

"Sorry, I gotta . . ." He cleared his throat and stood. "I need an answer on the house."

Another drink. Her vision blurred. *Don't cry.* "I'll do it."

He stopped by her chair and offered her shoulder a squeeze. "Thanks, bug. I really don't trust it to anyone else. You can have my pie, okay?"

Hannah closed her eyes as the first few tears escaped with the rattle of the front door. She stood and cleared the table. Now she had to find a family to buy this house who'd love it as much as she did. Fat chance. Maybe she should be happy if she could find someone other than Kensington willing to buy it.

• • •

Was he making the same mistakes as his father? Thomas pulled his coat tighter around him as a blast of winter whistled in the air and blew down his collar. It was almost ten. He could've gone to Hannah's for a cup of coffee, but then the questions would've started again.

What did Madison need? Are you really making the right decision?

He couldn't answer the second question, but as for Madison's request? The only thing he could figure was she was doing her best to lure him into staying the night. He didn't know how much longer he could be strong.

The streetlight above him flickered but stayed on as he reached for the diner's door. Thomas let the warm air laced with the aroma of beef Stroganoff wash over him as the familiar jingle announced his presence and drew the attention of the few late-night patrons.

"Sorry, grill's closed for the night." Uncle Donny's deep voice carried from the back.

"But is the coffee still hot for a nephew?" Thomas added a nickel to the antique jukebox in the corner and selected "I Walk the Line" out of habit. He needed a new favorite song. This one held too many memories of the one person he refused to let himself think about.

Thomas claimed his regular corner stool at the counter—the only one that didn't have a wobble

39

to it. He slid the red cupid crepe-paper decoration farther down the bar and out of sight. Maybe he should nudge it over the bar and into the trash below. Valentine's Day was over and—well, that was hideous. But this place was home and he'd sure miss it when he moved.

Uncle Donny's wide frame appeared in the doorway, a grin on his face and grease on his apron. What he had left of his hair was now fully gray, and by the lines on his face, the long days were finally catching up to him. He grabbed a hand towel that had been slung over his shoulder and wiped his hands. "What brings you here so late?" He lifted a mug off the shelf, poured a cup of the dark brew, and slid it in front of Thomas.

The rich aroma soothed his nerves. "Out for a walk."

Uncle Donny pulled out a second mug and filled it. "Want to talk about it?"

Thomas stared into his mug. Talk? About Madison's skills at manipulation? About why his heart had done a belly flop at the mention of Janie returning? Or maybe about how he'd felt the day he realized he could never have the life he'd dreamed of?

Uncle Donny nursed his coffee, waiting.

"How did you know marrying Aunt Lucy was the right decision?"

His uncle's balding head bobbed. "Your aunt told me you went and got yourself engaged. Congrats and all that. I guess if you cared enough to plan it and buy the ring then that's a good start."

Thomas rubbed his fingers against his pulsing temple. "I wouldn't say I planned it."

His uncle's brow creased. "You just happened to have a ring in your pocket?"

"More like we ended up at a ring store on Valentine's Day that happened to be next to the restaurant Madison picked out." Thomas drew a gulp of his coffee. Okay, that sounded bad, but what could he do now? What could he have done then?

"But you did ask her, right?"

Thomas glanced out the front window of the diner into the darkness. That whole night had been on fast-forward. Madison had been going on about how he was everything she'd ever needed, and the next thing he'd known he was handing over his credit card.

He turned back to his uncle. "That part's a blur."

Uncle Donny stared him down before he threw back the rest of his coffee. "But you do want to marry her. Right?"

Thomas shifted on the stool, his left foot tapping the floor. "Yes. Of course . . . I mean, why wouldn't I? She's . . . lovely."

His uncle's brow pinched again. "A marriage can't be based on a pretty face."

Thomas took another gulp and set his mug a

little too hard on the counter, sending a splash of the black gold over the edge. He reached for a napkin. "Well, we want the same things." *Or at least I can give her what she wants. Unlike Janie.*

Uncle Donny studied him a minute. He opened his mouth to speak but stopped short when another customer bid him a good night.

Thomas needed to cut this conversation off before it went any further. There were things he wasn't about to admit even to his uncle. Things no one knew. At least not in this town, and he planned on keeping it that way. In Heritage, if anyone knew . . . everyone knew. And this was one thing that couldn't get back to Janie.

Aunt Lucy appeared from the back room. Perfect timing.

"Hi, Aunt Lucy. Thank you again for the pie. You're awesome."

She wiped her hands on her apron. "Did you notice the new spice I added?"

His smile faltered. Surely God would forgive him this one lie. Then again, he hadn't been talking to God much lately. "It was a great change."

Aunt Lucy's eyes narrowed as she crossed her arms and leaned her hip against the counter. "I talked to Hannah."

Thomas laughed and raised his hands. "You caught me. But I'm sure it was great. I know only a few people who can bake like you."

Aunt Lucy gathered a plate left behind by a customer. "Few? Who else do you have baking for you?"

Janie flashed into his mind, but he'd keep that bit of information to himself. After all, it had been a long time since she'd baked for him. "How was Hannah when you called?"

Aunt Lucy reached for a cloth and began wiping down the counter. She discarded the moist napkin he'd used for his spill and lifted his mug to clean underneath. "Down, but she'll have to learn your wife will take priority."

Thomas gulped against his dry throat. Wife.

She paused mid-wipe and looked at him. "Is everything with Madison okay?"

He returned his attention to his mug. "She wanted to show me some job options she found in Muskegon."

"Are you leaving your job at Heritage Fruits? I thought you were happy there."

"Things have changed there since George Kensington died." He shrugged and cleared his throat. Once he'd thought he'd retire there. But as he knew, life doesn't always work out like you expect and plans have a way of dissolving. "And now the rumor is that they're making cutbacks and the first round of pink slips will be going out next week. I'm the low man on the totem pole, and since Madison is itching to move away from Heritage anyway, I sort of volunteered to be the first let go. So as of a week from Monday I am officially unemployed."

"I'm sorry about that. George Kensington would be sick to see what's become of his company since Dale took over." Aunt Lucy wiped her hands on her apron and sighed before shooting a look at her husband.

Uncle Donny nodded and turned back to the kitchen.

Aunt Lucy topped off Thomas's cup. "We got a call from Don's brother who's ill. Don wants to go for a long visit, but there's no way. There're few people we trust to watch the diner. And there was no way we'd ask you to quit Heritage Fruits. But if you're in between jobs anyway . . ."

He smacked down the mug, abusing the porcelain yet again. "Me? Run the diner?"

"Don't sound so surprised." Aunt Lucy handed him another napkin. "You're the best cook I know, other than Don. Plus you've been working here on and off since you were sixteen. You're perfect. And really . . . the only option." She twisted the towel in her hands, waiting.

Thomas tightened his hand on his mug. She had no idea what she was asking. Work the diner? Yes, he could do it—in fact, he'd thought about taking it over many times growing up. A pipe dream of sorts. Why else had he majored in business and taken evening classes in culinary arts?

Of course, he'd anticipated a fine restaurant,

not . . . this. But it was more than the place being a little run-down. After all, he could wield a hammer and screwdriver with the best of them. It was that the fantasy had always included Janie at his side. Living only half his dream might be more than he could handle.

"I don't think I can. I mean, who'd do the baking?"

She waved her hand to dismiss the problem. "I'll find someone to make a few fresh pies and help with the serving, but we need you to manage it."

Thomas shifted in his seat again. He needed a way out. "Madison really wants me to look for a job outside of town."

She leaned on the counter, her expression pleading. "It'd only be for a couple months. That will give you time to find a job that you like and not take the first one you're offered. Promise me you'll pray about it."

Pray. One thing he'd avoided doing at all costs lately. God seemed to be leading where he didn't want to go—where he couldn't go. "I'll think about it."

The ever-present twinkle in his aunt's eyes dimmed as she stood again. "That's all I ask."

She patted his hand and turned back to the kitchen. He didn't know if he'd disappointed his aunt more by not jumping at the chance or by not saying he'd pray about it. But she didn't understand. No one did.

God wasn't on his side.

Black-and-white photos tiled every inch of the wall above the counter, each a glimpse into Heritage's past. It was their own personal wall of fame—only there was nothing famous about the photos. Just locals who'd lived out a common life here in the small town. Madison wanted out of this common life. And soon.

One thing was for certain. Whatever decision he chose would make one of the women in his life very unhappy.

He didn't want to fail at one more thing. Luke hefted another shovelful of snow and chucked it to the side. He drew a breath of air, soaking in the scent of fresh snow. Salve for his soul. Snow made the world look new and mistake free. It hid past failures, and for a short season, his flower boxes were on par with the rest of the neighborhood's.

Too bad it couldn't erase the D- he'd gotten in web design.

He jabbed at the next scoop of snow a little harder. The afternoon sun sparkled off the fresh white blanket. It had stolen the chill from the air, leaving it almost too warm for the last week of February. He slid out of his thick down coat and tossed it aside. He wished he could wait for the snow to melt away, but the ten inches that had come down last night wouldn't disappear anytime soon.

The physical labor released some of the restlessness that had settled in his muscles since working so close to Hannah, since the mail arrived that morning, and since the numerous failed attempts to open that blasted box over the last week.

"You whistle a lot."

Seven-year-old Jimmy stood on the back of Otis. Coat unzipped and two sizes too big. But he had one that wasn't totally out-of-date—and that meant more than anyone knew to a kid. Life wasn't always easy in the foster care system.

Jimmy's *s* in *whistle* had disappeared in his missing front teeth. Had he been whistling? Maybe Hannah hadn't been completely off about—what did she call it?—his "worry-whistle." Not that he'd tell her.

The boy slid off the polished brass nose of the hippo and landed in the snow, his black hair flopping in his eyes. "I guess this new snow means Otis gets to stay longer."

"I've heard he doesn't walk in the snow." Luke chucked and hefted another shovelful of snow. "Then again, you know what they say—"

"Yeah, yeah. 'When no one is looking and the time is right, Otis walks to a new site.' " Jimmy squatted down. His dark brown gaze was eye to eye with the hippo. "But how does he really move?"

Luke had spent many hours as a kid contemplating the same question, as did almost every kid in town. "I don't know." When Jimmy gave him the stink eye he held up his hands. "Honest. I have no idea and I've never met a person in town who claims to know."

Jimmy leaned against the hippo, then reached down, scooped up a handful of snow, and packed it into a round ball.

"You aren't going to throw that at me, are you?"

The boy laughed, showing off the gap where his two front teeth had been a few weeks ago. "We could have a snowball fight."

Talk about an uneven fight. Then again, the kid was probably banking on using Otis as his shield. "How about first you help me shovel this walk and then we can have a snowball fight? You'll have to do this for your family someday."

The smile on his face melted away. "I don't get to see my family much."

"I know." Luke's chest tightened. Not just for Jimmy but for his own memories. "But it doesn't mean you won't someday." His words sounded weak even to his own ears.

Jimmy hopped over, took the shovel, and did his best to dig the blade into the snow. Luke set his shoe on the back of the blade and added a little weight until it disappeared in the drift. Jimmy hung on the handle, but it barely moved.

Luke gripped the handle. "How about you dig, I'll lift."

"Deal."

Luke emptied the shovel to the side and handed it back to Jimmy.

"You was a foster kid too, right?"

" 'You *were* a foster kid.' And yes. I moved into this house in the second grade and stayed until graduation."

"They adopt you?"

"It was only Mrs. Shoemaker—and no."

"Why not?"

Luke kicked at an ice chunk that clung to the step. "I don't know. Maybe she didn't want to be a mom."

It was what he told himself anyway. Somehow it never seemed to ring true. But it was easier than admitting he wasn't good enough for her.

Jimmy leaned in and wiggled the shovel until the red blade disappeared again. "Did you have visits with your mother?"

"Nope, my mom died when I was very young." Luke searched his mind for her. But like most things, the memories came back lacking.

"My mom yelled at me in our last visit." The boy dropped his gaze.

Luke didn't know Jimmy's entire situation, but the bits he'd learned weighed on him.

"All kids get in trouble sometimes." A vague memory floated up. "I remember once my mom had written my name in my clothes for something. Must have been in preschool or kindergarten. Anyway, after watching her I took the permanent red marker and wrote her name in her white blouse."

He could still see it, clear as day. A-N-N. He'd just learned his letters.

"Was she mad?" Jimmy stepped back to let Luke empty the shovel again.

He couldn't picture her face, only that he'd been sent to his room for the evening. "Yeah, she was mad."

Jimmy took off his mittens, then tossed them together in the air and caught them. "Did you have friends who lived close?"

Luke's gaze shifted to the Thorntons' house next door, zeroing in on Hannah's childhood window. When would he stop expecting her to appear and tap out their secret code? Two taps and a knock: *Meet me at the treehouse.* Tap, knock, tap: *I'm grounded. Call you tomorrow.* "Yeah, my best friend. She lived right there. Her brother lives there now."

Jimmy's eyes widened as a snarl bent his lip. "Your best friend was a girl?"

Luke laughed. "Don't worry. She didn't make me play dolls."

The boy tossed his mittens higher this time and only caught one. "Did she ever try and kiss you?"

Luke's hand stopped as his brain returned to that day in the treehouse their senior year. He'd never known a kiss could be like that. That ended up being their only kiss, but he'd never forget it.

With the few girls he'd dated in college, it hadn't felt like that. Then again, maybe his memory made it out to be more than it had been. He blinked the memory away and focused back on Jimmy. "Why?"

"There's a girl at school named Sarah who tried to kiss me at recess. Yuck."

A woman's voice called for Jimmy in the distance.

"I gotta go." He slipped on one of the mittens and looked around for the other.

"Rain check on the snowball fight?"

Jimmy's brow wrinkled. "You want to have a snowball fight in the rain?"

"No." Luke picked up the wayward mitten and held it out. "It just means we'll do it later."

"Deal." Jimmy took the mitten and studied Luke. "Mrs. Adams said not to bother you, but I told her we was friends. You're my friend, right, Luke?"

Luke swallowed against the lump in his throat. Vulnerability was written all over the kid's face. How many well-meaning adults had drifted in and out of his life, all with promises to be a mentor, friend, big brother? But life happened and schedules filled up. And it was the kid without parents who ended up alone at his big game, with no one to snap a photo after his first home run.

Luke cleared his throat. Maybe Hannah was right—maybe he did need more people in his life. And what could be a better place to start than with someone who needed a friend as much as he did? "Yeah, Jimmy. I'm your friend."

A grin stretched across the boy's face just before he took off in a sprint.

Luke scraped the blade against the concrete step to clear the remaining slush and moved on to the next.

Deep bass vibrated the air as a black Mustang pulled up in front of his house. Great. What did *he* want? At least Ted was in the car too.

"Hey, Luke." Ted gave an easy grin and leaned out the window as the radio's volume lowered. "Did you see Virgil Nell is retiring from his position as chief? My dad's taking it, which means one of the assistant chief positions is open. You should apply."

What was the point? Everyone knew it'd go to Ted. Luke's hand tightened on the shovel. "Probably not."

Ted brushed the mop of red hair from his eyes and offered what seemed to be a genuine smile. "Think about it. Derek and I are both applying."

"Maybe Luke knows he's not cut out for it." Derek Kensington leaned over from the driver's side, a smirk on his lips. He had been a thorn in Luke's side since elementary school and seemed to like playing the part.

Luke didn't acknowledge Derek's comment but focused on Ted. "Maybe I will apply."

The cocky grin on Derek's face only grew.

Shoot. Why had he let Derek goad him like that? Now he'd have one more thing to throw in Luke's face when he failed.

Luke nodded and stepped back, but Derek wasn't done. Of course not. "You and Hannah Thornton hang out a lot. You two a thing?"

He refused to react. "No."

Confidence tilted his lips. "She dating anyone?"

Hannah and Derek? No way. Not going to happen. "Stay away from her."

"Turned you down, did she?" Derek eyed Luke's house a moment and then focused back on him. "Maybe she's looking for a guy who has a bit more to offer."

Luke forced a calm exterior as he leaned on his shovel. "Heard from Jon lately, Derek? I got a postcard saying he was enjoying Italy. He didn't mention you were borrowing *his* car or staying at *his* house."

The blue in Derek's eyes turned to ice as the smirk dropped to a hard stare before he faced the road, the car's engine revving. Ted waved as the window rolled up, and they pulled from the curb.

What a jerk. Ironic that the jerk's cousin had been one of Luke's best friends growing up.

Luke's hand tightened against the plastic handle until the finger grips pinched at his skin. He jabbed the shovel back into the snow. Hannah was wrong. She wasn't his only friend. There was Jon—well, he was currently in Europe somewhere. And Mrs. Shoemaker's brother, Chet—but it had been at least three months since Luke had been to see him. Talk about a recluse—that was Chet.

Maybe Luke should ask him about that box. There was a good chance it belonged to Mrs. Shoemaker since he'd discovered a removable panel on the other side of the wall in the laundry room.

Maybe he could ask Chet about the assistant fire chief position too. After all, the man had been with Heritage's volunteer firefighters for decades.

The chances of Luke getting picked over Ted were slim to none in this town, but he had to try or Derek wouldn't let him forget. He just hoped he wasn't setting himself up for one more failure.

three

Six months in a foreign country should've been long enough for either Thomas to come to his senses or for her to get over him. Janie Mathews stabbed a green bean with more force than needed and shoved it into her mouth. Her mother's cooking soothed a bit of the homesickness she'd carried the past six months, but it didn't do anything about her still-broken heart.

Maybe when Thomas saw her—

"Earth to Janie." Her mother tapped her fork against her glass. A smile deepened the well-formed lines of her face. If it weren't for the graying at the edges of her black hair, no one would guess she was nearly fifty. "You were going to tell us about your trip."

Janie blinked at her family all wrapped around their long oak table. The closest in age to her was Olivia at twenty-two. But with Olivia taking after their father's Scandinavian heritage and her taking after the Italian in her mother, few guessed they were sisters. Between the seven kids, they seemed to have hit every possible genetic option.

The aroma of her mother's roast and potatoes filled the air, along with the tinkling sound of silverware on china. Her mother had insisted that her homecoming was a celebration. And it was. She had to stop this mental whining.

Janie dabbed her lips with her napkin and searched her memory for a good story.

"Did you eat snails?" Six-year-old Trinity's face twisted, her blonde pigtails swaying from side to side.

"I did." Janie leaned forward, forcing her eyes wide. "And I liked them."

"Ewww." The three youngest wrinkled their noses.

"I told you, Faith." Ten-year-old Caleb poked his sister in the shoulder, his dark blond hair in need of a haircut bristling out in every direction.

"But I bet she didn't eat them out of the garden." Faith shoved away his hand and tossed her dark curls over her shoulder. She had changed the most over the past six months, shifting from little girl to full-on preteen. "And I'm still not eating the one you found."

Her mom snapped her fingers at the younger two. "Gideon's working at the garage again."

Gideon tossed the hair from his eyes as he stabbed another piece of meat. "It's a good job and I need money for college next year."

"It had nothing to do with Danielle?" her mother added with a wink.

Subtle, Mom.

His face blanked as his fork paused halfway to his mouth. "Dan? She's like one of the guys."

"I think she's adorable. She just needs more girls in her life to help her bring out her feminine side." Her mother sent a pointed look at sixteen-year-old Ellie, who had always been the girliest of them all. Even for tonight's dinner she had a full face of makeup and her blonde hair styled in perfect beach curls.

Ellie held up her hands. "Don't look at me. I don't do makeovers, and frankly, the girl scares me."

"Dan's cooler than any of your friends." Gideon sent her a smirk then pointed his fork at Janie. "But I don't like her like that."

Janie suppressed a laugh. She'd missed this. No way did she want to move away from Heritage and miss seeing everyone grow up. She had to find a job here.

Ellie leaned closer. "Did you find a European boyfriend?"

"No way," Trinity piped up. "She's gots to marry Thomas."

"She can't marry Thomas." Caleb shook his head as he shoveled another spoonful of potatoes in his mouth. "He' ma-we-in Mad-a-nin."

"Caleb," her father snapped. He rarely talked and never snapped. "Don't talk with your mouth full."

She glanced at her dad but he just stared at his food. She scanned the table. Three forks hovered halfway to the intended mouths. She locked eyes with Olivia. Her best friend, her confidante. "What did he say?"

Olivia set her fork down and reached for her napkin. "Thomas . . . is engaged. To Madison Westmore."

Engaged. To someone else.

Janie stood, knocking her chair back. Her legs shook as if they might give out. "Excuse me." She raced toward the stairs as the room erupted with voices, most yelling at Caleb. Poor kid, it wasn't his fault.

Her vision blurred as she pushed through her bedroom door and collapsed on her bed. She buried her face in her Pooh Bear, letting more tears flow. The bear Thomas had given her. Thomas. She huffed and whipped the offending toy at the door just as it opened.

"Hey." Olivia caught the bear and set him on the dresser. "No need to take it out on me . . . or Pooh."

"I want to be alone." Janie flopped back on her pillow and rolled to face the wall.

"The great thing about being a Mathews, you never have to go through anything alone. Even if you want to." Olivia's bed squeaked as she settled in.

"How can he be . . ." The word lodged in her throat, making her want to heave.

"Do you want to gorge ourselves on ice cream, watch a Nicholas Sparks movie, and cry all night?"

"Maybe." Janie stared out the window, the moon almost full. "I was so sure God had a plan for us."

"He does."

"This plan stinks. I want a refund." Janie stared at a pile of mementos on her desk that Thomas had given her over the years.

"I didn't say Thomas getting engaged to Madison was God's plan, but He does have a plan for you, and it may or may not include Thomas."

"I don't want a plan that doesn't include Thomas." Her voice softened as she blinked back the tears.

"You say that now. Just remember God's in control and—"

"Don't say that!" Janie bolted upright and tossed a throw pillow at her sister. "God's not in control of Thomas right now. I know it from the way he talks. He's running from God and I can't stop him."

Her sister threw the pillow back. "You're not supposed to, and you can't fix whatever is so broken in him right now that he's acting like an idiot." Olivia stared out the window, then brushed a lock of blonde hair over her shoulder and focused back on her sister. "And I didn't mean God's in control like He's controlling things. Or that any of this is what He wants. Maybe it is, maybe it isn't. But God is never out of control. He isn't up there freaked out by Thomas's choices, wondering what to do next. God's still got this."

Janie wanted to believe that was true. She lay back on her bed and stared at the ceiling. The watermark from the roof leak last summer still snaked across the white surface. It really needed painting. A lot of the house needed painting, but her parents were pretty maxed out on time and money. "Why does being a grown-up have to be so hard? Love. Money. I need a job."

"Good luck with that. Even the diner isn't hiring right now."

"I don't want to move, but I can't keep mooching off Mom and Dad, and I don't really want to watch Thomas marry Madison and settle down with a dozen kids."

Olivia grunted, reached for the basketball next to her, and shot it straight up, then caught it and tossed it again. "Rumor is they're selling the house and moving."

"That's what's so idiotic about this." Janie rolled on her side to face her sister. "Thomas always wanted to raise his family in Heritage."

He'd been so excited the day he signed the papers to buy Hannah's half, making him full owner. Fourth generation in that house. Maybe he was running from more than just her.

Olivia tossed and caught the ball again before turning on Janie with wild eyes. "Maybe he's been taken over by aliens."

Janie laughed and brushed away a tear. "I think I'd prefer that."

Her mother's head poked through the door. "I don't want to interrupt, but you mentioned earlier wanting to get a job. I don't want you to feel rushed."

Mentioned earlier? More likely her mom was listening through the vents. Got to love this old house. But Janie didn't fault her. There were few people she respected more.

She offered her mom a smile. "I appreciate that."

Her mom stepped into the room with a magazine in hand. "I found this article about how to turn cake making into a business."

Cake making? That sounded promising. Janie sat up and reached for the magazine. Wow, these were incredible. She could make cakes that tasted amazing, but they looked like cakes. These looked like animals, a purse, a teapot. Was that a book? She couldn't create cakes that looked like these. She'd failed art for a reason. Really, who fails art?

Olivia studied the page over her shoulder. "That's a cake?"

Janie didn't want to crush her mother's idea, but she knew her limitations. She pushed the magazine back toward her mother. "There's no way I could make these."

"You're the best pastry chef I know." Sitting on

the edge of Janie's bed, her mother wrapped her arm around her shoulders. "You'll never know if you don't try. Just the thought of you moving away again . . ."

She opened her mouth to say no but couldn't bring herself to deny the hopeful look in her mother's eyes. "Thanks, Mom."

Her mom set the magazine aside and placed a kiss on top of her head. "We'll get through this, baby girl. You'll see." Moisture tinged her eyes as she stood to leave. "One day at a time."

Janie studied the design in the magazine again. "These ducks look easy enough."

Olivia dribbled the basketball a couple times and then tucked it under her arm. "It's either that or moving."

Janie sighed and dropped back on her pillow. "I guess it's time to try tapping into my inner Martha Stewart."

If Janie said she was leaving town too, Hannah might pitch a fit. Her friend would be struggling to find a local job now that she was back, but Heritage without Janie wouldn't be the same. Hannah scanned the room of familiar faces for her best friend. No luck. The buzz of the lunch crowd filled the diner, and Hannah snagged a booth by the front window before they were all gone.

The salty scent of fresh-out-of-the-pan fries and grilled burgers permeated the air. Hannah's stomach rumbled in protest of her missed breakfast.

A too-familiar set of wide shoulders appeared at the counter. "Is my carryout ready?"

Hannah wadded up a napkin and tossed it at his back. "Did you get that box open?"

Luke retrieved the napkin and slid into the seat across from her. "You've got to stop throwing things at me."

"Maybe you should stop deserving it."

"What'd I do this time?" He dropped the napkin in the middle of the table.

"You haven't told me about the box." Hannah snagged a glass of water off Olivia's tray as she passed by. Olivia rolled her eyes and tossed a straw at her.

"Well, Miss Nosy, I'm headed out to Chet Anderson's now. Hoping he might be able to help with the combination."

Aunt Lucy appeared next to them and placed a to-go order in front of Luke. "Ready to order, Hannah?"

She drew a long sip of her water. "Can I owe you?"

"What about your emergency money?" Luke laughed and reached for his carryout.

Hannah pressed her lips together. "That's for emergencies only. No one is dying. It stays hidden in my purse."

He shook his head, pulled a few napkins from

the dispenser, and added them to his bag. "I'm not sure anything will ever be important enough for those three hundred dollars. You'll die at ninety-nine with that money still clutched in your hand."

"Luke, did you want to eat here?" Aunt Lucy shot Hannah a wink. Yeah, that was discreet. "I can put that on a plate for you."

Luke stood and grabbed the food. "Wish I could, but I need to get out to Chet's."

Aunt Lucy waited until he was out the door and then dropped onto the bench across from Hannah. "Here I thought you two finally had a date."

"If your niece is looking for a date, I'm here. How about Friday night?" Derek Kensington slid into the booth next to Hannah and offered a charming smile. Too charming. With his black hair, blue eyes, and a face that could grace the cover of *GQ*, Derek could date almost any girl he wanted. And he knew it too. His designer shirt pulled tight on his muscled shoulders as he dropped his arm on the back of the booth.

"No thanks." Hannah slid a little farther from him. "Don't worry, though. I'm sure you have a backup already in place. Probably several."

He pressed his palm against his chest. "You wound me."

"Of course I do." Hannah removed his arm from behind her and shoved his shoulder with a laugh. "Now return to your harem. I'm waiting for Janie and you're in her spot."

"I'll concede for now." Derek stood and leaned on the table. "But I'm not giving up." He sauntered back over to his friends at the counter.

Aunt Lucy glared at Derek before focusing back on Hannah. "Janie's coming?"

"I ran into her this morning, but we only had time for a few hugs." Hannah tapped at her phone screen to see the time. "I hope she doesn't take too long. I've got an appointment to show a house in an hour."

"The Fergusons' house again?" Her aunt's brows pinched.

"The twentieth time is a charm, right? Maybe we need to get more businesses to move in. We just lost the WIFI, but we still have the insurance agency, the bank next door, and a few others like this diner we can count on."

Aunt Lucy dropped her gaze to the table and slid her aged hand across the smooth surface.

"We still have the diner, right?"

When her aunt looked up, the reassuring twinkle was absent from her eyes. "Uncle Donny's brother is quite ill. Donny needs to go see him. There's someone we've talked to about taking over while we're gone, but if they say no . . . the loss may be more than we can handle to keep it open."

Hannah leaned forward. "Who? I'll hog-tie them into agreeing."

"Which is why I'm not telling you. Just pray

whatever is best will happen. And pray I find a baker. That's proving harder than I thought."

"Sorry I'm late." Janie appeared next to the booth with a box in hand and smiled at Aunt Lucy. "Are you joining us?"

Aunt Lucy stood and offered Janie a hug. "Welcome back. Hannah and I were just chatting. I don't need to interrupt your time."

"No interruption. I've missed you too. I've missed everyone."

"I can't tell you how much we missed you." Hannah offered a side hug as Janie slid next to her. "Don't ever leave again."

"That's my goal—which brings me to this." Janie pulled the top off the pastry box and moved it to the center of the table.

"Lumpy yellow cupcakes?" Wait—did that one have eyes? Gracious, these were terrifying.

Janie dropped her head in her hands. "I knew this was a bad idea."

Aunt Lucy slid back into the booth and turned the box around. "What is it?"

Janie pulled out a magazine and dropped it on the table. *Reader's Weekly*? She thumbed through a few pages and shoved it in front of Hannah. Cute yellow ducks topped the cupcakes across the magazine spread.

"They're supposed to be cute. Not . . . that."

"Maybe you should try a different one." Hannah scanned the pages, but the ducks definitely looked like the easiest option. She thumbed through a few more pages before she froze and blinked at the headline.

SEARCHING FOR AMERICA'S BEST SMALL TOWNS. $250,000 PRIZE TO SPRUCE UP YOUR TOWN.

"This is perfect."

Janie scanned the ad. Her nose wrinkled. "Really? You think we'd qualify to be one of the best small towns in America? And how does that help me with a job?"

Aunt Lucy claimed the page and scanned it. "Heritage needs something like this."

"We could win," Hannah said. "I just have to find the right way to present us."

Janie reached for one of the distorted cupcakes and peeled back the paper. "Behind a veil—a thick veil."

"It says that the town must invest ten thousand dollars and complete an improvement project. Those projects will be judged and the top five will move on to the semifinals. One great project could revive this town."

"What project would do all that?" Aunt Lucy reached for the magazine again.

"I don't know, but I'll figure it out." Hannah jabbed the page with her finger. "We can do this."

"We?" Janie held her hands up in front of her. "Oh no, I need to find a job. Or figure out a way to sell these."

Hannah grabbed her aunt's hand across the table. "I've got it! Hire Janie."

Janie sat up straighter. "You're hiring? Olivia said you weren't."

Aunt Lucy's mouth dropped open. "Uh . . . well, not a waitress. We need a baker."

Hannah pulled a cupcake from the box and shoved it into her hand. "They may be ugly, but I bet you haven't tasted better."

Aunt Lucy, who wasn't sharing their excitement, raised the cupcake to her mouth. "It *is* good."

"Good?" Hannah lifted one eyebrow.

"Fine, it's the best I've ever tasted." Her gaze darted between the two women before she shook her head with a laugh. "It's only for a couple months, but if you want the job it's yours. If you promise no fancy animal things on top."

"Promise." Janie jumped to her feet. "I need to go call my mom. I'll be right back."

"Don't forget this means you have to help me with the town project," Hannah yelled after her.

Aunt Lucy stared her down.

"What?" Hannah claimed another cupcake. "Janie's great. You said so the other night."

"But the cook I asked to fill in is Thomas."

"What? Oh . . . that'd be—"

"Yup." Aunt Lucy covered a laugh with her hand.

"What are you going to do now?"

She patted the back of Hannah's hand and slid out of the booth. "Pray harder than ever. And hope my nephew doesn't kill me."

"Are you going to tell him?" Hannah popped the rest of the cupcake in her mouth.

"And give him a reason to turn me down? Besides, an aunt can hope." She winked at Hannah and walked toward the kitchen.

Hannah picked up the magazine and read the article over. She had to find a project the board would invest ten thousand dollars in to win that contest. She stared at the run-down, vacant buildings across the street. Maybe Janie was right. She needed a veil. A thick veil.

Luke had seen many girls fall to the charm and money of the Kensington family over the years, but he'd never thought he'd have to worry about Hannah. Shifting into a lower gear, he turned onto the old dirt road that led to Chet's, a dust cloud stirring up behind him.

He'd always thought—hoped—that once he got his life together, it would be him and Hannah together. She deserved the whole American dream, and he wanted to be the one to give it to her. But a successful job in the white-collar world didn't seem likely if he couldn't even pass that class.

Maybe he should have spent more time studying, but he had work. Then there were all the hours he was putting into his house—the house that in its best shape wasn't near what Derek had to offer.

The guy had actually looked right at Luke out the front window of the diner as he slid his arm around Hannah. Was this some sort of game to him?

Luke's fingers tightened around the steering wheel as he pulled into Chet's long dirt drive. The three voice messages he'd left on Chet's phone hadn't produced any answers. Time to see if good old-fashioned bribery would.

He grabbed the Styrofoam container of biscuits and gravy in one hand and the metal box in the other and headed for the house. He eyed the dilapidated building with its peeling paint and a shutter hanging off one hinge. Had it been this bad a few months ago when he'd been here, or had the winter taken a big toll?

A pop and a crack split the silence as the first step gave way. Luke caught himself against the rail, nearly spilling the food in the process. He pulled out his foot and scanned the rest of the porch, choosing the spots that appeared most sound.

The front door flew open as a wrinkled face leaned out. "I don't want any—Luke?" The frown transformed into a grin as Chet attempted to smooth the mess of gray hair that probably hadn't seen a comb in over a week.

Luke needed to check on the guy more often. "Afternoon, Chet. I brought lunch." He lifted the food container.

"Come on in." Chet waved his leathered hand over his shoulder and disappeared back inside.

Luke followed him through the entry toward the living room. "I left you several messages on your voicemail."

"I still haven't figured out that crazy phone. Technology will be the death of me."

As run-down as the house's exterior had become, the inside was the polar opposite. The furniture, straight out of the Sears catalog from 1962, was clean and in good shape. Alex Trebek spouted questions to three contestants on an old analog TV that sat in the corner, a converter box propped on top and rabbit-ear antennas sticking out the back. Chet wouldn't replace anything until it was completely worn-out.

The place smelled of mint and pipe tobacco from the man's one vice, although he claimed he was quitting. He'd been claiming that as long as Luke could remember.

He set the food on Chet's ever-present TV tray and took a seat on the brown tweed sofa, setting the black box on his lap.

Chet sank back into a plush brown recliner and reached for the container. "What's this?"

"Your favorite." At least it used to be.

The wrinkles in Chet's cheeks doubled with

his grin as he lifted the top. "Don hasn't lost his touch."

"Go ahead, eat while it's hot." Luke offered him a napkin-wrapped plastic fork and knife from his shirt pocket.

"Don't mind if I do." He took his time with his first bite before he looked back at Luke. "They're hiring an assistant fire chief."

"Yup."

"Applying?"

"They'll give it to Ted." Luke flipped the numbers on the box.

"Ted?" Chet shoved another bite in his mouth. "That kid wouldn't make a good leader if you cracked him in the head with the fire hose."

"Ted's a good guy. And third generation in the department." Luke, on the other hand, was a man without. Without connection. Without family. Without a past.

"You should apply." Chet forked another bite.

If he didn't, he'd be letting Derek believe he'd gotten to him. "Maybe."

"What's that?" Chet pointed to the black box and reached for the remote. *Jeopardy!* went silent.

"Found it in the wall of the house. Did your sister have a lockbox?"

Chet's blue eyes narrowed on the box, the fork halfway to his mouth. Then he set the food down and wiped his mouth with the napkin.

"Whatever's in it can't be worth all the trouble of opening it."

Luke swallowed. Maybe he was more like Chet than he wanted to admit. A rock settled on his chest.

He slapped the box. "I want to get this open. Are you going to help me, or am I going to have to try over a million combinations?"

Chet studied him as he pressed his lips into a thin line. "Fine, although I think it's a bad idea to go digging into the past. Nothing good can come of it."

What did he mean by that?

"If it was Lottie's, let's try dates: birthdays, anniversaries." Chet pushed out of his recliner, shuffled over to a bookshelf, and withdrew an old Bible. He slid back into his seat and opened the cover, his wrinkled finger sliding across the page.

"Generations of births, weddings, and deaths of my family are recorded here." His eyes grew glassy. "Only one date left to enter. Generations of Andersons—and I'm the last."

What was he supposed to say? Luke would have loved to become a member of the family, but that had never happened. Not legally.

Chet cleared his throat and rattled off a set of numbers.

No luck.

Five attempts later, Luke shook his head. "You sure it's a date?"

"Nope. But if it's not, I don't know where to start." Chet stared down at the page. When he spoke again, his voice was husky. "Let's try Timmy's birthday."

"Her husband?"

Chet's eyebrows lifted. "Her son. But I guess she never talked about him to you, did she? Her husband and Timmy died in a boating accident about ten years before you came to live with her. That's why I encouraged her to take you in. Thought it might help her heal."

An ache grew in his chest, sending pain down his arms and legs. "I guess it didn't work."

"But it did. You were good for her, whether you saw it or not."

His mind flashed to the day he'd seen the adoption papers in the trash. He'd never been good enough for her even after he'd spent twelve years trying.

Chet's voice rattling off a set of numbers shook him out of his thoughts. He dialed them in and pushed the button. As the latch flipped up, a cool sensation washed over his nerves. So it wasn't that she hadn't wanted to be a mom—just not *his* mom.

"Going to open it?" Chet eyed him with an unreadable expression.

Luke nodded and lifted the lid.

Papers. Lots of papers.

The breath Luke hadn't realized he'd been

holding escaped in a whoosh. He leafed through the documents, but nothing stood out. He picked up the first one and opened it. Mrs. Shoemaker's wedding certificate.

"The box belonged to her, that much is settled." He glanced up at Chet. The man studied his every move.

Luke lifted the box to pass it to Chet when his own name caught his eye. He reached for the paper and unfolded it. His own birth certificate. Or at least a copy. He smoothed it out. He had the original somewhere in the files the state had released to him when he turned eighteen, but it'd been a long time since he'd looked at it. Talk about the last of the family line. Perhaps Chet was right. History was best left as history.

He studied his father's name, trying to feel some sort of connection to his heritage. Then he found his mother's name. His heart paused and then picked up double time.

Sarah Eleanor Johnson.

Sarah? His mother's name was Ann. Wasn't it? Or had he muddled that memory in his head too? He closed his eyes, still picturing the bold A-N-N in red letters on the white blouse. Maybe he couldn't even count on the few memories left in his head.

Something wasn't right. But was it the memory or the paper?

"What's that?" Chet's gruff voice broke into his thoughts.

"My birth certificate." He passed the box to Chet. "The rest seems to be your sister's personal documents."

The tense muscles that had creased Chet's forehead eased as he took the box. "I'll figure out what to do with them."

"Mind if I take this?"

"Nope, it's yours." Chet slammed the top of the box and set it on the far side of the chair. "I'm beat. After that good meal, I think I'm going to take a nap if you don't mind."

"Of course." Luke stood, scanning the certificate again as he walked back to the door.

"And take this." Chet followed him and held out an envelope. "It's a letter of recommendation for you for the assistant fire chief."

"How did you—"

"I typed it up as soon as I heard about the position. A lot of people believe in you, Luke. You need to learn to believe in yourself." He offered Luke a firm pat on the shoulder. "Now promise me you'll apply."

Believe in himself? If it were only that easy. Maybe he'd be more confident if he knew more about who he really was. He wasn't even sure of his mother's name.

His hand tightened on the birth certificate. Or maybe it was time to stop looking to an empty past to tell him who he was, and instead grab ahold of his future.

Luke shoved the birth certificate in his pocket and extended his hand to Chet. "I'll apply."

four

If ever she needed a cup of hot coffee, it was today. Hannah resisted the urge to rub the sleep out of her eyes as she slammed the door of her car. She walked toward the diner as she pulled out her phone and checked her messages. Still no leads on the Ferguson house. Her shin rammed into something solid, sending a sharp pain up her leg.

She caught her balance and rubbed her leg. "Hello, Otis. Decide to stake out the diner for a while? A little warning next time might be nice."

Hannah sidestepped the hippo and pushed through the door of Donny's. The scent of hamburgers and chili filled the air, bringing a rumble to her stomach. Maybe she should stay for dinner. She slid behind the counter and reached for a mug. A benefit of being the niece—no waiting.

She'd been up past midnight brainstorming ideas to save the town but still had nothing. How was she going to get the town behind a worthy project if they had no project?

"Mind topping me off?" Al Mathis's gravelly voice shook her out of her thoughts. His scruffy gray beard had grown to the point that it now hid his familiar toothy smile.

She filled up his mug, passed two sugars in his

direction, and leaned a hip against the counter. "How's retirement?"

"Short-lived." He lifted his cup, the steam rising in front of his face. "I'm doing PI work these days."

"Is there a large market for that in Heritage?"

"Nah. Most of it's out-of-town work." His eyes softened as he studied her. "If there's anything you need, anything at all, you let me know. Your daddy and I served on the force for twenty years together. That makes us nearly family." He pulled out a card and slid it to her across the counter.

Hannah swallowed down a sharp lump as memories of her dad and Al laughing together at this very counter floated through her mind. She nodded, picked up the card, and dropped it in her purse. "Thanks."

"Hannah darlin', can we get fresh coffee over here?" The jovial voice of Harold Jameson, town mayor, was unmistakable. That, and he was the only one who ever referred to her as Hannah darlin'. He'd been doing it since he'd started meeting for coffee with her father every Tuesday back when she was four years old.

Hannah made her way over to the table, coffeepot in hand. "Evening, gentlemen."

The mayor lifted his cup to her. His smile, which was tucked behind a thick mustache, doubled his round chin. "Thank you."

Another cup slid toward her. "Sell any houses lately?"

Dale Kensington. He looked so much like his son, only the black hair had aged to more of a salt-and-pepper, and the blue eyes weren't so much cocky and harmless as calculating and shrewd. Her hand tightened on the handle of the pot, but she added some of the fresh brew to his mug as well. "Nope. Destroy anyone's legacy lately?"

He leaned back and drew a sip, keeping his eyes on her. "You have me all wrong. Or maybe you're just sensitive about the Fergusons selling to me."

Warmth drained from her limbs. He had to be lying. They had an appointment with her tomorrow.

A smile tugged at his lips. "Hadn't you heard? I bought the property this morning."

"How could you?" Her voice cracked, and it took all her strength not to dump the whole pot on him.

"I gave them a more-than-fair price—just like I'll offer a fair price for my new town project." He motioned to a map sitting on the table. Wait, was that supposed to be Heritage? Heritage with a strip mall in the center?

The mayor looked up from his coffee and smoothed the little bit of comb-over that he had left. "Nothing is final yet. We're just considering options. This has seemed like the best option. But your aunt told us you've got a great new idea for the town."

"Did she?" She forced a smile. So much for the surprise factor. *Thanks a lot, Aunt Lucy.* Not to mention she'd only read about the contest three days ago. She was not prepared for a meeting.

"Tell us about it. Unofficially, of course." The mayor offered her a wink.

Unofficially? A lot was done in this small town unofficially. She'd thought they'd have learned after her mother, but Heritage tended to run things "small town" through and through.

"If the Manor were restored—"

"Can't afford it." The mayor shook his head. "We've looked into it. Can't even afford to tear it down. Any other ideas?"

"I'm working on it."

Kensington shook his head and added a packet of sugar to his coffee. "What we need is new, modern, commercial."

Hannah set the pot down on the table hard enough to splash some of the black liquid over the edge. "We need to restore the history of this town, not build a new one with discount stores and strip malls."

The mayor grabbed a napkin and dropped it on the spill. "We'd all like that, Hannah, but the money just isn't there."

"And we have the money for a strip mall?"

"There's an investor who'd back that project." He focused on his mug.

No doubt Dale Kensington was using his brother's company as this investor. "The prize money is 250,000 dollars. Think of all the good that money could do for this town. Money *we* could decide how to spend, rather than an investor."

"That would be something, wouldn't it?" The mayor gazed off into space as he took a long drink of his coffee.

Kensington smirked and shook his head. "But winning that prize is a long shot."

"A long shot, but not impossible." Hannah snatched up the pot again, her fingers pressing into the plastic handle. "I'll have a plan all laid out for the meeting."

Mayor Jameson nodded as his brown eyes lost a bit of their usual joy. "We'd like nothing more than to do this, Hannah, but only if you can come up with a solid idea and at a cost this town can afford. Perhaps you should sit down with Kensington here. He has a business mind for things."

"Why would you want to hang out with an old guy like my dad?" An arm dropped on her shoulder as Derek smiled down into her face. The aroma of his expensive cologne surrounded her. "I have a business degree. I'll help you out." Leaning closer, he added in a low voice, "I'm not the ogre my dad is."

She shrugged off Derek's arm with a laugh and stepped back. He was paying way too much attention to her lately. "I'll keep that in mind. Gentlemen." She nodded at the group, set the pot back on the counter, and grabbed her coat. So much for catching dinner here.

She needed space. To breathe. To think. To come up with a plan. She pushed out the door and marched toward her car. She pulled her phone out and texted Janie that she was on her way, then tapped Luke's name as she climbed in.

Luke answered on the third ring. "Hey, Hannah."

"Mr. Kensington might as well be named Mr. *King*sington." She flipped on the heat but was greeted with a frigid blast. She pulled out of the parking lot, heading west of town.

"What happened?"

"He wants to drop a strip mall in the center of town. Right in the middle of the historic district." Hannah whipped the car down a dirt road. Janie really did live in the middle of nowhere.

"We have a historic district?"

"The old buildings in the middle of town."

"The condemned ones?"

"Not all of them are condemned. Those houses could be great again. But it gets worse." Hannah swerved around a puddle. The weather had taken its toll on this road. Monster truck arenas would be an easier place to navigate.

"Worse?"

"The mayor suggested I work with Kensington of all people." Her hand flew into the air but she grabbed the wheel again. "I don't need his help. I don't need anyone's help."

Hannah swerved back and forth, doing her best to avoid the worst of the road. But the brights weren't working on her car and the road disappeared into darkness twenty feet out.

Pothole. Rut. Pothole. Dog.

DOG!

Hannah slammed on the brakes. The car slid on the mud and slush and drifted to the left. *Move, doggie!* "No!"

"Hannah?"

Her phone had dropped into her lap as she white-knuckled the steering wheel. Why wasn't the dog moving? She'd almost come to a stop . . .

Bump.

Oh no. Did she really hit a dog?

"Answer me!" The faint voice traveled up from her phone.

She picked it up. "Luke." Her voice came out squeaky and unrecognizable. "I need your help."

Hannah had assured him that he didn't need to call 911, but a thousand-pound weight still lifted from Luke's chest when he turned the corner and her car sat in the road and not wrapped around a tree. He hopped out of his truck and approached. Hannah sat perched behind the steering wheel, and a dog lay in front of her car. She hadn't run over it.

He knocked on her window and waited as she rolled it down. "Are you okay? Why didn't you answer when I called you back?"

She held up her phone. "Battery died."

Why could she never remember to charge her phone?

He stepped back to the front of the car, knelt down to get a closer look, and coughed against the foul odor rolling off the dog. It had the face of a Lab but the coloring and ears of a shepherd. Its chest moved up and down in a slow but steady motion.

Super. Now what? He couldn't leave it to suffer, but he didn't relish having to put down an animal in front of Hannah, or at all for that matter.

He peeked at her again. Her mouth dropped open as she hopped out of her car. "Is it still alive?"

"Why don't you—"

"Let's take it to the vet."

"The vet? It has no collar. It's skin and bones, half frozen, and probably full of disease. This isn't someone's pet. It was close to death when you hit it—if you hit it. The thing could've fallen over on its own. It might be best if we . . ."

Tears clung to her lower lids. He couldn't say it. He didn't even want to think it. But what was the alternative? This animal could be feral and maybe even rabid. It didn't look as though it was long for this world, so why make it suffer a long car ride only to die upon arrival? Wouldn't putting it out of its misery be more humane?

She fisted her hands at her sides. "Just because it's seen better days doesn't mean it's worth giving up on."

"Hannah—"

She held up her hand. "We're taking it to the vet. I know you aren't one to get attached, but do you really want to off the dog because it needs a bath?" She opened the trunk of her car and started rummaging around inside.

Not get attached? He was here, wasn't he? And he wasn't trying to off the dog. He was trying to protect her. Didn't she see how dangerous this could be?

Hannah returned to his side with a blanket in hand. She laid it on the dog and started to wrap it around the body. The dog, although skinny, had to weigh over forty pounds. Not to mention it could wake up any minute, and then where would she be? Who knew what diseases might be just one bite away?

"Give me that." Luke knelt down and finished arranging the blanket for her. He lifted the dog from the ground, eyeing the bundle for any movement. He carried it to the bed of his truck and laid it inside.

Hannah pointed to the passenger seat.

"No way. I'm not having a feral dog wake up next to me as I'm driving down the road."

Hannah walked toward her car. "Fine, but I'm riding with you." She ran to her car, pulled it to the side of the road, and turned on her flashers.

Luke pulled out his phone and sent a message to dispatch that he'd be out of the area. He'd been trying to be available as much as he could. He needed to look fully committed if he had any chance at the job. But Hannah's safety was more important.

"Can I borrow that?" Hannah reached for his phone. As soon as he handed it over, she hopped in his truck. Probably calling ahead.

For her sake, he hoped the dog would be okay. But then she'd be faced with the problem of what to do with it. No way could she keep a dog in her apartment.

The animal still hadn't moved by the time they arrived at the vet. Not a good sign.

"You grab the dog. I'll hold the door." Hannah was out of the car by the time he had his truck in Park.

Luke picked up the dog and carried it inside. Half the lights were off and the gray reception desk sat empty. Hannah rang the bell and snatched up the check-in clipboard.

"Luke Johnson? Is that you?" A silky-smooth voice filled the room. Chin-length black hair, heavy makeup, and low-cut blouse.

This couldn't be happening. "Cindy . . . I didn't know you worked here." He didn't even have to look at Hannah to know her eyes were burning into the back of his skull.

"It's a new job since Ray and I split." Her lips twisted and she dropped her chin. "But there's an upside. I can date again." She leaned closer and tapped her black fingernail on his left hand, which still held the dog. Her perfume wafted toward him, competing with the stench of the dog. "I see you're still single. Maybe I should see if they're hiring at the lumberyard. You still working there? We had a few good times working together. Remember?"

Good times? He wasn't sure he'd call them that, but he did remember. Only because a certain brunette wouldn't let him forget. He drew a breath and chanced a peek at Hannah. Big mistake. He'd underestimated the fury that could pour out of two normally beautiful hazel eyes.

He stepped between the women, blocking Hannah's view of Cindy. "The dog is kind of heavy. And stinks. Where can I lay it?"

Hannah stepped around him and slapped the clipboard on the counter.

Cindy blinked at Hannah. "I'm sorry, I didn't see you. You went to school with us too, right? Anna, wasn't it?"

"Hannah."

"Of course, my mistake." Cindy picked up the clipboard and glanced over it.

Luke could see that Hannah had put her and Luke's names down as contacts. But she'd left his number blank—no, viciously crossed out.

Cindy's chin dropped again as she fixed her eyes first on him, then on Hannah, then back to him. "Are you two an item now?"

Hannah shrugged and laid a possessive hand on his arm. Her warmth soaked through his sleeve and climbed up his arm. He stared at it a moment, uncertain of what she might do next and even more uncertain of what he wanted her to do next.

He glanced at her face. The women were having a stare down and this was nothing more than a power play. He took a half step back and her hand dropped off his arm. "Where can I put this dog?"

"Carry it back to the first room on your left." Cindy held the door for him before disappearing behind a set of swinging white doors.

Luke blinked against the bright lights of the room. A large metal table sat in the middle, a sink in one corner, and a few chairs off to the side. He placed the dog on the exam table as Hannah entered behind him.

"Cindy hasn't changed much," she mumbled.

Luke walked over to the sink and added a generous amount of soap to his hands. He scrubbed up to his elbows, letting the fresh smell replace the dog stench left behind. "Neither have you, it seems." He reached for a towel, then another.

"What do you mean by that?"

"What was that out there? Or am I wrong and we really are an item now, which would be interesting news to me. But hey, I'll go with it." He tossed the paper towel into the trash and stepped toward her until she was forced to take a step back.

The confidence evaporated from her face. "I . . . I never said that."

"You didn't deny it. So maybe I should assume . . ." He took another step, backing her into the wall.

Her wide eyes searched his face. He'd started this as a joke. Something to teach her a lesson not to use him like that. But now that he stood inches away, his plan grew blurry as he was thrust back to the last time they'd been this close.

He leaned closer. The only things left in focus were her wide hazel eyes and cute freckled nose. When her gaze slid to his lips, his heartbeat doubled in volume.

Cindy popped her head into the room. "Dr. Gascho will be right in."

Hannah ducked under his arm and hustled over to the dog, leaving her back to him. "Did you get that box open?"

He sank into the nearest chair. What was that?

He'd nearly kissed her. Kissed her until they both forgot why it hadn't worked last time. Adrenaline still rushed through his veins, but who knew if it was from relief or disappointment.

They'd always had an unspoken no-touching rule. Now it seemed that had been a good plan.

Luke lifted his head. Hannah stared at him. Waiting. Had she asked him something? Right— the box. "Just some papers of Mrs. Shoemaker's."

"Bummer." She leaned against the wall and stared at the dog. "I was sure it was going to be something more exciting."

Like his birth certificate that contradicted the only memory he had of his mother? He should tell her about that. Why didn't he? Why couldn't he get the words past his lips?

He would tell her. Later. After he had more answers. He ran a rough hand through his hair. "What are you going to do with the dog if it lives?"

She spun around and looked at him, her teeth tugging at her bottom lip.

He knew that look. "I'm not taking the dog."

Madison didn't get it, but he had to help Aunt Lucy and Uncle Donny. Thomas parallel parked in front of the diner and hopped out of his car. Never hurt to be a little early. He also hadn't wanted to stay and listen to Madison shout at him anymore. She may not want him to take this job now, but when he could afford to take her out again she'd change her tune. Not that he'd have much time to go out.

Besides, this was his one opportunity to do what he'd always wanted. Which was why the offer had plagued his thoughts all week. No doubt once he was married, nothing but a corner office at a high-profile company would please Madison. But that was fine with him. He'd gotten used to tossing his dreams aside for reality—that was what growing up was all about. But today he'd live his dream.

Thomas slowed as he approached the diner. Then there was the fact he'd have to work with Olivia day after day. He could only take so many glares. Maybe it would be different with him being the boss and all. But knowing Olivia, probably not. Not that he blamed her. Just as long as Janie didn't visit often.

He'd managed to avoid her since her return. Both for her sake and his. This was one occasion where the tight fit of a small town wasn't to his liking. In a city, the chances of crossing paths with an ex were slim.

He pushed through the door and scanned the room. No Olivia. See, the night was on his side.

Aunt Lucy's face lit up as she greeted him. "You don't know how glad I was to get your call. We can't thank you enough."

"My pleasure. So, what's first?"

His aunt's eyes darted about the room. "Why don't you take a seat in the corner booth? The baker should be here soon."

She swallowed and glanced at Uncle Don, who'd stepped up beside her. Thomas's eyebrows shot up as his uncle turned away with a chuckle.

That was weird.

Thomas made his way to the booth. His phone rang as he slid in, and he pulled it out. Madison. He tapped the screen. "Madison, listen—"

"I'm sorry." Her voice was soft. Had she been crying?

"What?"

"I'm sorry I yelled at you." Her voice hitched. "You're right to help your aunt and uncle. Just promise me when this is all over, we'll leave."

Thomas rubbed his hand over his face. Few people really understood Madison's need to start new. But being the daughter of the town bum couldn't be easy. Growing up under the stigma of his mother's "legacy" had been hard enough. "It's only for a couple months, Madison. It won't change anything."

"Promise?"

His heart pinched. "Promise."

"Thank you, Thomas."

"For what?"

"I know I can be . . . difficult. But you seem to be one person I can depend on."

Thomas swallowed. Whether it was his idea

or not, their engagement was a good thing. She needed him, and he'd be the kind of husband she needed. "I'll always be there for you, babe." A figure approached from the corner of his vision. "I gotta go."

"Okay, bye. Love you."

"Love yo—" The words died on his lips. Janie stood next to the booth.

"Tommy?" All the tenderness in Madison's voice had disappeared.

He cringed at the nickname and turned away before he mumbled into the phone, "Love you too, bye."

He turned back, but the unshed tears that formed in Janie's eyes testified that she'd heard him. He clenched his fists under the table. He hated hurting her, but she'd never have the future she wanted with him.

Janie blinked back the tears and glanced around before sliding into the booth across from him. "Hello, Thomas."

"Welcome back. How was Paris?" Could they sound more formal? This was Janie, his best friend for nearly a quarter of his life, and they talked as if they were strangers.

"Fine." She looked anywhere but at him.

"Fine?" He'd talked with her for countless hours as she planned the trip, the places she should see, the people she'd meet, and all he got was *fine?*

"Fine." She leveled her stare at him. "I hear congratulations are in order. How is Madison?"

His gut twisted as he swallowed. "Fine."

Okay, perhaps *fine* was an appropriate response for the time. Could this be more awkward? Why had she even sat with him?

He could have kissed his aunt when she appeared next to the table. Her gaze darted from him to Janie and back again as she twisted her fingers in front of her. "I know this may be awkward. But we're all adults and this is business."

Janie appeared as lost as he was.

"I think you're going to have to spell it out for them." Uncle Don walked up and gave her a squeeze around the shoulders before moving toward the register.

Spell it out? Thomas darted one more look at Janie. They wouldn't.

"Thomas, Janie is your baker. Janie, Thomas is the chef and manager." His aunt released a breath as if the information had been bursting to get out.

"I don't think—"

"There's no way—"

Thomas and Janie spoke as one, but Aunt Lucy held up both hands. "Listen. You're both adults, you both need jobs, and Don and I both need you. I'm sorry things didn't work out between you romantically, but this isn't about that. Can we all agree to be grown-ups?"

Thomas glanced at Janie, who nibbled at her lip with her teeth. Her telltale sign she was ready to bolt. Not that he could blame her. But if she left, where would that leave Aunt Lucy and Uncle Donny? Or him? There was no way he could do this on his own.

His aunt didn't have a mean or manipulative bone in her body. She'd never have put him in this position unless there was no other option. And she had a point. He didn't know Janie's situation, but he needed a job, and if Janie was looking, the pickings were slim in town.

"Okay." Thomas somehow kept the waver from his voice.

Both of the women turned wide eyes on him. "Okay?"

He turned to his aunt. "You need us. We need jobs. No matter how I feel about it, there's only one option."

Janie studied him across the table, then looked at Aunt Lucy. "I guess he's right. I'll . . . do it. I mean, how bad could it be?"

Thomas locked eyes with her before he darted his gaze away. Right. How bad could it be? "It's only two months, right?"

"Yes. Probably." Aunt Lucy clapped her hands together. "Janie, why don't you come with me, and Uncle Don will be back in a minute to go over the books and purchasing with you, Thomas."

The women disappeared into the kitchen.

What had he just agreed to? It was bad enough to get a taste of half of his dream, but working side by side with Janie? He rested his elbows on the table and dropped his head in his hands.

Then there was Madison. She was not going to be pleased with this turn of events.

five

Kensington had to be wrong. The Fergusons wouldn't have sold to him. Hannah straightened her shoulders and knocked on the solid oak door. Sure, it needed a good sanding and refinishing, but they didn't make doors like this anymore—with time and craft. The door creaked open.

Hannah stared into the aged eyes of Mrs. Ferguson. "You sold to Kensington?"

The twinkle faded a bit as she nodded and stepped back. "Please come in."

Hannah followed the woman through the foyer and sat in the offered chair at the dining room table, surrounded by box after box of memories ready to be taped up and carried away.

Mrs. Ferguson poured two cups of tea and placed one in front of Hannah. "This teacup belonged to my grandmother. It was one of her only frivolous things that survived the Great Depression. Everything else had to be sold. Even the silver platters her mother had brought on the boat from England."

Hannah ran her finger along the pale flowers that edged the rim of the ivory cup.

The woman's eyes turned glassy. "I asked her once if she regretted having to sell so much. She said that stuff was just . . . stuff." Her aged eyes shifted from sad to determined. "It was time to sell the house, Hannah."

Hannah set the cup down. "But I could've found you a buyer. One who'd love this house."

Mrs. Ferguson's wrinkled hand landed on hers. "My oldest son, Evan, took his first steps right in that doorway. The same doorway where his father first kissed me under the mistletoe when we were just sixteen."

"Then how can you let this all go?"

Her hand squeezed tighter. "It's been a good house to us. But in the end, stuff is just stuff. Stuff that will pay for a nice retirement house near our grandkids. Kensington is offering more than we could hope for from a different buyer."

Hannah nodded, not trusting her voice.

"You're a dear and I thank you for trying, though. Don't get too attached to things of this world, Hannah. Everything eventually passes away." The woman patted her hand one more time and stood. "I'd love to visit more, but I need to get back to packing."

Hannah followed Mrs. Ferguson to the door but paused by an old drawing hanging on the wall. "Is that the Manor?"

"My mother drew that in high school. Now that was a beautiful house back in the day."

Hannah ran her fingers along the aged frame. "That it was."

"Would you like it?"

Hannah yanked her hand back. "Oh, I couldn't. It was your mother's."

"And junk to my children. If you like it, please take it. It will do my heart good." Mrs. Ferguson lifted the picture from its hook and held it out to Hannah. "And I think I have some old town archives in the attic. When I find them, I'll pass them along as well."

"Thank you." Hannah hugged the woman's slight shoulders and then made her way to the car and angled the picture onto the passenger seat. She couldn't save it all. She'd be lucky if she could save her own childhood home or the Manor.

A few minutes later, Hannah pulled into the parking lot of her apartment building and eased the drawing from the car.

"What's that?"

Hannah spun around.

Janie leaned against her own car with two coffees and a bag of donuts. "First you ditch me for a mutt and then you miss running this morning."

Hannah cringed and accepted one of the cups. "Sorry. I went to visit Mrs. Ferguson."

Janie followed Hannah into her one-bedroom apartment. "Did they really sell to Kensington?"

"Yup." Hannah leaned the photo against the wall in the living room. Living room? She supposed one could call it that. In this little apartment, the main room became the Swiss

Army knife of rooms. Living room, dining room, office.

"I'm sorry." Janie put one of the donuts on a plate and held it out.

Hannah took the plate and settled onto her gray IKEA couch. "You have no idea how much I need this."

"Have you heard from the vet?" Janie plopped in the worn leather recliner and tucked her feet beneath her.

"No." Hannah's voice caught. How could she be so attached to a dog she'd only seen conscious for less than ten seconds?

"Did the vet think it would live?"

"He could only tell me that it was a male dog, riddled with fleas, underfed, and suffering from a case of worms. He said he'd know more when the dog woke up—if he woke up."

Janie's face wrinkled. "Worms? Leave it to you, Hannah, to pick the most pathetic creature in the world for a pet. What are you going to do with him if he does live? You can't have him here."

"Assuming when he does wake up that he's more like Lassie and less like Cujo, I was hoping Luke would keep him for me, but he said no."

"I'm sure you can think of ways to convince Luke to take him." Janie wiggled her eyebrows at Hannah.

"Stop. Luke made it clear years ago that we're only friends, and he hasn't seemed to change his mind." The words came out more clipped than she'd intended.

Normally, Hannah let Janie's teasing about Luke roll off her back. But today . . . today was different. Today still had Luke's scent imprinted in her memory and the warmth of his breath seared on her skin.

Hannah drew a large swallow of coffee then set it aside. "Here's news. Cindy Monroe works at the vet down in Muskegon."

Janie's eyes popped wide. "As in—"

"The very one." The past burned through her memory just as much as it had the other night.

Janie blinked twice. "Wow. That must have been . . . awkward."

"You could say that." Hannah stared back at her donut. She wasn't hungry anymore. The memory of the way Cindy had been fawning all over Luke still turned her stomach.

"What did Luke say?"

"What does Luke always say? Nothing."

Janie leaned back and stared at the ceiling. "Take it from me, Hannah, you two need to learn to talk it out before one of you ends up engaged to someone else and there's so much left unsaid. Oh, and then you end up working together. Did you know about that little detail when you foisted me on your aunt?"

Hannah held up her hands as a shield. "No, I swear. But . . . it could be a good opportunity—"

"Don't, Hannah." Janie flicked her gaze to Hannah, redness rimming her eyes. "He's moved on. If I didn't need a job, I'd quit now." She laid her head back and closed her eyes again. "But if you're really not interested in Luke, maybe I'll ask him out?"

"What?" Hannah's voice cracked.

"See, not as much fun when others mess in your business, is it? Just admit you're in love with him already and be done with it."

Hannah dusted the sugar from her hands. "Isn't that a cool old drawing of the Manor?"

"Nice redirection." Janie studied the drawing. "It looks so much better without the old run-down vet houses in the next lot."

"Vet houses?"

"Yeah, my dad said they were built by the government during the housing crisis after World War II. They need to be torn down."

Hannah stared at the picture. "That's it. We may not be able to fix the Manor up yet, but we could clear the area around it to make a park. Then the money we win could be used to turn the Manor into a museum or library."

"That'd be cool, but how will you remove the houses?"

Hannah's phone vibrated. "Hello?"

"This is Cindy. Dr. Gascho has cleared your dog and he'll be ready on Wednesday." Her short, clipped voice offered no warmth.

"Wednesday? Okay, so he's healthy?" *And not like Cujo?*

"The doctor will explain all the details when you pick him up." With that, the line went dead.

She owned a dog.

Now to convince Luke to take that dog and figure out how to turn this idea for the town into a plan before the next council meeting. But what did she know about coming up with an impressive business plan?

Derek's face floated into her mind. As much as she hated it, maybe it was time to ask him for a little help.

Six hours ago she'd been ready to quit, but at this rate she'd be lucky if they didn't fire her before the two months were up. Janie ran her hands under the warm water and added some soap. The sweet scent of strawberries and cream surrounded her, doing its best to soothe her tattered nerves.

She'd messed up the cinnamon rolls and the coffee cake first thing. Lucy had said not to worry about it, but how could she not? She'd just completed six months of baking with some of the finest teachers in Paris and couldn't even get basic measurements right.

She tried to blame it on switching back from the metric system, but she knew the real reason had less to do with measurement conversion and more to do with a six-foot dark blond who breezed by her about every ten minutes, leaving a lingering musky familiarity. Every whiff took her back to another memory.

Maybe she'd buy him a new bottle of cologne. One that smelled like . . . mint. Her grandfather smelled like mint. It was comforting but definitely wouldn't take her mind places it shouldn't go.

"You must be Janie." A girl who redefined the word *petite* stepped into the kitchen and loosened the knot on her apron, her words flying a mile a minute. "I'm Noel. There're a few other servers who pick up an odd shift here and there but for the most part it's Olivia and me. I remember you from school but I was a few years younger than you so you probably don't remember me. I'm off now but it was nice meeting you. I don't work tomorrow but I'll see you the next day."

Janie blinked at her, mentally decoding the fire hose of words that had just come at her. "Did you say your name is Noel?"

"I know, right? I was born with bright red hair and green eyes and my parents named me Christmas. Or the equivalent of. I guess I should just be glad I wasn't born with blue eyes or they might have named me America or maybe Liberty." She pulled open the back door. "Anyway, gotta go."

The door slammed, and Janie stared at the rattling panes of glass.

Her sister pushed into the kitchen. The moist

106

fine hairs around her brow testified to her long day as well. "You look like you've been Noeled."

"Does she always talk that fast—or that much?"

"Honestly, I don't understand half of what she tells me, but we seem to get along just fine. Just smile and nod." Olivia fanned her face with a menu and leaned against the counter. Her pale blonde top bun brushed against the shelf. She was tall even without heels. "That pie of yours is selling like hotcakes. Please tell me you're making another."

"Nope. Bread." Janie dried her hands and started gathering ingredients.

"Uhhh, you're killing me."

If the pie had been a flop too, Janie might have thrown in her apron then and there. But she'd finally gotten something right and Lucy seemed more than pleased. Of course, she'd made the pie when Thomas was taking a break. No matter. She just had to get the first-day jitters out. Now she was on a roll.

The ring of a bell split the air.

"Sounds like someone is ready to pay." Olivia turned back through the door. "Hurry up with the bread. Dinner rush will be starting soon."

Janie checked the time on the wall clock. Twenty-five after four. Great, Thomas would be—

The kitchen door swung open as Thomas breezed in, snagged his apron, and walked back out.

—back soon.

Janie focused on the bowl. She was the pastry chef and a doggone good one too. She could make a loaf of bread. She just needed to mix this up, then she could leave the kitchen while it rose. She combined the ingredients, flipped on the mixer, and watched the dough hook do the hard part.

After a few minutes, she pulled the bowl away from the mixer, covered it with a cheesecloth, and set it near the warm oven to rise. She wiped her hands on her apron and marched toward the main door.

Thomas stepped through, nearly colliding with her. He caught her by the shoulders to steady her and then snapped his hands back. "Sorry."

The warmth left by his fingers remained, and it took every ounce of strength not to reach for him. She steadied her nerves and looked up with her practiced indifferent expression.

Why was he looking at her like that?

Come to think of it, she'd practiced the expression in front of the mirror, but she really should have run it by Olivia. She'd hate to think she looked as if she were in pain.

His focus stopped on her lips. Or maybe he—

"You have flour on your chin." He stepped past her, taking care not to even brush against her.

"What?" She swallowed hard.

"Flour on your chin. I thought you'd want to

know before you went out." He snagged a few tags from the ticket holder, pulled a few patties from the cooler, and dropped them on the grill. The sizzle of the meat filled the air and cut off all other communication.

Janie glanced in the mirror by the sink and wiped her chin. Thomas having second thoughts? She had to get over herself. He wasn't interested. Done deal. Move on. She pushed through the door into the main diner.

"Finally." Olivia shoved a tray at her. "Take these fries to table nine!"

"Nine?"

Olivia grabbed her shoulder and pointed to a booth by the window. "The one with Pastor Nate."

Pastor Nate?

She eyed the three possibilities at the tables. One was a woman, so not Pastor Nate—unless Nate stood for Natalie. But she'd guess not. The other two were men. One wore a three-piece suit and had a graying beard, while the other had a tattoo peeking out of his collar. Pastors did suits, not tats, right?

"Pastor Nate?"

The first man glanced up from his tablet and shook his head.

"Over here."

Janie spun and faced the tattooed man. "Your fries?"

"Thanks." He accepted the fries then extended his hand. "You can call me Nate."

He couldn't be that much older than she was. His hair, nearly black, was a little long for her tastes, but with his scar from an eyebrow piercing and a few days' worth of scruff across his square jaw, it suited him. Like a bad boy of Hollywood.

"Do I have something on my face?" He rubbed his hand across his chin.

"No. I'm sorry. You're just not what I expected for the pastor in Heritage. LA maybe. A lot did change while I was gone."

"I wasn't quite what the town was expecting either." He motioned to one of his tattoos. "And I'm guessing you're Olivia's sister who was in Paris."

It all came back to her. "Yes. And you're Leah and Caroline's cousin."

An unreadable expression crossed his face as he glanced toward the counter. Janie followed his gaze. Olivia eyed them before she pushed back into the kitchen. What was that about?

He focused back on her, but some of the smile had dimmed from his eyes. "So, can I count on seeing you Sunday?"

"Absolutely. You have a good meal—uh, fries."

The bell jingled and Madison breezed through the door and walked directly back to the kitchen.

Janie held up her hand. "You can't go back—"

Madison's icy glare silenced her. She bit back

a string of words that came to mind. The order window offered a perfect view of Madison rising on tiptoes to plant a kiss on Thomas's neck.

She had to get out of here, but where? She eyed a side door by the cash register. Today was as good a day as any to explore where that went. Even a closet would give her a moment to compose herself.

Janie turned the deadbolt in the door and stepped inside. Light shone through butcher paper that had been taped on the front windows. Iron chairs rested upside down on their matching tables, all lined up opposite an antique-style counter. This had to be the business next door.

"Isn't it great?" Lucy appeared in the doorway. "Don and I bought it fifteen years ago when we were considering expanding, but when the economy went south so did our plans. We've put it up for sale several times but haven't had one bite."

"I love the counter." Janie reached out to the wood but stopped. A thick layer of dust covered every surface.

"It was a candy shop. They had the best truffles, but like many businesses in this town, they didn't make it." She stared at Janie, then wiped her thumb across her cheek—no doubt a smudge of flour Janie had missed. "Are you sure you can do this for the next couple months?"

Janie shifted her weight to the other foot. "I don't know. But he's moved on. I can too."

"I explained to Madison she isn't allowed back in the kitchen during hours of operation. But I can't promise that will keep her away." Lucy dusted her palms across her apron.

"I can do it. I will do it." Janie forced back the tears. "Time to check the bread."

By the time Janie returned to the kitchen, Thomas was nowhere in sight. She lifted the cheesecloth covering the dough. Her heart dropped. The dough remained in a small, dense lump. It hadn't risen one bit. She closed her eyes and ran through the recipe in her mind. She'd measured it all right, of that she was certain.

Yeast. She'd forgotten the yeast. Janie blinked several times, forcing herself not to cry. Why did she ever think this job was a good idea?

Luke had witnessed Hannah doing some crazy things over the years, but this one outdid them all. When she'd called and announced she needed to drop by for a chat, he'd expected she'd try once again to convince him to take the dog.

He'd spent the last hour making a mental list of all the reasons he couldn't and wouldn't let the dog stay with him. And if the list failed, he'd shift the conversation to his birth certificate, which he still hadn't found a way to talk to her about. But all his plans flew from his mind when she started talking about something even crazier.

He watched her across the table. Her lips were

still moving, but he'd stopped listening after the words "set the middle of town on fire." Maybe she'd finally lost her mind. Well, if she hadn't, he was about to.

Luke raised his hand. "Hannah, stop. You can't set the town on fire."

"Not the whole town." Hannah huffed and shook her head. "Just three houses."

"That's better?" Luke gulped his coffee. Cold. He stood, dumped the black brew in the sink, and poured himself another cup. He needed all his synapses firing for this conversation.

She pulled a piece of scrap paper from the recycling bin and a pen from the drawer. "Just stay with me."

Like that was an easy goal.

Hannah mapped out the center of town but left out the row of condemned houses. "Just imagine the Manor standing alone in a park in all its glory."

"Its glory?"

"Not yet. But it will be. And around it—a beautiful park." She added bushes, trees, and a swing set to the drawing. "Every town needs a center point of gathering, like in Stars Hollow, where they had that great gazebo. For Heritage, it will be the Manor."

He turned to offer Hannah a cup of coffee but thought better of it. The girl didn't need caffeine right now. "Stars what?"

"The town in *Gilmore Girls*? The television show." Hannah dismissed his question with a wave of her hand.

He sat and took a gulp from his steaming mug. "So, you want to knock down a bunch of condemned houses to make another condemned building the gathering point?"

"The Manor isn't condemned. That's a vicious rumor. The vet houses were condemned ten to fifteen years ago. The owners didn't want to pay to demolish them and didn't want to pay taxes, so all were eventually reacquired by the town because of unpaid back taxes. The Manor was donated to the town. The only reason the vet houses still stand is that it's too much money and too much hassle to get rid of them."

"I'm not surprised." He tilted his head and lifted his cup to her. "But why would the Manor be a place to gather? Condemned or not, it's no place to hang out."

She leaned her elbows on the table and stared at him. "The park will be the place to hang out. And when we win the grant money we can make the Manor a community building for events. Maybe add a library or museum. With these other buildings gone, it will open the whole block up."

"Then why not knock them down? You don't have to set the town on fire."

"That's what I thought, but Derek looked into it and the closest dump is across county lines. We'd have to pay major fees due to some of it being hazardous waste."

"What about the fees for burning hazardous waste?"

"For the fire department to burn them we have to have any asbestos removed. But the rest is controlled by the town so if the board approves, they just have to sign off that they won't fine themselves. Trust me. The buildings need to be burned. If you think they're bad on the outside, you should see the inside—"

"Inside?" Luke choked as he attempted to swallow. "They're condemned. Who let you in?"

"Janie and I just walked in."

He set down his mug and gripped the edge of the table. "The doors are locked."

"Fine, we walked in through a window." She crossed her arms in front of her. "Just the first one. The window is missing. It was in bad shape with nasty old furniture. They're a lawsuit waiting to happen."

Luke growled. "That's why people are supposed to stay out. Including you."

Hannah stared at him before turning back to the rough map she'd drawn. "Anyway, Derek gave me a bunch of research about other towns using such buildings for training burns."

"That is the second time you've mentioned Derek. Are you spending time with him now?"

"No. The board suggested that he give me some

help with my plan, and since I need the board's approval for this project, I agreed to his input. That's all it is." She dismissed the idea with another wave of her hand. "Even you have said before that the Heritage Fire Department needs more training. Well, set the houses on fire and train."

She was dead serious. She had no idea how dangerous it could prove to be. It would have to be an all-hands operation with the surrounding fire departments standing by. With so many buildings in a row, the challenge would be controlling the burn. If they got more than one hot at a time, it could end up decimating the whole town. And if she wanted to save the Manor, this wouldn't be a walk in the park.

Luke ran his fingers through his hair and dropped his elbows on the table. "So if Ted, his father, and the town council agree—and that's a big if—you really think this will win you the grant?"

"The article said it's looking for towns that are ambitious and ready to do what it takes to turn over a new leaf. What's more ambitious than burning the middle of town?" Hannah glanced at her watch. "I told Aunt Lucy I'd help them pack the car. I'm telling you this is it."

Luke groaned and shook his head. "And here I thought I was going to have to talk you out of bringing me that dog." He leaned back in his chair and downed the last of his coffee.

Hannah moved to the door and paused with an impish smile. "Right, the dog. He'll be here Wednesday. See you then." She dashed out, slamming the door before he could even swallow.

Luke bolted to it and whipped it open. Her car was already pulling away from the curb.

He wasn't taking that dog.

Jimmy's red rider bike lay discarded in front of his porch. Luke hopped off the steps and peered under the porch. Jimmy huddled in a ball, shivering, with tearstained cheeks and red-rimmed eyes.

"Hey, bud, what's up?"

Jimmy brushed his wet cheeks with the backs of his hands, leaving dirt streaks behind. "Nothin'."

"Really? Hmm. Then why are you under here? Let's go shoot hoops."

The boy shrugged. "Okay, somethin'. But you can't help."

"Try me." Luke shifted his weight and leaned against the side of the house.

The boy stayed mute as if waiting for Luke to give up and leave. Wasn't going to happen.

Jimmy sighed as he wiped his nose across his sleeve. "Mrs. Adams is all-ee-geric to dogs."

"Were you hoping for a dog?"

"I asked for one for my birthday. Always wanted a dog. Mom always said she didn't need another mongrel to feed. What's a mongrel?"

117

Luke ruffled the boy's hair. "Guess what? I'm getting a dog on Wednesday."

Where did that come from? That was not what he'd meant to say.

The boy's wide eyes filled with hope. "Really? Can I play with him?"

No going back now. But perhaps this was the next step in learning to be there for someone, even if it meant stepping out of his comfort zone. And this step might look like a four-legged, slobbery mess. "Yup. Anytime you want."

Jimmy let out a whoop and jumped up. "Can we play ball now?"

"Sure thing."

See, opening up wasn't so hard. Luke forced down the anxiety building. He'd do it one day at a time.

six

If Luke tried to turn her away, she might have to get down on all fours with the dog and beg. Hannah opened the passenger-side door of her Volkswagen Bug, grabbed the leash, and offered a gentle tug. Nothing. With a slow hand, she patted the dog's head and scratched by his ear. He leaned into her hand and closed his eyes. Who'd have guessed that under all that dirt the dog was almost blond with a white underbelly?

Stepping back from the car, she gave the leash another gentle tug as she patted her leg. The dog inched backward until he was pressed against the far door. The air had cooled with the setting of the sun, and the dog seemed to prefer the warmth of the car. Like she didn't.

"Wrong way, pup." Hannah pulled with a bit more force. "Come on, doggy." She needed to come up with a name.

The vet had said the dog was underweight, but she'd be willing to debate that at the moment. She could control a fifty-pound dog. After all, she weighed more than twice that. Although doing this in a skirt wasn't her best choice.

She'd set another meeting with Derek, and she had just twenty minutes to get there. She was behind on laundry, so it was a skirt or her ratty jeans and a sweatshirt. If she wanted to be seen as a professional, she needed to look professional—the skirt won out. But if she'd known she was going to have to wrestle this dog into Luke's house, she'd have opted for the jeans.

"Come here . . . Rover? Spot?"

No luck—and a dumb name for a dog with no spots.

The door behind her creaked open, causing the dog's ears to perk. A high-pitched whistle followed by a few claps filled the air. *Really, Luke?* Did he think she'd brought him Lassie, who'd just come on command?

Another whistle split the silent evening.

She glared at him, ignoring the little hop her heart did at the sight of him barefoot in jeans and a white tee. "That's not—"

A mass of fur flew past her legs, sending her tumbling into a patch of remaining gray snow. She glanced up in time to see the mutt bound up the old porch steps and into the house.

Maybe she'd call him Brutus.

Hannah stood and brushed away the grit embedded in her kneecaps. So much for looking professional at the meeting.

She grabbed the bag of supplies, slammed the car door, and followed them into the house. The dog may be staying here, but it'd still be her dog.

Hannah dropped the bag on the table with a thud. "How'd you do that? I couldn't get him to move an inch."

Why did she sound so angry? Maybe because he'd done something she couldn't. Maybe because her left knee ached. Or maybe because, if she didn't stay just a little irritated, she'd be tempted to cancel the meeting with Derek and spend the evening with Luke.

"I have the touch." Luke rubbed the dog's ears and held something up to the furry snout.

"You have bacon?" Maybe she'd call the dog Mooch.

Luke offered a half grin. "Yeah, bacon helps too."

"Cheater." Hannah dug into the bag. Where were the pills the vet had given her?

"Resourceful." Luke paused from scratching the dog's ears and took in the full length of her, his gaze lingering a touch longer on her legs. "Do you normally dress up for a dog drop-off?"

That look was not going to help her state of mind. Janie's words floated back. *Just admit you're in love with him.*

She broke eye contact and focused on the bag. "I have a meeting, and you aren't supposed to feed him people food. He'll get overweight. I bought him this food for now until I can get to a pet store for the brand the vet recommended. I also bought a few toys."

"A house showing?" Luke peeked in the sack and pulled out a tug rope, brushing her hand in the process.

Hannah jumped away and pulled out the medicine. "Just a meeting. He needs to take this three times a day."

He set the rope aside, then took the medicine. "All right."

Hannah knelt to ruffle the dog's ears. "I really appreciate this. I'm not sure what I'd have done with him if you hadn't agreed."

"I don't think I technically agreed." Luke looked at the dog sniffing around the kitchen. For more bacon, no doubt. Spoiled already.

"Well, you didn't disagree, so that sounded like an agreement to me."

"Sort of like I didn't disagree about the controlled burn?" He lifted an eyebrow at her.

"Okay, no. You really disagreed with that. But I believed—*believe* it is a good idea, and I'll convince the town council I'm right. I'll show them the figures and the plan for the space. I also have testimonies of three other small towns that handled the old vet houses in a similar way. Of course, they burned them over twenty years ago. But a fire is a fire."

His hand tightened on a chair as he leaned on the back of it. "That's where you're wrong. Fires aren't all the same, and they can be dangerous. And I don't like the idea of starting one in the middle of town."

"Fire is the best method since it's free and—"

"It's only free as long as it burns just what

you're planning on burning." He shook his head. "And what about the asbestos removal?"

"That is a cost, but I found a company that will do it for about a thousand dollars—give or take, depending on how much is there. But it's a small investment for cleaning up the center of town. It's something that's needed to happen for a long time. This is the perfect way to do it. Trust me."

Luke's intense gaze burned into hers as he reached for the ball she'd bought for the dog. "I trust you."

Hannah broke eye contact and reached into the bag again, but it was empty. "Don't forget the pills. They're very important. And the follow-up instructions on the bottle."

"Pills. Got it."

Luke bounced the ball a few times and the dog came to attention. Luke tossed the ball through the doorway to the living room. Nails scraped across the wood floor as the animal scrambled after it. A few thuds followed by a loud crash. The dog bolted back into the room and squeezed between the chairs under the table. A yellow-tinted puddle spread across the floor.

"You've got to be kidding." Luke's voice shook as he flexed his hand.

Hannah's gaze darted from the dog to Luke. If he kicked them both out, where would they go? She couldn't take him to her apartment or they'd both be homeless.

The muscle in Luke's jaw twitched as he drew a calming breath. "I guess potty training is first on the list."

"So, he can stay?"

"For now. But I'm still not convinced this is the great idea you think it is." Luke gestured to the floor. "Case in point."

Hannah stepped over the puddle to the counter and pulled off a hefty amount of paper towels. She'd have to add that to her next shopping list. She pulled out the chairs and did her best to contain the mess.

"At least you haven't redone the floors yet." She offered Luke a half smile. His blank stare didn't change.

Luke would see she was right about the dog. And eventually he'd see she was right about burning the houses too.

Thomas stretched his neck and sighed as the long hand touched the twelve. Nine o'clock. Kitchen was closed. He flipped off the grill and scraped the spatula across the surface, taking care to leave no stray bits. He grabbed a clean, wet rag and ran it over the smooth metal. Steam billowed and moistened his face.

After hanging his apron on the hook, he ran his hands under hot water and added a fair amount of soap. Overall, it had been another successful day, but he still couldn't forget the hurt that had flashed in Janie's eyes when Madison stopped to see him.

Thomas chalked it all up to one more reason it'd be good to get out of Heritage. The more he let the idea sink in, the more he found himself longing for it. Starting fresh where no one knew his past failures or had their own personal expectations for his future. Hannah hated the idea, but she'd see in time it was best for him, Madison . . . and Janie.

He stepped over to the soda fountain and filled a cup with Mountain Dew. A few of the regular late-night stragglers remained. Wait. And a couple not so regular. Hannah and Derek? Together?

Derek patted her hand across the table, offered her a playful wink, and stood to leave. She laughed at something he said before looking back at the papers in front of her.

That was . . . interesting. Thomas waited until Derek was gone before moving in. "What're you doing with Derek?"

Hannah slid out of the booth and shoved the files in her bag. "You of all people are going to lecture me about who I'm spending time with?"

He grabbed a box she was trying to balance. "Give me that."

She surrendered the box but marched out ahead of him.

Thomas nodded to one of the waitresses walking by. Noel, was it? "I'll be right back. Janie is here if you need her."

The cool evening air hit him in the face as he pushed out of the diner. Hannah paused at her car, which was parallel parked in front of the diner, to unlock the door. A scowl still pinched her face.

He leaned against the door to keep her from pulling it open. "I'm just looking out for you. You know Derek is the love-'em-and-leave-'em type, right?"

Hannah pushed him out of her way and yanked the door open. "It was a business meeting, nothing else."

Thomas eyed her yellow skirt as he handed her the box. "Oh really? Is this your normal business attire?"

She tossed it in and slammed the door. "It's laundry day and I wanted to look professional."

"Just be careful. Derek is used to getting his way."

"We're only meeting one more time tomorrow night and then I think I'll be ready."

Thomas leaned against her car again. "What's Luke think of you spending time with Derek?"

"Why is everyone asking about Luke lately?"

He lifted one eyebrow. "Everyone?"

"You, Janie, Aunt Lucy . . . you."

"You can't count me twice."

"I can if you're bugging me about it twice as much." A series of unidentifiable emotions crossed Hannah's face as she leaned on the car next to him. She focused on the sidewalk and

126

toed a two-inch crack with her foot. "Do we stink at relationships?"

Thomas's gaze flashed back to the diner where Janie stood in the window talking to a customer. She never smiled like that for him anymore and probably never would. Not that it mattered. "Nah, we've just had a few bumps. But you can find someone. I found Madison."

"And that's really what you want? I mean, my opinions about the girl aside, I have the feeling you haven't gotten over someone else."

Thomas shoved his hand in his pocket, shook his head, and focused on his shoes. "I'm trying. I love Madison. I do. She needs me. But with Janie back . . . it's much harder than I anticipated. I've heard it said that you never forget your first love. I have a feeling for some, that's true."

"Why did you break up with her? Tell me."

He kicked at a piece of broken sidewalk. "It didn't work out."

Hannah jabbed her finger in his shoulder. "I want a real answer this time. According to Janie, things were perfect, then you started acting weird and within a week you'd just ended it. Did . . . you cheat on her?"

"No." How could she think that? He rubbed at the spot on his shoulder.

"Did you stop being attracted to her?"

"She's beautiful." The last word came out in a whisper and he cleared his throat.

Hannah paced away from the car. "Then what? Were you weirded out that she bears a strange resemblance to that photo of Grandma Ethel?"

Why couldn't she let it go? He clenched his fist then stretched his fingers. "Seriously? Hannah—"

"If she *was* related to Grandma Ethel, you could be concerned that your kids could come out all—"

"I'm infertile." Ugh. Why did he say it? He hated that word. Even if she was just his sister, it was humiliating.

He pushed away from the car and crossed the sidewalk to Otis. Dropping down on the brass back, he leaned forward on his elbows, burying his head in his hands before he looked at his sister.

Hannah stared at him wide-eyed, mouth opening and closing but no sound emerging.

"Stop that."

"How . . . why do you know that? I know it happens, but don't people usually find out *after* they try to have kids?" Her eyes bugged out. "You two weren't—"

"No! Stop. You're seriously bad at guessing." Thomas shoved his hands through his hair. This was why he hadn't wanted to talk about it in the first place. "Do you remember when I had that cancer as a kid? Well, one thing they warned Mom and Dad about was that the treatment could make me . . . ya know."

"Infertile?"

Thomas cringed. That word again. "Yes."

"Wow, that's tough." She stared into space before looking back at him. "So, why did you break up with Janie?"

"Janie wants kids. Lots of them."

"Have you talked to her about this?"

"No, and you can't either." He darted a glance at the diner. The idea of her hearing through the window sent a chill through him.

Hannah dropped next to him on the hippo. "Thomas, she may say that given the option, she'd choose you. Trust me."

He shook his head. "Exactly. Choose me and give up what she wants. You accused me of making the same mistakes as Mom, but I'm not. Dad married Mom knowing she never wanted to live in a small town, thinking he could change her mind. I won't make that same mistake. I know what Janie wants and I can't give it to her. I refuse to strap her to a life she doesn't want."

"So, adopt."

Like it was that simple. Thomas shrugged. "Maybe. But Janie wants it all. Remember when we went to her big Memorial Day family reunion? She went crazy over her cousin who was pregnant. 'What's it feel like? I can't wait. I want a daughter who looks like me, a son who looks like you . . .' I made an appointment with a specialist the day we got back from the reunion. I knew

129

from my records it was a possibility, but it's not like I'd ever been tested."

Hannah laid a hand on his arm. "You've got to tell her."

He shook off her pity. "No, I don't. This is best."

"Where does Madison fit in?" Hannah's lips twisted. "Are you just using her?"

"No." Thomas stood and paced a few feet away. "I told you, I love Madison. I really do. It may look different than it did with Janie, but not all love looks the same."

"You told Madison then?"

Thomas sighed and shook his head. "No. But she doesn't want kids. She's been clear about that."

"So you'll never have kids?" Hannah's eyebrows arched.

He didn't blame her. The concept had been hard for him to take at first too. He shrugged again. "She might change her mind, and there's always adoption, but we'll see."

"You should definitely have that conversation before you get married."

"We will." He dropped back to the seat next to her. "And you be careful with Derek."

"Oh my word." Hannah punched him in the arm. "Drop it already."

"Fine." He laughed and rubbed his arm. "You punch like a girl."

"Good, because girls are tough." Hannah lifted

her fist, threatening another hit, but she couldn't hide her smile.

He grabbed her wrist with his hand. "Just try."

Hannah leaned her whole 130 pounds into him, but he just pushed her away, almost sending her sliding off Otis. She laughed and pulled back. "Fine, I yield." She leaned her head on his shoulder. "I'm sorry."

"It's not your—"

"No, I'm sorry you've had to go through this alone, and I'm sorry I've been so hard on you. I can see you're trying to do the right thing for Janie. But you need to talk to her. I won't tell her. I promise."

"Thank you." Thomas's throat pinched as he spoke. He could see Hannah's point, but she was wrong. Janie deserved the best guy, and he couldn't be that man.

With the way his mind was spinning, there was no point in attempting to sleep in. Luke kicked aside his blue comforter and rubbed the sleep from his face. The morning chill drifted into the room from between the windowpanes. He needed to find time to install the new windows he'd purchased, but his renovation list already took up two notebook pages. And was that a new crack on the ceiling? Perfect.

He pushed up to a sitting position and reached for the manila folder that had plagued his thoughts and restless dreams. He flipped it open and stared at the pitiful contents. He'd done a basic internet search for both Sarah Johnson and Ann Johnson, but that proved fruitless. Who knew that Johnson was the second most common name in the country, only behind Smith? Sarah and Ann? Might as well be named Jane Doe.

The birth certificate provided a little more information on Sarah, but unless he knew where to search it didn't matter. And really, his investigation skills didn't exceed that of Google. He could hire someone, but letting a stranger or even a friend dig into the void of his past was more than he could take.

He ripped off a piece of yellow lined paper from the legal pad and scrawled in caps across the top, *Who was my mother? Who am I?* He underlined it several times and drew a line dividing the page left from right. He wrote *Ann* at the top of the first column and *Sarah* at the top of the second. Under Ann he wrote *memory*. Under Sarah he wrote *birth certificate*.

He paused and scanned the paper. That was all he had. A memory and a piece of paper. Why was he even fighting this? The paper had to be right. It was his birth certificate, for goodness' sake.

Then why couldn't he let go of Ann?

He ran his finger along a photo of him and his father that he'd unearthed among his belongings in his search. He must have been about four. Was it so terrible to want the memory to be right? Because if the memory was wrong, then he didn't even have that little bit of his mother. He had nothing.

He forced down the lump in his throat, slammed the file shut, and tossed it on his nightstand. Maybe he'd go for a jog before he started on the construction this morning. He might just be able to get the bathroom tile down before his evening shift at the lumberyard if he hurried.

A wet nose nudged at his hand with a whimper.

The dog had attached to him quicker than he'd expected. He had to have been someone's pet before, but all the searches he'd done for missing pets had come up void as well.

"I'm okay, boy. Feel like a run?" He reached for his shoes and made his way to the kitchen. "But first, coffee for me and bathroom for you."

Luke let the dog out and then hit Start on the coffeepot. Probably not the healthiest choice before a run, but the caffeine was required this early.

The scanner blared to life as a high-pitched squeal filled the kitchen. *"Attention, Heritage Fire Department. We have a reported structure fire at 523 McCain Road. All available units, please respond."*

He dropped his shoes by the kitchen table and grabbed the boots he kept by the door. Then he turned off the coffee maker and held the door long enough for the dog to run in as he rushed out, snatching his coat off the hook as he went. "Sorry, boy. When I get back."

He took a deep breath and slid into the driver's seat. The truck's engine roared to life before he'd even shut his door.

He headed south down Henderson Road then took a right on Richard Street. Jimmy waved at him from the sidewalk as he sped past. Luke made a quick left on Chapel Road and then pulled into the station.

He arrived first at the firehouse and ran toward his gear. Most of the guys would meet them at the fire. It was his job to pick up the truck, but he had to wait for another rider first.

Luke stepped into his gear and then slid into the cab. He started the engine and slid on a headset as Derek pulled into the parking lot. Luke refrained from rolling his eyes. Awesome.

"Not quite how I wanted to spend my Thursday morning, how about you?" Derek jumped in the cab and grabbed his own headset. "I had a pretty late night."

Luke ignored him as he pulled out on the road. He flipped the siren and waited for an update from dispatch.

"More reports of the structure fire have been—"

"Did Hannah tell you we had a date last night?" Derek cut off the report. "It was our second date, actually."

"You wish, Kensington. Now be quiet, I'm trying to listen." Luke bore down on a car and blared his horn. The car pulled to the shoulder.

"Closest structure is fifty feet, but woods are located to the south. The draft tank—"

"I take that as a no." Derek let out a snicker.

Warmth seeped through him as the image of Hannah dropping off the dog last night assaulted him. She'd said she had a meeting but refused to say more. The memory of her in that yellow skirt flooded his mind. He shook the distraction away. He had to focus on the fire right now, not Hannah's legs.

"Engine One, I want you to set up—"

"You should want what's best for her. That best is me."

Luke darted a glare at Derek. "How would you know what's best for Hannah? She's your choice of the month and now you talk like you know her. Just shut up. We missed our orders." He pressed the button to the repeater. "This is Engine One. Could you repeat that?"

Derek took advantage of the three-second delay. "We got to know each other pretty well last night."

"Engine One, approach from the south. Luke, run the pump, and Derek, pull a line. Nate has already done a 360. There's a cutoff road just past the tree line—take it and follow the second left."

Luke gazed to the left at the first break in the

trees. Smoke billowed into the air from a field. His knuckles whitened as he gripped the wheel and turned onto a private dirt road. Please let it be the one the chief had been talking about.

"Face it. You can't offer Hannah what I can."

He pulled the engine to a stop and stared down Derek. "Stay away from her."

Derek just smirked. "We have another date tonight."

Luke flung his door open and jumped to the ground. He marched over and started pulling the line.

"Luke, what're you doing?" Chief Grandy came around the side of the truck. His brown beard covered most of his face, but the part that Luke could see didn't look happy. "I said to run the pump. Derek's got that covered. And why did you park your truck there? I said the south side, man."

"Sorry, I'll move it."

"Leave it." The words were clear even over the roar of activity. Chief Grandy's voice seemed set on double volume at all times. "Ed already grabbed the pump, so get on tools and get your head in the game, man." He strode away, shaking his head and shouting into his radio.

Luke retraced his steps toward the cab and accepted the ax that Thomas held out.

He had known better than to get into it with Derek, but he'd let the guy get to him. Now he was left looking like the idiot who couldn't follow instructions. He marched toward the truck and gave silent thanks he was on tools. If there had ever been a time he wanted to bust a few things up, it was now.

seven

There was no way she was waiting outside in this rain. Hannah lifted the pot of long-dead geraniums by the door and snatched the key, faint whimpering of the dog greeting her from the other side. She edged the door open and paused. The dog stared at her and tilted his head to one side. Was he still Lassie or was today the day he went Cujo? The pup walked over and licked her hand. Lassie it was.

"I've got to stop thinking of you as Lassie." *Or Cujo.* Hannah carried the water dish to Luke's kitchen sink. Did the guy not know how to wash a dish? After filling the dog's bowl she set it down and filled the sink with hot, soapy water.

"What should I name you?" Hannah debated several names as she washed, rinsed, and dried. She knelt and rubbed the dog's ears. "Don't worry, we'll find the right name."

The dog yawned and leaned into the scratch. See, owning a dog was fun.

According to the chart on the wall, Luke hadn't given him medicine yet today. She could do that. She was the owner, after all. Hannah opened the bottle and dropped a large brown pill in her hand. The dog's ears sank back and he turned his face away. The vet had just placed the pill in the back of his throat. She reached a slow hand out toward his snout, but he scrambled to his feet and bolted up the stairs.

Great. Now what? Hannah had been in this house countless times, but she'd never ventured up the stairs. Mrs. Shoemaker had strict rules when they were growing up, and after the woman had died, keeping that boundary seemed the right thing.

"Puppy. Doggy-dog." She had to come up with a name. She placed her foot on the first step. "Rover," she tried with a firmer voice. Nothing.

The wood creaked with each step. She wouldn't be sneaking up on the dog. At the top of the stairs, the narrow hall had four doors, only two of which stood open. That helped narrow the options. She peeked in the first room. Nope. Just tools, small pieces of insulation, and a stack of new windows resting against one wall.

She made her way to the second room. A sheet had been nailed over the lone window, casting a soft blue light around the room. It had to be Luke's—the scent of his body wash lingered in the air. With her big toe, she poked at a pair of sweatpants puddled on the floor and resisted the urge to hang them up. She didn't want him to think she'd been rummaging around his bedroom.

A gray T-shirt had been tossed across the unmade bed. Other than the sweatpants and his bed the room was tidy. The guy wasn't much for clutter. An old, dusty Bible sat between his alarm clock and a handful of Stephen Lawhead novels on his nightstand.

She trailed her fingers across the navy stripes in his comforter as she moved to his desk. A loose photo of her and Luke leaned against a Little League trophy. It had been taken their senior year, a week or so before Luke had kissed her. A week before everything had fallen apart.

She lifted it and brushed away the dust. Luckily her style had simplified. But Luke hadn't changed at all. He still wore gray T-shirts. Still had those same soulful eyes. And he still had that lock of hair that didn't want to stay tamed.

She shook her head. She needed to find the dog and get out.

She glanced under the bed. A bundle of blond fur lay tucked about as far back as he could go.

Maybe she could lure him out. If only she had one of those tennis balls—or bacon. She scanned the floor and paused. A file lay facedown next to the bed with the contents spilling out. The dog must have knocked it off the night table as he rushed under.

Hannah picked it up to set it back on the nightstand, but something slipped out. Grabbing the runaway paper, she started to slide it back into the folder but stopped.

It was a photo of a man holding a little boy about age four. It was slightly yellowed with age, but she could easily make out the boy's familiar curly brown hair and that dimple in the left cheek.

She opened the file to set the photo inside when Luke's scrawled note stopped her.

Who was my mother?

"What are you doing in here?"

Hannah jumped to her feet as Luke entered the room. His tone was casual, but Hannah's gut still coiled like it had in the fourth grade when she'd gotten caught peeking at the Christmas presents. Sure, for him the steps didn't creak.

Adrenaline flooded her as she took in his soot-covered face and the acrid odor of charred wood. He'd been to a fire. His eyes, red from the smoke, blinked at her.

The dog popped out from under the bed and went over to greet Luke.

He knelt down and scratched behind the pup's ears. "What are you doing under there?"

"Had to chase him. He needed medicine. Ran under there." Why did she sound like a robot?

"I hide it in bologna." His eyes shifted from the dog to her hands then hardened.

Right, the file. "Luke, what's—"

"I need to take a shower." He strode over, pulled the file out of her hand, and slid it into a drawer, slamming it shut. He turned toward his closet without another word.

"What?"

"S-H-O-W-E-R. Water shoots from above. Washes away this stink." He sat on his bed and pulled at his boots. He chucked them in the closet, where they landed with a thud.

"Not a 'what did you say' what. What in the world was that about?"

He stared at her, his jaw twitching.

"Seriously? You're going to pretend I didn't see that and you want me to play along? Is honesty so hard?"

"Me?" He pushed off the bed and took a step toward her. "How was your date last night?"

Last night she didn't have a date. Last night she'd—oh, Derek. Her stomach plummeted. How did he even know?

"Meeting? Really, Hannah?" He reached into his drawer for a clean T-shirt and then slammed it shut. "Your boyfriend was too happy to let me know all about it on the way to the fire."

Boyfriend? She crossed her arms over her chest. "Derek isn't my boyfriend. He was helping me with the town project. Which is more than I can say about you."

He stood up straight, losing any remaining softness from his features. "Then I guess he's perfect for you."

"You're being ridiculous." She pushed past him as she stepped out of the room. "I'm taking Rover for a walk." She called the dog but it didn't move.

"Rover? His name is Spitz."

143

"What? It's my dog, I'll name him what I want. Besides, what kind of name is Spits? Like, he drools?" She clapped her hands and beckoned the dog. "Come here, Rover."

"No, with a *Z*. Like Mark Spitz, the Olympic swimmer. He loves water. It's better than Rover."

The dog barked and sat by Luke's feet.

"Spitz?"

The dog darted a look at Hannah and barked again.

"Why not just name him Phelps?" She crossed her arms in front of her and wrinkled her nose.

"Phelps is a dumb name for a dog."

"And Spitz isn't? It's my dog. I'll name him." Hannah stomped her foot. "And why won't you talk about that file?"

He leaned against the door frame and stared at her. "Why won't you talk about your date?"

"It wasn't a date." Her hands shot in the air.

"Fine." He mimicked the gesture. "It wasn't a file."

"Really?" Hannah tried to go back into the room, but Luke still stood in the doorway. Why did his shoulders have to be so wide?

"Let it go. This isn't something you need to fix." He crossed his arms over his chest. "I wouldn't even be questioning these things if you hadn't insisted that I open that stupid box."

"You said the box was just old papers of Mrs. Shoemaker's." Hannah took a step back.

"It was . . . mostly."

"What else?" When Luke didn't answer, Hannah stepped toward him again. "You're always pushing."

"And you wonder why when you break into my house and go through my stuff."

"I didn't break in. I used the key, and I came to feed the dog, not go through your stuff. The file was an accident."

"Were the dishes an accident? Or did you do that to lessen the guilt for your date?"

"Why would I feel guilty about a date? We're only friends . . . right?" She marched toward the stairs.

"So it *was* a date." He followed her down the hall.

Hannah growled and turned back at the bottom of the stairs. "You know what? Perhaps it's time for a little space between us."

"Fine." He stopped at the top of the stairs. "Enjoy your non-date tonight."

"I will. You enjoy your secrets. And maybe I'll find someplace else for my dog. Come on, Rover."

The dog whimpered and laid his snout on Luke's foot.

"Rover," she tried again, but the dog didn't move. She cast a final glare at Luke before she let the door slam on her way out. It seemed the key to Luke letting you close was having fur and a tail.

Let him have his private little world. Let him have the dog. She was done trying.

• • •

He should have told Hannah about his past long ago, but shutting people out had become his default. Luke wedged the crowbar between two aged boards of Chet's porch and leaned his weight into it. The squeak of nails protesting the movement filled the crisp afternoon air. His hand flexed against the ache in his fingers. Not quite cold enough to turn numb, but cold enough to object to the hard work in the wind. Whoever said spring started the twentieth of March didn't live in Michigan. He tossed the broken board to the pile he'd started in the yard and tapped his hammer on different boards, testing for any other bad spots.

You can't offer Hannah what I can. Derek's words bounced back and forth in his head. But Derek was wrong. Sure, Luke didn't have a lot, but he had a house, and once he had it fixed up they could build a life together.

The look on her face as she'd stomped out of his house flashed through his mind. He'd screwed that one up good. Whether she liked Derek or not before, he might have just pushed her toward him.

Maybe he'd overreacted to Hannah and the file—okay, there was no *maybe* about it—but it hadn't helped that it all came on the heels of listening to Derek spout off. He'd never liked the guy, but the idea of him and Hannah . . . ugh.

Luke slammed his hammer down, sending a spike of pain up his arm. That board was still good.

The phone in his pocket vibrated and he snatched it out. Unknown number. Not Hannah. He sighed and slid it back in his pocket. When the voicemail chimed he picked it up again and tapped the screen to listen. Cindy? Great, she'd tracked down his number after all. He tapped Delete but saved the number. He'd keep screening his calls if she was trying to get ahold of him.

Shoot, he was supposed to call to follow up on Spitz after ten days. Maybe he'd leave a message after hours.

The front door squeaked as Chet emerged, holding two steaming mugs of coffee. "Need a break?"

"Don't mind if I do." Luke tossed the hammer aside and accepted the mug.

"Hear anything about the job?"

"I turned in my paperwork and now I wait for an interview." Luke took a long swig of his coffee. Strong and bitter. Man coffee, Chet called it. Maybe a dose of man coffee was just what he needed. "I'm not sure what you put in that letter, but I swear—ever since I dropped off that paperwork, Dan Fair, Tim Lacy, and a few of the other guys on the team look at me differently. Talk to me differently."

"I doubt I told them anything they didn't already

know. My guess is that the change isn't in them, it's in you." The steam from Chet's mug billowed up into the chilled air. "You used to show up, do your job, and then leave. But now I hear you've been arriving early and staying later. If people are treating you different it's because you're treating them different."

Maybe community wasn't so much about your pedigree but more about what you put into it.

Luke finished off the mug and set it aside as he reclaimed his hammer. "Did you ever notice that I whistle?"

"Who do you think taught you how to whistle?" Chet reclined a bit in his chair.

"Was there a specific song that I whistled more than others?"

Chet tipped back his mug to claim the last of his coffee. "Yup. Didn't know the tune myself, but Lottie and I talked about it several times. Why do you ask?"

"Hannah mentioned it." Luke reached for the next board and laid it in place. "The birth certificate I found in that box . . . I started looking for information on my mom."

"Any luck?"

Luke claimed a nail and held it in place. "Nothing to give much hope. And a few days ago, Hannah found my research. She started to ask me about it and I . . . overreacted."

"What's the big deal? She knows your history."

148

He coughed and spun his empty mug in his hands.

Luke drove the nail in with three solid hits and reached for another. "That's the crazy thing. It should've been easy to show her."

"You think she'll only like you if you have it all together?"

Luke lined up another nail and drove it in. "I don't know if she'll ever like me even if I can manage to get it all together. I failed one of my classes last semester."

"I don't think she'll give a dag-gum about your class. But I'm guessing you didn't tell her about that either." When Luke didn't comment, he stared him down. "Why the business degree?"

"Jon said when he got back from Europe he'd get me a job at Heritage Fruits."

"And you want to spend your days behind a desk, typing in numbers?"

"You did."

"And I loved it. But we aren't talking about me. We're talking about you." Chet shook his head and focused his attention on Luke's work on the porch. "I've got a feeling you're much more comfortable with a hammer in your hand than a computer mouse."

Luke dropped the hammer and stood up straight. "A few handyman jobs here and there aren't really anything to raise a family on."

"You are capable of more than being a handyman. You should get your contractor's license.

The work you've done on that house in a short time is nothing short of amazing."

"That's still—"

"—not as prestigious as a white-collar desk job." Chet stood and stretched then tapped Luke's chest. "That is all in your head."

"Hannah deserves more."

"Hannah deserves what she wants. And that girl wants you. I'd bet the house on it."

Tell that to Derek and his two dates. "There may have been a time, but that was long ago. I messed that up too."

"How?"

What was this, confession time?

Luke turned away. "We dated in high school . . . or almost did."

"Almost dated?"

"We kissed in the treehouse, then stayed up talking for hours. When we went back to school on Monday . . . It was the way she was trying to fix me in subtle ways."

"Fix you?"

"I told her I couldn't afford a tux for prom and she said she'd pay for it. My car broke down and she wanted to pay for that."

"But your pride wouldn't let her."

"It felt like I was *almost* the guy she wanted to date, but not quite. So we fought. Rumors started about another girl at school and me. Hannah called me a few names I won't repeat. It was a bad

150

summer. We did manage to patch up a semblance of friendship before she left for college, but it wasn't the same."

The pain from that time in his life resurfaced. He'd never known emptiness like that.

"Now you're friends?"

Luke shrugged away the memory. "When she was home from college one summer, we mended some fences, but we've always avoided the dating subject."

"What changed?"

He slid the next board into place and reached for his hammer again. "I thought I'd eventually get over her. I was wrong."

Chet pointed a gnarled finger at him. "But you still believe you aren't good enough."

Luke shrugged. "I thought if I could fix up the house, then I'd have something to offer."

"You're making this too hard. You just need to answer one question. Do you love her?"

Did he love her? Luke stood with a stretch and stared at the distant woods. Could he let her in?

Chet shuffled to the door. "There's more coffee in the kitchen if you want it."

Luke set the hammer aside, gathered some stray nails that had spilled, and grabbed his mug. He pushed through the front door and headed toward the kitchen. The black box rested open on the dining room table with the contents laid out in careful piles.

Luke's eyes skimmed the papers as he passed. His gaze paused on one of them. *The Will and Trust of Lottie Shoemaker.*

She had a will? Had Chet known about it?

He scanned the document but stopped at the words, *I leave my house to the town of Heritage.*

To the town. Not to Chet.

If Chet didn't own it, then he couldn't sell it to Luke.

If this was true, then that rent-to-own contract sitting at home was nothing better than fancy scrap paper.

eight

She was confident, capable, and ready to do this. Hannah's heels clipped against the sidewalk as she approached the town hall with an armful of papers, proposals, and charts. A lawn mower rumbled in the distance, filling the warm breeze with the sweet smell of cut grass. It was a new day, a new season, and this proposal had to work.

Her phone chimed, and she dug it out of her bag as she walked. Luke. Her hand gripped the phone a little harder. It had been eleven days since they'd talked. Eleven long days. She hated not seeing him, and she hated that she hated it. Why did he have to have such a hold on her?

She paused outside the community building and tapped the screen. "Hey, Luke, what's up?" That sounded casual enough.

"Hi. Um . . . the thing is . . . can I stop by?"

Hannah dropped down onto a bench by the door. "I was just heading into the town council meeting. Can I swing by after?"

A long pause filled the air. "That's the thing. I think you should reconsider the burn."

That's why he was calling? Not to say that the past eleven days had been as hard for him as they had been for her. Not to say he was sorry. Not even to wait for her to apologize. No, all

he wanted to do was tell her she was wrong—
again.

Hannah straightened her shoulders and tapped
at the bundle of charts in her lap. "I've done my
research and Derek—"

"You're trusting Derek over me now?"

Hannah forced a smile at a man walking by and
dropped her voice. "No. I don't trust him more
than you. Would you let me finish? Derek and
Ted went out and did all the measurements. I
have the paper right here. The buildings are far
enough apart with a margin to spare. It isn't a
problem."

"Yeah, well, I went out and measured them too.
I'm not sure where they got their numbers, but
there's no margin, and someone could argue that
the two southern buildings are too close."

Hannah bit her lip. The burn had been Derek's
suggestion to begin with. But he wouldn't fudge
the numbers, would he? The guy liked things to
go his way, but that'd be dangerous. Still, Ted
had been with him. She might not always trust
Derek, but she could trust Ted.

Luke cleared his voice. "Trust me, Hannah. The
houses are too close. Sure, you could make a case
for it, but if they all caught at once—"

"Luke, I can't do this right now." Hannah
scanned her watch. "We aren't going to burn
them all at once. I've got to go. I have to get in
there."

"Are you even going to consider what I said? We'll find another way. Trust me."

How could the plan work without this? "I'll . . . think about it. I gotta go."

Hannah slipped the phone into her purse before yanking the door open. Ted sat slumped in a chair, his unruly red curls flopping in his eyes. He fiddled with his phone while Derek scanned the crowd. The moment his blue eyes found her, his ever-present cocky grin tilted his mouth as he patted the empty chair next to him.

Hannah slid into the spot next to Derek and leaned toward Ted to whisper, "Are you sure the fire isn't a concern for the town?"

"My dad said he's done several training fires like this." He dismissed it with a wave, never taking his eyes off the phone. "That's how us volunteer teams get training."

She held up the paper with the measurements Derek had given her. "These numbers are correct, right? You both checked them all?"

Ted shot a look at Derek and then looked back at Hannah and swallowed, his green eyes appearing uncertain for the first time. "Yeah."

"Luke said—"

"Luke?" Derek's hand landed on her shoulder. "Luke is full of it."

She shrugged off his hand. Maybe a different seat would be better. She started to stand when Cindy slid into the end chair, crossing her legs and blocking Hannah's way out. Her black-rimmed eyes traveled around the room.

Hannah dropped back into the chair. "Luke's not coming."

Cindy cast her a quick glare before a smile tugged at one corner of her lips. "I know. If you see him, tell him I'm sorry I missed his call the other night. But I got his message."

A bang of the gavel declared the meeting open, and Mrs. Jarvis, Heritage's town secretary, read the minutes from the last meeting.

Missed his call the other night. The words echoed in Hannah's head. She might be sick.

She peeked at Derek and Ted out of the corner of her eye and then focused on her presentation. Did she trust them more than Luke? There was no contest. She trusted Luke—hands down. But that didn't mean he was always right.

Her name over the crackling speakers pulled her out of her trance.

Derek patted her knee. "Knock them dead."

The guy did know business.

Hannah set her papers on the podium and fisted her hand to keep it from shaking. What presentation was she going to make? "Ladies and gentlemen, Heritage has a long, rich history. However, with the economic downturn, it has fallen on hard times. Right now we have the opportunity to revitalize our town at *Reader's Weekly*'s expense. They're holding a contest for towns just like ours that want to turn over a new leaf. Start fresh. And with a little help, I believe we can win that money."

Applause filled the air. Hannah nodded at her supporters.

"What does the contest involve, Miss Thornton?" The mayor laced his fingers on the desk in front of him.

"We need to prove to *Reader's Weekly* that we're the most worthy town. We need to show them that we have ambition and don't just want to receive but give as well. After some research, I believe the best way to stand out is to embrace both who we are and who we want to become."

More applause.

Hannah relaxed her fist and turned the page on her notes. "We're the town of Heritage, and I believe it is time to live up to our name and embrace our roots. And what cries 'Heritage' more than the Manor?"

Murmurs rippled through the room.

"I know it isn't much to look at now. But we can change that. If we invest ten thousand dollars in renovations—"

"You think ten thousand dollars will renovate the entire Manor?" Bank owner and council member Bo Mackers leaned into the microphone. "Ten thousand dollars won't even cover fixing up the exterior."

"No, but if we clear the area around it for a park,

it will prove that we're serious about change, growth, and pride in our town."

Hannah went on to describe her plans for the square, the future of the Manor, and all the benefits it would bring to the community.

When she finished, applause filled the room once more. People were actually behind her on this. This was going to work.

"What is required to enter the contest?"

She wasn't sure which committee member had asked, so she tried to make eye contact with each. "The town must invest a minimum of ten thousand dollars into this renovation project."

The applause dwindled into an unsettling murmur.

"And if we don't win, that ten thousand will be gone." Dale Kensington leaned back in his chair and laced his fingers across his chest.

"The *Reader's Weekly* Project would come at a cost to the town, but it'd also provide a space to recoup that cost with a giant fundraiser."

"So you have a fundraiser planned?" Mayor Jameson's face lit up.

"I can add that to the plan." Hannah forced the quaver from her voice.

"And how do you propose to rid that property of the abandoned houses?" Dale Kensington gave her a knowing smile. But how could he know? Derek promised he wouldn't mention it to his father.

Trust me. Luke's voice echoed in her head.

"If we were to demolish them—"

"Too expensive." Kensington's smile dimmed as he tapped his pencil against the desk. "The closest dump that can handle that much debris is across the county line, and did you know they charge extra for hazardous waste? Just fees and equipment would max out your funds, with nothing impressive to show *Reader's Weekly*."

The town council members nodded in turn.

The mayor sighed and tapped his glasses against his chin. "We'd all like to see a few changes, but we aren't sure if this is the best investment of the town's money."

She was losing them. She should stop and think. Maybe even pray about it. But she didn't have time. She had to act. Besides, God had given her a brain, and her brain said she needed to fix this now.

The mayor reached for the next paper on his stack. "We'd like to help you, Ms. Thornton, but we don't see this working out at this time."

"Wait."

They paused and stared at her.

A drop of sweat ran down beside her ear. "There's another option that's free."

"Free?" Mayor Jameson's bushy eyebrows rose. "That's something we'd consider."

"A controlled burn." She glanced at Ted and Derek. Ted smiled and nodded, but Derek looked at his dad. Were they in cahoots about something? Unease traveled down her spine. Maybe she was reading too much into it.

"Hannah?" The mayor looked at her expectantly.

Maybe she should wait, do more research.

Derek stepped up beside her with his own folder in hand. "Ted Wilks and I have measured, and his father already signed the report about the benefits and risks of using a controlled burn to clear the square."

He had a report?

Derek passed out stacks of paper, then returned to the microphone and began answering questions about the process. The guy had a way with people. Within minutes he had everyone on his side. He should've been a politician.

Luke's face flashed in her mind, but she shook it away.

The mayor's face creased in a grin. "Well, Ms. Thornton, it looks as though you have a solid plan. All in favor of investing ten thousand dollars in the *Reader's Weekly* Project in the care of Hannah Thornton, with the understanding that this fundraiser you've planned for the new square will pay back half that loan, say aye."

A round of ayes went up.

Hannah's breath paused. Was this really happening?

"All opposed?"

Silence.

"Well, there you have it. And with any luck, this will pay off in your contest and we can finally restore that Manor."

Hannah swallowed. "Yes, sir." She reclaimed her seat as they moved to the next item on the agenda.

She'd done it. This was what she'd wanted. Wasn't it? She shook away the question. It was time to move forward.

She had to think of a fundraiser. She'd never be able to raise that kind of money at a fair by selling cupcakes. Her teeth tugged at her lip. Worse, she had to tell Luke they were going forward with the controlled burn and hope he'd still talk to her.

Who'd have guessed he'd enjoy running this place as much as he did. Thomas flipped off the neon "Open" sign, pulled down the shade in the front window, and clicked the lock into place. They'd only had a handful of customers since seven thirty. Not enough to justify four employees. If he owned this place there were a few things he'd change, like earlier closing. Then there was re-covering the booths. And the counter—he shook away the thought. No way Madison would let him buy this place. He couldn't let himself go there.

Working with Janie had been easier lately. He was moving on, and she would eventually too.

The door rattled behind him. Hannah stood smiling and pointed at the lock.

He shook his head and waved. "We're closed. Go away."

She rattled the door again. Her voice was muffled through the glass. "I know where you sleep and five different ways to break into that house."

He reached for the lock and opened the door. "You may not want to yell that through the town if you're really trying to sell the place."

"Then maybe you shouldn't move."

He wasn't getting into this here, again. "Janie is at the back booth filling saltshakers with Olivia and Noel."

Thomas moved to the kitchen and set to cleaning the grill, doing his best to ignore the giggles from the other room. The bell on the front door chimed. Shoot. He'd forgotten to lock the door after he let Hannah in.

He wiped his hands on his apron and marched out. "Sorry, we're closed."

"Of course you are." Madison went up on tiptoes to kiss him. He flinched. He'd worked at keeping all affection to private time. He snuck a quick look at the booth out of the corner of his eye. Janie continued to laugh and carry on.

He grabbed a tray of clean silverware and set it on the table between Hannah and Janie. "When you're done there, you can start wrapping silverware. We're getting low."

"Might as well." Olivia laid a napkin in front of her and reached for a fork. "Hannah wants us to figure out a fundraiser to raise five or six thousand dollars for the town. We could be here all night. Any ideas, Thomas?"

Fundraising? Like he knew anything about that. "Sell cookies."

"Sell ten thousand cookies to a town of two thousand people?" Hannah leaned back and crossed her arms. "That's the crux of our problem. If we wanted everyone here to pay the ten thousand dollars, we could just ask for donations, but no one in this town has extra money right now. What we need is something unique that will draw people from the outside."

"A fair," Noel piped up as she topped off the last saltshaker. "Sell food and crafts. There's a lot of local talent around here. People would be willing to donate their time to do something for the town."

"A fair might work." Hannah tapped her pen on her lip. "But that's still a lot of carnival games for one town. What we'd need is something large to sell. A big-ticket item and a crowd pleaser to draw people from other towns."

"Like winning a car for a half-court shot at a basketball game." Olivia dashed for her phone when a chime filled the air.

"Exactly. Except we don't have a basketball court or a car to give away. Buying one might defeat the purpose." Hannah massaged her temples. "We need to sell something that the town already has."

"Relationally stunted men?" Olivia mumbled as she pitched the phone back into her purse.

"That's it!" Madison clapped her hands together. How had he forgotten she was here?

She took a step closer to the table. "Don't you remember when the town of Gilbert did that a few years ago?"

"They sold relationally stunted men?" Olivia paused, the silverware in her hand half wrapped.

"They did a bachelor auction." Madison started digging through her giant red purse. "They aren't much bigger than us and they made almost six thousand dollars."

"You think women would pay money for a date with the guys in this town?" Hannah lifted an eyebrow.

Madison pulled out a pad of paper and grabbed a pen from the counter. "I did in Gilbert."

Say what?

Okay, the conversation had just gone a direction Thomas no longer needed to be a part of. He reached for Madison's hand. "We're out of here."

Madison dropped his hand. "I can think of at least forty guys off the top of my head. You could average fifty to a hundred dollars a date, and some could bring in more than that—trust me. I'd pay that. That's two to four thousand dollars right there."

Had she just said—

"I mean I would bid if I weren't engaged." She patted Thomas's hand.

That was better. Well, kind of.

Madison pulled up a chair and started scribbling a list of guys' names.

"I think . . ." Janie looked from Hannah to Olivia.

Good. At least Janie would have enough sense to put a stop to this.

"I think people would drive to see that even if they weren't sure they'd bid. Then, while they're here, they could buy some food, a craft, even play a carnival game. It's a great idea." Janie leaned over to look at Madison's list. "Add Ted—he'd do it."

Ted? Thomas had heard enough. "You think you're going to find guys willing to do this?" He snatched Madison's list and started reading it. He gripped the paper tighter as he got farther down the list. No doubt most of these guys would agree. But they weren't the kind of guys he wanted his sister dating—or Janie, for that matter.

He stopped at Luke's name and tossed the paper back on the table. "Luke will never agree."

Janie nudged Hannah's shoulder. "I have faith that Hannah can convince him."

His sister's face reddened as she sent Janie a glare.

Thomas studied Janie. Is this what she really

wanted? A bachelor auction? What would he do if she were to start dating one of these town jerks? He shifted his gaze and found Olivia's eyes on him. Caught.

He turned to Madison but she was leaning over, adding more to the list of names. How many guys did she know?

"How about this?" Olivia pinned him with her focus. "If Hannah can convince Luke to do this, then you let Janie off on Friday night for a date."

Janie's head jerked up. "What?"

He stared at Janie. "You have a date Friday? With who?"

Olivia winked at her sister before looking back at him. "I didn't say it was this Friday. She wouldn't say yes if she had to work. But if Luke agrees then she gets a Friday night off."

"Hey, don't go writing checks that my charm can't cash." Hannah laughed and reached for the list.

Olivia turned to her. "It's not a bet. It's just a friendly agreement. Thomas thinks he knows everything, but I disagree."

Did Janie really have a date or was Olivia just calling him out? He'd call her bluff. Janie wouldn't date any of the guys around here. The only one worthy of her was Luke, and Hannah might have a thing or two to say about that.

He shook his head. "Janie doesn't have a date."

Janie's eyes hardened. "I can have a date you

don't know about. I got a new apartment. Did you know that?"

Thomas pressed his lips together. Had she already moved on?

A cocky smile spread across Janie's face. "Didn't think so. So what is it? Yes or no?"

His confidence wavered but he couldn't let that show. "Yes."

The girls nodded and smiled.

Hannah turned to a clean page in her notebook and scribbled the words *Bachelor Auction* across the top. "Okay, we'll need to call a meeting."

Had Janie moved on? That was what he wanted. Right?

Thomas clenched his teeth and turned back to the kitchen, grabbing Madison's hand as he went. "Come on."

She yanked her hand back and waved him off. "You finish up. I'll stay and help them."

Thomas shook his head as he pushed through the kitchen door. The whole world had gone crazy. And if Luke agreed to this, Thomas might just lose his mind too.

How long could it take them to read a few pages? Luke forced his attention away from the rest of the men filling the diner's corner booth and reached for his water. He grabbed a napkin to wipe up the ring left on the green Formica. Since his house legally belonged to the town—

or would once the will was made public—Luke had decided to go straight to the source and talk to the mayor. After all, Harold Jameson was a reasonable man. The rest of the council? That was still to be seen.

The diner wasn't really the place he'd wanted to lay this all out, but when he'd called the mayor about the will, the man had mentioned that several of the council members usually met for dinner once a week, so this made it simple. When Luke questioned whether that was allowed, Mayor Jameson had laughed it off and called it "a small-town perk."

Luke could only hope that handling this all without involving the authorities would also fall under "a small-town perk." He didn't know if they could arrest Chet for what he'd done, but if he made it through this meeting without the town taking sides against his old friend, he'd consider it a success.

He reached for his water again as he shifted in his seat, the cracked red vinyl protesting the movement. The dinner crowd had died down some, but a steady stream still came and left—usually with a piece of Janie's pie in hand.

Luke dipped his head to shade his eyes from the evening sun that poured through the diner's front window, highlighting the painted words and casting strong shadows across the floor. They'd been reading the papers for fifteen minutes. He drummed his fingers against the table, causing the silverware to rattle and earning a glare from Dale Kensington. He stilled his movements and sat back.

The mayor looked up from his reading. "How long have you known about this?"

"A week."

Bo Mackers's furry eyebrows pinched into a V. "I've never known Chet to be anything but honest."

The last thing he wanted was to drag Chet down with this. "Chet knew Lottie was torn between leaving the house to me or the town. I also believe him when he says he didn't have any idea what happened to the will or what she'd decided. When the house legally fell to him, he tried to make both happen. He gave me a deal I couldn't refuse and then passed my payments on to the town."

"That explains the eight hundred dollars cash we've been getting every month." Gerald Atkins leaned back and shoveled a bite of pie in his mouth. "So, what are you proposing, boy?"

Luke swallowed against his dry throat. Maybe Olivia would come by with more water soon. "I'll just make payments directly to the town."

The mayor flipped through the pages again. "I don't see why not."

"Hold on." Kensington slapped the paper down on the table and jabbed his finger at the amount paid for the house. "That property alone is worth more than this price."

"But he's put a lot of work in it." Bo pulled out his bifocals and examined the figures again.

"Understood." Kensington nodded as he held up both hands. He continued after a dramatic pause. "But I think it's only responsible, considering the current tight finances of the town, to see if there's someone out there willing to offer more."

As if Kensington cared about the town's best interests.

"Is there a booming housing market here in Heritage I'm unaware of?" Gerald laughed before he forked another bite of pie. It was amazing the guy was still so thin with the way he ate.

Kensington leaned his elbows on the table. "I'll buy it."

If it wasn't one Kensington, it was his father. With George gone and Jon off in Europe, the whole rest of the family was out to get Heritage.

Kensington tapped his finger on the deed. "Kensington Corporation has been acquiring properties in the downtown area for some time. I want development. It just so happens that this house is a property I've had my eye on for some time."

"Since when?" Luke smacked the table, causing the glasses to rattle.

"Now, calm down." The mayor patted Luke's arm. "We aren't going to come to an easy conclusion today. This will be discussed at the next town meeting."

The men agreed as Kensington shot Luke a smirk. He'd already calculated his win. Luke could see the writing too. If he had to bid against Kensington, he didn't have a prayer.

The men stood one by one, leaving Luke and the mayor alone at the table. The older man's smile seemed forced. "I was hoping to make it easy for you, Luke, but if I'm shooting straight, Kensington may offer us a bid we can't refuse."

"I know." Luke leaned his forehead against his steepled hands.

"I hope we can figure out something." He pulled out his wallet and dropped a few bills on the table. "I heard you were applying for the assistant fire chief position."

"Yes, sir."

"That position comes with a spot on the board. Did you know that?"

"No, I didn't." Luke sat up straighter. Talk about community respect.

"I think you'd be good at it. Hang in there." Mayor Jameson slid out of the booth and squeezed Luke's shoulder before heading to the door.

"Wow, you look like you've seen better days." Pastor Nate slid into the seat across from him.

"Hey, Pastor."

"I'm like a year older than you. Call me Nate."

Nate gathered a few of the discarded dishes and stacked them. "What's on your mind?"

Luke laced his fingers behind his head. "You ever feel like you don't quite fit in?"

Nate's deep laugh filled the air. "You're kidding, right? Five tattoos and a motorcycle don't really say 'Midwest small-town pastor.' I think the church lost over half the congregation the day I showed up to preach my first sermon. Of all the places God could call me to serve, Heritage didn't even make the bottom of my list."

"Why did you come? I mean, there are churches everywhere."

"When I first moved here I thought God brought me because of family. My cousins Leah and Caroline Williams used to live in town and run the WIFI. But after they left and my biggest supporter, George Kensington, died, I have questioned why God has me here more than once. But God asked me to come *here*. To do His work *here*. He doesn't always call us to do the easy thing or the thing that makes the most sense." The leather of Nate's jacket whispered in protest as he rubbed the back of his neck. "Is your family nearby?"

Luke blinked at the question. Everyone in town knew he was an orphan. Everyone except the new guy. "They died when I was young. Grew up in foster care."

"How bad was it?"

"Could've done without the first couple stops, but I landed with a caring lady. Stayed with her from about seven on."

"That's one deep GP."

"GP?"

"Grace point. The gospel is full of images and analogies, but sometimes one hits home more than the rest. The Bible says God sent His Son so we could become his children through adoption. He's now your dad. You're not an orphan but God's child. That's from Galatians 4. My own personal paraphrase." Nate lifted his hand to motion to Olivia but seemed to change his mind before she turned in their direction. He leaned forward, focusing back on Luke. "I love those verses, but having never been an orphan, it's an abstract concept to me. But you? You read that and the gospel isn't just a story but your greatest dreams come true. You've been adopted by Christ. You have a new heritage."

Olivia paused by the table and handed Luke his check without looking in Nate's direction.

Luke pulled out his wallet and drew out a twenty. "It's a good thing I was an orphan?"

"Never. But God can use it. Have you ever cost someone, well, a lot of money, and deserved nothing more than to be kicked to the curb? But instead, that person not only gave you a second chance but helped pay the debts you owed?"

"I don't think so."

Nate balled up a leftover straw wrapper. "I have. Long story, but my dad showed me what grace is really all about." He tossed the wrapper onto the pile of plates. "So when Colossians tells me that through the cross Jesus forgave all our sins and canceled the debt we couldn't pay, believe me, it's more than abstract good news. It hits me like a tidal wave. That's my GP."

Luke leaned back and crossed his arms over his chest, doing his best to take it all in. "Your grace point."

Nate slapped his hands together and pointed at him. "Exactly. Do I think it's a good thing I got myself into that situation? Nope. But like Joseph said, 'What was intended for evil, God meant for good.' Your lack of family can be an anchor dragging you down, or you can let it be your—"

"Grace point." An anchor was exactly how he'd always seen it. Could it be his grace point? His own GP?

"The person I'm meeting just showed up." Nate stood and waved at someone at the door and then dropped his card on the table in front of Luke. "Call me if you want to chat more. Or stop by on Sunday. Maybe I'm not as bad as everyone says."

Luke laughed and picked up the card. "I didn't stop going because of you. Life got . . . complicated."

"Happens. But that's usually when we need God to step in and uncomplicate things."

174

Luke examined the small card before sliding it into his wallet.

Adopted by God. A new heritage.

There was no doubt he believed in God, but could He uncomplicate Luke's life? The house, Hannah, his mother . . . His faith might not reach that far.

nine

Luke's opinion didn't mean much in this town, but he'd always thought it meant something to Hannah. He scanned the paper in front of him that outlined Hannah's plans for renovation, including the controlled burn. He resisted the urge to wad it up and march out of the room. At least he'd chosen a seat by the door.

The wooden pews, brown Berber carpet, and stained-glass window all brought back memories from his younger years. It had been a while since he'd been in the church. Not as long as some of these guys, but still, long enough.

Lottie Shoemaker had been diligent about Sunday attendance and he'd always gone, hoping to be that son she'd wanted. Probably not the best motivation to seek God, but something during those years stuck. His gaze traveled to the end of the altar on the left. In eighth grade he'd knelt there, committing his life to God. He huffed. What had he known about life in the eighth grade?

Still, he couldn't deny what a difference God had made. A peace. A home. Nate's comment returned to his mind. What had he called it? His grace point. Maybe there was something to that.

He'd walked away in college. Not a run of defiance. Just a slow wander until he couldn't remember why he'd wanted to go to church in the first place. He hadn't remembered until now. He stared at the altar again. Maybe home wasn't a house after all. He'd have to think on that.

The wooden pew creaked next to him as Nate sat down a few feet away. He didn't seem any happier about being here.

Nate nodded at him. "You know what this is about?"

"Nope." Luke shook his head. "But it got me to church."

Nate settled back and stretched out his arms. "Not quite what I meant. But I'll take it."

"Hey." Thomas slid in on his other side.

Luke did a double take. "What are you doing here? The notice said 'all single men.' "

"Do you know what they have planned?" Thomas nodded to where Hannah, Olivia, and Janie stood talking to the left. "I'm offering support to anyone opposing it."

That didn't sound good. Luke scanned the crowd. About thirty-five guys in all, give or take. He turned to Thomas to ask more, but Hannah stepped up to the front with Janie and Olivia at her side. She scanned the crowd until her eyes collided with Luke's. Her smile faltered. Maybe his mood showed on his face more than he'd meant it to.

"First, I want to thank you all for coming." Hannah's shaky voice rose above the crowd. "I know the signs, posters, and phone calls were a bit vague, but we wanted you to hear us out."

"Well, since you were asking for all single guys," Tony Evens shouted from the middle of the sanctuary, "we assume you three ladies are looking for dates."

Hannah's face reddened as a few whistles echoed in the room. "No."

"Please. I'd take a date with any of you three," a voice yelled from the crowd, and everyone laughed.

"Or all three," another deep voice added.

Luke's shoulders tensed. If he could tell who was talking, he'd give the guy a piece of his mind. Or a piece of something. Then again, the last thing he needed to do was start a fight in a church.

Nate's hand clenched until his knuckles whitened. Was he bothered because he was a pastor, or because he was interested in one of those three women?

Thomas leaned over and said with a harsh voice, "Exactly why this is a bad idea. Those girls don't know the guys they're dealing with."

Hannah ignored the comments. "Many of you have heard about the plans to restore the center of town. When it's done, the Manor will be an icon of Heritage and the surrounding park a great place for us to gather. The problem is all of this costs money."

"You want us to give you money?" That had to be Derek.

Hannah bit her lip, locking her eyes with Luke again. "No, we want to sell you off for money."

Luke blinked. *Come again?*

Hannah held up her hands to quiet the murmurs. "We want to hold a bachelor auction on the Fourth of July on the steps of the Manor. It'll be part of a larger bazaar to raise funds. The auction will be the main event."

"You think there are enough women in this town who will spend money on us?" Doubt laced Ted's voice.

"I knew no one would go for it." Thomas lowered his voice as he sat back and crossed his arms over his chest.

Janie stepped up to the mic. "We plan to promote this to the surrounding towns through social media and news media outlets. We hope to pull in tourists over the holiday weekend."

Derek stood, quieting the crowd. "You want us to agree to onetime dates from desperate women who could be from anywhere and who we'll probably never see again."

"That's not how I would put it, but . . ." Hannah swallowed, her hand gripping the paper tighter. "Yes."

The room erupted in cheers and laughter. A few

180

high fives. Luke shot a glance at Thomas and Nate. No high fives in this row. He leaned over and jerked his head toward the door. "I'm getting out of here."

He'd just reached the back with Thomas and Nate when Hannah's voice echoed in the room. "Wait!"

He paused with his hand on the door.

"I know that . . . some of you may have your doubts. But think about it, please."

Luke pushed out of the room as Hannah said something about needing portraits. Awesome. More reasons for her to hang with every single guy in town.

He kicked a rock down the sidewalk. "If I'm frustrated with Hannah . . . and Thomas here is still trying to convince himself he doesn't love Janie—"

"Hey—" Thomas sputtered.

"Whatever, dude. We both know it's true." He turned toward Nate with an eyebrow raised. "You'd better be in a bad mood about Olivia or there might be more of a problem than we realize."

Nate eyed him back. He stood a little taller as he crossed his arms over his chest. "I'm not inter-ested in Hannah or Janie, but I don't want to talk about it."

"Good. We specialize in repressed emotions." Luke rubbed the back of his neck. "Want to get out of here?"

181

"You play basketball?" Nate reached in his pocket and pulled out his keys.

"Yeah, but the only decent court around here is at my friend Jon's house and he's in Europe." Luke searched his brain for something else close by.

Nate jingled the keys. "Unless you're the new high school basketball coach."

"Nice." Thomas slapped Nate on the back. "I think this is the start of a beautiful friendship."

"Meet you there in fifteen." Luke turned toward his truck. "Thomas, you want a ride?"

"Sure." Thomas followed him to the truck and slid in. "I rode here with Hannah and I'm not waiting for her."

The church faded in his rearview mirror, along with Hannah and one more of her crazy ideas.

Jimmy skipped down the sidewalk with a girl. Maybe it was Sarah. Luke honked and waved, laughing at the memory of their conversation as they shoveled snow. *Watch out, kid, they'll break your heart.*

"Is that the Adamses' foster kid?"

"Jimmy."

"What do you think of adoption, Luke?"

Luke turned down Henderson Road. "I think I'm too old now, but thanks for the offer."

"No, would you adopt?"

"It'd have to be the right situation, but if that's what I felt was right, I wouldn't hesitate." He pulled the truck into his drive and cut the engine. "Why? You thinking about adopting?"

"Just thinking."

That wasn't an answer.

"How do *you* feel about adoption?"

Thomas shrugged. "I don't know. Would they feel like my kid? Or like I was just raising someone else's kid?"

A familiar weight settled on Luke's chest. That's who he'd always been to Mrs. Shoemaker. Timmy had been her son. Luke had just been someone else's kid. He pulled out the keys and flipped them in his hand. "Relationships are what you put into them. Mrs. Shoemaker never felt like my mom because she chose not to be my mom. But Chet always felt like an uncle, or what I guessed having an uncle would feel like. I wasn't any more related to Chet than I was to Mrs. Shoemaker, but it felt different because Chet made it different."

I hate it when you push me away. You push everyone away. Hannah's face flashed in his head. But that was different. Wasn't it?

Enough of this. Luke hopped out and slammed his door. It'd feel good to play ball.

How long was she expected to wait? Two weeks and Luke still hadn't signed up.

A distant banging interrupted Hannah's steps to the porch. She followed the sound around the back of the house to the treehouse. Their treehouse. Man, it had been a long time since she'd been up there.

"Luke." She stared up the ladder and the banging stopped.

He stared at her from the trapdoor. "What?"

Direct had always been best with Luke. "I don't have you signed up yet for the auction. I need—"

"I'm not doing it." He disappeared again.

"What?" A few others had said no, but Luke had to sign up. It wasn't just Olivia's bet with Thomas. Luke always had her back.

The hammer started again.

The last time she'd been in that treehouse was in high school. The day they'd kissed. Their only kiss.

She kicked the base of the tree. "Luke!"

He paused his work but didn't look at her again. "I'm not changing my mind."

This wasn't working. She dropped her bag by the trunk, shoved the papers she needed him to sign under her arm, and reached for the first rung of their homemade ladder. When no cracking wood followed, she climbed until she could reach the rope to pull herself inside.

The place was smaller than she remembered, and with Luke taking up two-thirds of the floor the only place for her to go was right next to him.

Afternoon light flooded the windows and illuminated the walls they'd decorated over the years. All the photos, drawings, and graphite still

184

remained, but they were weathered and faded. She ran her fingers along the low ceiling that Luke had painted for her. Cobalt blue with stars dotted everywhere. He'd known she'd loved the stars, and after her mom left he'd painted it just to cheer her up.

"I'm not changing my mind." Luke positioned a board into the corner that had been damaged in a storm a few years back.

Hannah dropped her hand from the ceiling. "Please, Luke."

"No." He grabbed a nail from a box, held it in place, and drove it in with three solid hits.

When he reached for another nail, she pulled the box out of his reach and shut it. "Why?"

Luke stared at the box, then shrugged, sat back, and reached for his Coke, taking a large gulp from the can.

Hannah dropped the box back on the floor, and the ring of shifting nails echoed in the confined space. "That isn't good enough."

He rolled the pop can back and forth in his hands. "Why does it matter, Hannah?"

"It just does."

"You have plenty of guys signed up." He downed the rest of the soda and set it aside. "Why do you care if I do?"

Why did she care? Her fingers picked at the weathered wood floor. "You're a big part of this town."

He let out a humorless laugh and reached for his hammer again. "Not really."

"You are, and this town looks up to you. We need the money and you're one of the . . . best-looking guys in town." She turned away. She'd kept her tone casual enough, but one look at her flushed face and he'd see right through her.

"Not buying it."

Was he serious? She pushed the papers toward him and pulled a pen from her pocket. "Well, it's true, and I need you to sign up."

He pushed them back toward her. "No, you don't."

"Please."

"Give me one good reason."

"I need to have someone to bid on!" Hannah had never wanted to suck a sentence back into her mouth more in her life. If only she could hide right about now. But where could she go? They were in a four-foot-by-four-foot box.

He stilled and leaned back, studying her with an unreadable expression. "You're going to bid on me?"

She focused on the papers in her hand again. "I mean, if I bid on anyone else, it would start rumors."

He didn't say anything for a long time. Then took the papers and started reading.

She stared at the ceiling again. That was a mistake. How could she keep her emotions in check? It was here under her starry sky that she'd fallen for him. Not the day he'd painted it, but one day at a time. And it was under her starry sky that he'd kissed her.

Hannah's eyes flicked back to Luke. His eyes burned intensely, and something in his expression stole Hannah's breath. But she had to remember the days that followed that kiss, when he'd given up on them, on her. Just like her mom.

She broke eye contact and handed him a pen.

Luke scrawled his name at the bottom. The air seemed to have grown thicker and warmer in the space of two minutes.

A photo pinned to the wall wiggled in the slight breeze. The corners curled in and age had yellowed it, but it was still one of her favorites. She reached up and pulled it off the wall for a closer look. It had been taken their junior year after a football game. She'd been smiling at the camera and Luke had been smiling at her.

This photo had given her hope for the first time that the humongous crush on Luke that she'd been nursing for years wasn't as one-sided as she'd always thought.

He held the papers back out to her with a teasing grin. "Are you going to break out your mad cash to bid on me?"

She yanked the papers from his hand. "Don't call it that. It's emergency money, and you've got to be crazy to think I'd bid three hundred dollars on you. Besides, I never said I was planning to win the bid."

"Wait, so you got me to sign before you told me I could end up with anyone?" Luke leaned back and started gathering his tools, dropping them in his toolbox.

"No backing out now." Hannah gripped the rope and lowered herself down.

"Do you have a second? I want to show you something."

"Sure." Her voice wavered a little and she resisted the urge to kick the tree again.

They made their way to the porch without a word, and Luke disappeared through the door for only a moment before he reappeared with a folder in his hand.

"My birth certificate was in the box that we found in the wall." He extended the file to her. "I'm sorry I didn't let you see this."

Hannah took the folder and opened it. "Don't you have a copy already?"

"Yes, but the other day I remembered my mother's name was Ann—I could swear. But the name on the certificate is Sarah, and I was trying to see if I could find anything on it. It didn't work." He shoved his hands in his pockets.

Hannah glanced at the information, pausing on the photo. "You were so cute."

"Were? You just said I was one of the best-looking guys in town."

"I should have never told you that." She pulled out his birth certificate and read it over. "You know, if you hired—"

"No." Luke pulled the file from her hand. "I can't afford to hire anyone. And I won't let you spend your money on it either. So don't ask. Besides, I'm still deciding how much I want to invest in this search. My mother died when I was a kid, no matter what her name was. That's the end of the story."

Her smile faded as his hand tightened on the file. No matter how strong Luke was for her or tried to be for others, part of him was just a young boy who'd lost his parents, lost in a big, lonely world.

"That's all. Thanks for listening." He checked his watch and turned back toward the house. "I have to go get ready for work. I'll see you around."

Then he was gone before she could say she was sorry, ask questions, or even offer him a hug. Then again, the way her mind was going today, a hug might have been a bad idea.

Hannah pulled out her phone and tapped Janie's name.

"Hello?"

"Luke's on board. Tell Thomas you need Friday off." Hannah fished in her bag for her keys but found a card instead.

"I don't have a date, Hannah."

"Thomas doesn't need to know that." She pulled the card out, flipped it around in her fingers, and studied it. *Alfred Mathis, Private Investigator.* "It'll be good for him. He needs to know you've moved on."

"You want me to lie to him?"

"No. You don't have to tell him who you're going out with. You simply tell him you want the night off to go out, and his imagination will do the rest." Hannah slid into her car.

"I don't know."

Hannah tapped the card against the steering wheel. "Sometimes those closest to you can't see what's best for them. Besides, you need a night off. You never said you were going on a date— Olivia did."

"I . . . suppose."

"Just think about it." Hannah ended the call and lifted Al's card again. Luke might not want to investigate his past, but she knew he'd never really be free of it until he did.

Besides, he only said that he didn't want her to spend her money on an investigator. Al's offer was free of charge. Like she'd told Janie, sometimes people can't always see what's best for them.

Janie's date didn't bother him. Not one bit. Thomas smacked the frying patties with his spatula a little harder than necessary, then pulled a basket of onion rings out of the fryer and hooked it to the grease drainer. Their savory scent traveled through the air. He forced his mind to Madison. They had a date later. Maybe they'd watch the latest Bond movie. See, he had good dates too.

It was Uncle Donny's call earlier that was really bugging him, not Janie. His uncle said they wouldn't be back until June, and now he was stuck in this town an extra month.

If Janie wanted to go out with every guy in town in that time, it wasn't his business. He reached for a stack of plates and laid them out on the prep table, each clanging against the metal. He reached for the buns and worked on the twist tie. She could go out every night and it wouldn't bother him as long as she was here to do her job when it was time. He was her boss, nothing more.

Why wasn't this untying? He studied the wires. They were curled into knots. Maybe he'd twisted too far. He started to work it back but that didn't help much. He grabbed the side of the plastic and pulled. Buns spilled out across the prep table. Awesome.

He separated the bottom buns, dropped them on the plates, and started adding the burgers.

Janie pushed through the door, hung up her apron, and washed her hands at the small sink. "I'm leaving in about ten minutes. It looks like it will be a slow night for you."

"Actually, it's busier than I expected it to be, so

I think I need you to stay." Okay, so maybe her date bothered him a little.

Janie's brows rose as she eyed the five customers. "Noel is out there. Between the two of you, I think you've got it covered."

"What if a crowd comes?" He waved his spatula in the air. "Did you think about that?"

"A crowd? In Heritage? At seven o'clock?" She reached for her purse, slung it over her shoulder, and pulled out her keys. "But if a big crowd does come, make sure you only let sixty-five in at a time. Any more than that and we'd be over fire code."

The bell above the door chimed.

Janie's eyes sprang wide. "That must be them now. The hordes arriving for your burgers and my pie." She turned her back on him.

"Who is it?" Thomas blurted out the words before he could stop himself.

Her brow wrinkled as she peeked through the window in the door. "Mr. Fair, and he appears to be alone. You're saved from the masses a little longer." She put her hand on the swinging door. "Now, if you don't mind, I—"

"No. Who's your date with?" His voice cracked, and he cringed at how weak he sounded.

Janie stood motionless. Her back to him. After what seemed forever she turned and stared at him with a hardened expression. "Does it matter?"

His pulse thudded. It didn't. Not really. He

squeezed his eyes shut. But it did. He focused on her again. "I just asked who it was. You owe me that."

Janie marched across the kitchen toward him, fire in her eyes. "I owe you what?"

Her words were whispered, but with the venom they were delivered with, she might as well have been screaming.

"Uh, I just mean—"

"No." She jabbed a finger in his chest as she clenched her jaw. "I owe you nothing. Five years we dated. Five. Then you up and dump me with no more of a reason than 'It's the right thing to do, Janie.' And then you're engaged to Madison before I even return from Paris."

"All I said—"

"No." Tears welled in her eyes. "You broke my heart, Thomas. I owe you nothing. I can go out with every guy in this town if I want and I don't have to tell you about any of it." She turned and flew out of the kitchen.

He stared at the swinging door until Noel pushed her way back through. "Fire on the grill!"

Thomas whipped around. Flames licked across the grill, dangerously close to the wall. He'd let too much grease pile up. His pulse soared as he snatched the fire extinguisher from the wall and snuffed out the few threats. White foam covered the metal and carried to the prep table. He eyed the burgers and buns covered in fluff and shook his head. Maybe Janie's dating bothered him more than a little.

Noel stood in the same spot, wide-eyed, mouth hanging open.

"Tell everyone that we're sorry, but the grill will be closed tonight." He eyed the time before running his fingers through his hair. Who knew what the health code required after spraying fire retardant on the cooking surfaces? "And make a sign for tomorrow too. I have a feeling it will take me all day tomorrow to fix this."

But that was just it. He couldn't fix this. The problem wasn't the grill. The problem was Janie was dating again and he couldn't do a thing to stop her.

ten

Hannah rubbed her fingers together for some warmth as she hopped out of Thomas's truck and approached the first condemned house. She pulled her coat tighter and expelled a sigh. Twenty days into April should not be cold enough to freeze water. Where had this front come from?

Of course, rising at dawn didn't help. But she wanted to catch the houses with the morning sun. Her fingers shook as she withdrew a set of keys from her pocket and found the right one. The metal bit into her fingers as she forced the lock to turn. The creaking door and dim room added to the creep factor.

"Boo."

Hannah screamed and whipped around, nearly smacking Janie in the process. "Really?"

"Payback for getting me up on the first Saturday I don't have to open." Janie followed her in, rubbing her arms. "Why did you want to come back here?"

"I'm creating a photo journal so the judges can appreciate how much demolishing these houses benefits the town." She lifted the camera that hung around her neck and eyed the room through the lens. "I need to get some shots before the asbestos removal crew comes through."

195

"You want photos of an old stained couch with a melon-sized hole chewed out of it? And let me say, whatever made that better be long gone." Janie released a shiver. "And don't forget the lovely scent of rot and mildew mingling in the air. You should make the photos scratch and sniff."

Hannah pulled back the curtain to let in more light. She lifted her camera, adjusted the aperture, and snapped a few pictures. She flipped on the display and held it out to Janie. "See?"

Janie shoved her hands in her pockets. "Why did you drop your art major? I assumed you'd just lost your passion for art, but now it's clear that isn't the case."

Lost her passion? If only she could. Hannah stepped over a broken chair and ignored the crunch under her foot. "My mom didn't find much use for her art in Heritage."

"You've let the fact that your mom left hang over you too long. When we hold the broken pieces of our lives too close, they'll cut us up inside."

Hannah squatted to see the room from a new angle. "I should just forget?"

"Give the pieces to God. See what He can do with them."

Just give them to God? Like it was that easy.

"Don't you think I've tried?" Hannah moved an old pop can out of the way. Then lined up the next shot.

"Do you wait on Him, or do you push forward with your own answer?"

Is that what she did? Hannah snapped a photo, then another.

Janie leaned against the wall, but a slight creaking sent her scampering back toward the door. "Why do you have Thomas's truck, anyway?"

Hannah ran her hand across the back of the faded green couch that screamed 1949. "I didn't know if there'd be anything I'd want to keep in here."

"In here?" Janie dusted off her hands. "That's being optimistic. I've got to go soon. Are you almost done?"

Hannah nodded and followed Janie out. The second house wasn't worth their time. The last house on the end had more junk than the rest, more stench than the rest, and even a metal spring sticking out of the side of an old wingback chair. "Maybe I have enough photos."

Janie clapped and hopped off the porch. "I agree."

Hannah started to close the door when a black metal stove nestled in the corner caught her eye. "What in the world?"

"No, Hannah. Come back. You said we were done." Janie's voice carried in from the front lawn.

Hannah stepped over a broken pot and ran her hand across the old cast iron. She was no expert on antiques, but it looked old.

Janie leaned in the front door. "We're done. I heard you say it."

Hannah waved her over. "It looks like the stove from the photos of the one-room schoolhouse that I saw at town hall. Then again, there's a chance all potbelly stoves from this era looked somewhat similar."

Janie dodged a dresser that had been tipped on its side. "You want a picture of it?"

"I want to keep it." Hannah gripped the cold metal and leaned into it. It was bolted down, but one of Luke's tools would take care of that. "We could put it in the Manor when we make it a museum."

Janie glanced at her watch. "I have to run and change and then get to work. How about we do this later?"

"Go. I won't be much longer."

"You sure it's worth it?" Janie's face wrinkled as she eyed the room.

"Yes. Now go. I'll be fine." Hannah waved off Janie as she evaluated the distance from the stove to the door. If she could get a few people to help move it, she could stick it in the bed of Thomas's truck. But she needed to make this as easy as possible, or she'd have a lot of people who saw it like Janie did—not worth it. And heavy, cold metal was hard on the hands. At least she could make a clear path to start.

Hannah flexed her fingers against the numbness setting in. It wasn't like she could turn on the heater. Or could she? She had a space heater at home, but that required electricity. Her dad had owned a portable kerosene heater he'd used to warm the garage. Thomas still used it occasionally. She could grab that and be back and still have time to get the stove out before the house showing this afternoon.

Twenty minutes later, she'd returned with the heater.

She slipped out of the truck as Jimmy skipped toward her on the sidewalk, his coat unzipped and his shoes untied. Luke walked a few paces behind, his cap pulled low and his hands deep in his pockets.

Hannah leaned against the bed of the truck. "What are you two up to this morning?"

Luke's head snapped up and a slow smile curled his lips.

Hannah's heart offered a little hop, and she chastised herself. Since the treehouse, she had lectured herself over and over to keep her thoughts in check. They were friends. Period. But as she looked at him now with those faded jeans low on his hips and the gray sweatshirt emphasizing the width of his shoulders, her brain was ready to check out.

Luke eyed the house behind her. His expression revealed nothing.

"I beat Luke in basketball, and now he owes me

ice cream." Jimmy ran farther down the sidewalk to the corner and jumped on the back of Otis. The hippo had moved there last week, facing the row of houses as if he'd come to say goodbye.

"Isn't it too cold for ice cream?"

"It's never too cold for ice cream." Jimmy slid down the hippo's shiny nose.

Luke's gaze followed Jimmy. "Careful." He turned back to Hannah and opened his mouth as if to say something but paused.

"Come on, Luke." Jimmy waved him over from where he stood on Otis's back.

Maybe she should ask him to help with the stove.

"Be safe." Luke nodded once at Hannah and turned away. He jogged to catch up with Jimmy, then the pair crossed 2nd Street to Donny's as Jimmy rattled off his favorite flavors.

Maybe she'd call him once it was warmed up inside. Hannah pulled the heater from the truck and carried it into the house. Five minutes later it was lit, and the musty odor had been replaced by the sharp scent of kerosene. Could she get carbon monoxide poisoning from a kerosene heater? She wasn't taking any chances. She opened a window a crack to let a little fresh air in, then held her hands over the warming stove. Her fingers thanked her as the warmth seeped back into them.

She'd have to give the cast-iron stove a bit

of time to warm up, but if she timed it right, it should be warm enough about the time Luke passed by again. Maybe she'd text him to make sure she didn't miss him. She pulled her phone from her pocket. Dead battery. She'd forgotten to charge it again.

She leaned over and gave the couch a shove. It moved an inch. She coughed again and stood. Maybe Luke could help move that too.

She stepped into the other room. This unit definitely had more unique junk than the others. An old wringer washtub sat in the corner, a broom and rags sticking out the top. Maybe they could save that too. She snapped a few photos before dropping the camera back around her neck.

An unfamiliar, bitter odor filled the air and stung her eyes as a haze thicker than the dust swirled in the room.

What in the world? Hannah hurried to the main room and froze. The breeze from the partially opened window had blown the bottom half of the threadbare cotton curtains over the heater. Orange and yellow flames licked up the material, reaching out and igniting the peeled-back edges of the wallpaper.

Fire!

Water!

Wait, there was no water in the house. She yanked her phone from her pocket, but it tumbled to the floor as her fingers shook. She crouched and felt around for it. Her stinging eyes refused to stay open. Had her phone slid across the wood floor? Not that it mattered. It was dead.

Across the room, orange flames crawled across the ceiling, and a section of ignited wallpaper dropped on the old couch.

Stop. Think. People died because they panicked. She couldn't fix this. Couldn't stop the fire. She had to get out. She coughed against the thickening smoke. She had to get out fast.

Hannah covered her mouth with the collar of her jacket, staggered to the front door, and then bolted across the road and shoved through the double doors of the bank. "Call . . . 911." She drew a gasp of air. "Fire . . . across . . . street."

Smoke leaking out one of the windows of the house was now visible through the bank's front window. The trail lifted skyward, growing by the second. She'd wanted the old houses to burn, but not like this. Luke's words of warning flooded her mind. This was no longer going to be a controlled burn.

He hated leaving Hannah to work in those houses alone, but there was no way Luke could bail on Jimmy to help her. This kid needed to know some adults could be trusted.

Ice cream dribbled down Jimmy's chin and a line of hot fudge rimmed his lips.

"Are you sure you can finish that?" Luke picked

up his spoon and pretended to reach for the mess of a sundae.

Jimmy pulled it closer as he offered Luke the evil eye. "Don't even think about it. I won fair and square."

Luke laughed and dropped his spoon. Fair and square? Well, that was a matter of perspective, but he wouldn't let Jimmy know that he may have been a little off on his game on purpose. At least for some of the shots. For others he'd really been off on his game. No doubt a certain brunette and the mixed signals she'd offered the other day had something to do with it.

What had she meant when she'd said she wanted to bid on him? The conversation had echoed through his mind on repeat ever since, and he still couldn't make sense of it. Did that mean she wanted a date with him? Then again, she'd also followed up with the fact that she hadn't planned on winning the bid. So maybe he was reading too much into it.

He eyed the front door, willing her to walk in. Partly because he wanted to see her and partly because he wanted to know she was out of those houses. If she wasn't done by the time he walked Jimmy home, he'd drag her with him. Why she needed to record every detail with her camera was beyond him. But arguing with her when her mind was made up was pointless.

"Call 911!" Olivia shouted as she pointed out

the front window. "There's a fire across the street in one of those old houses."

Luke jumped to his feet and bolted toward the door. Halfway across the diner, he paused and pointed back at Jimmy. "You stay put until I come for you." Locking eyes with Janie as he passed, he added, "Watch Jimmy. Hannah's over there."

Luke shoved through the diner's door and scanned the area. No sign of Hannah anywhere. He broke into a sprint and closed the forty yards in a matter of seconds. "Hannah!" he yelled into the house. But the roar of the fire muffled his words.

The front door of the house stood open as black smoke billowed out, but it had been standing open when he'd walked by earlier, so that didn't offer much hope.

He couldn't lose her.

He drew the corner of his shirt over his face and bent low to avoid the worst of the smoke, not that it helped much. Why couldn't fire offer more visibility, like on television shows? Real fire was unbearably hot, and real smoke was an oppressive, lung-torturing blackness.

He plunged in and dropped to his knees. If he found Hannah now, she'd be passed out on the floor. His hope started to rise when an initial search of the first ten feet revealed nothing but increasing darkness and heat. But another swipe connected his hand with her phone. No way would she leave her phone.

Luke's stomach churned as he resisted the urge to call out to Hannah. Doing so would only expose his lungs to more smoke. Even so, his lungs burned as if the fire was inside his body, his thoughts muddled. If only he'd been in full gear with a mask and an oxygen tank. Luke gave one last desperate swipe across the wood floor, gritting his teeth as a piercing pain ripped through his arm into his shoulder. Sticky liquid covered his hands.

He struggled to stay conscious. He couldn't leave Hannah. But what good would he be if he passed out in here? It'd slow the rescue efforts. If she even still had a chance.

She couldn't be gone! He needed her. He loved her. Why hadn't he ever told her? Financial differences and social classes suddenly seemed beyond silly in the face of this fire and death.

If he didn't get out soon he'd die himself. But which way was out? Clinging to his last shred of control, he willed aside the surging panic and forced his eyes open once more.

Was that light?

It could be a window, and if he couldn't break it, then he was a goner. But he had to try. Luke scrambled across the floor, finding the phone again. This had to be the right way. He gripped the hard plastic and continued his crawl until the dim light grew to the bright blue of the sky.

He'd barely made it to the porch when muffled shouts met his ears. He crumpled onto the grass, but hands lifted him to his feet once more. The words people were saying didn't make sense. He tried to stand up and ask about Hannah, but his lungs wouldn't work. Even in the open, he couldn't find enough air.

Shaking off the paramedic, he scanned the house again. The structure was fully engulfed now, and the flames were running up the side of the next house.

"Hannah." All that came out was a hoarse wheeze, followed by another coughing fit that dropped him to his knees. The ache in his chest dwarfed the rawness of his lungs.

A couple sets of hands tried to lift him onto the stretcher. He pushed them away with every last ounce of strength he had left.

"Luke, calm down. You need oxygen," Ted's voice shouted from his left. "And they need to look at your shoulder."

His weakened muscles gave way. "Person . . . in . . ."

Ted turned to face the buildings. "Hannah Thornton assured dispatch they were empty."

Hannah called them in?

Then her face appeared among the gathering crowd. She'd made it out safely.

Luke closed his eyes. Pain settled in as the

adrenaline faded out. Hannah was safe. Wonderful Hannah. Beautiful Hannah. Alive. Safe.

Thomas had backed his truck away from the houses, then started to suit up. By local law, they had to have four men to work a fire. By the time enough of the crew was there, the second house was fully ablaze.

Chief Wilks's voice came over the radio of the paramedic next to Luke. "We're going to let them burn, boys. Might as well save us time later. Let's just keep the third one from catching. Two is enough for now."

The world grew dark as a plastic mask was dropped over Luke's face.

The chief's voice burst through the speaker again. "Get those people back. The wind is shifting. We need to clear the street."

The explosion of glass echoed through the town as the flames reached higher into the sky. The heat grabbed at them, and the paramedics scrambled to back up the equipment.

Hannah may be safe, but the town wasn't. Flames licked at the side of the third house as hot cinders floated toward the Manor. If that old wood caught, it could burn the whole town down.

Lord, help us.

Janie could pretend all she wanted, but she was far from over Thomas. Her heart had stopped the second he'd run out the door to help with the fire, and it wouldn't restart until she could see with her own eyes that he was safe. Until then, she'd continue the never-ending game of UNO with Jimmy.

She dropped a yellow 6 on the stack, trying not to let her eyes swing to the door one more time. It didn't work. The diner's once beautiful awning dangled, covering the picture window like a charred piece of Swiss cheese. She shuddered. It had been close.

When the wind had shifted, they'd evacuated 2nd Street, Richard Street, and Teft Road. All Janie could think was to keep hold of Jimmy. The next hours had been a nightmare. The men battled to keep the wind from carrying the fire across 2nd Street as all three houses burned with a vengeance, showering the downwind buildings with embers. They'd even called in two neighboring departments for backup.

"Uno." Jimmy added a yellow 3 and eyed her as he peeked behind his remaining card. He'd taken the day in stride, and when they gave the all clear for the road again, Janie had brought him here. What else was she supposed to do? Who knew when his foster parents would get home? She'd left a note on the door that Jimmy was here, but according to him, they'd be out of town the whole day.

Janie tossed a blue 3 on the pile.

"You forgot to call Uno. That's two cards."

Janie blinked at her one card. "You caught me."

Her phone rang and she snatched it up. "Hey, Mom."

"Have you heard how Luke is?" Her mother's soothing voice came over the phone.

"Hannah followed the ambulance to the hospital, but no word yet."

Her mom hesitated. "And Thomas?"

"I've heard he's fine." She sent a reassuring smile toward Jimmy, who stared at her instead of his card. "I gotta go. I'll call you later."

"Out. I win." Jimmy tossed his last card down. "Did Luke go to the hospital?"

"Yes." She gathered up the cards and added them back to the box. "You want an ice cream sundae?"

"I already had one today."

Janie patted his hand as she stood. "Some days are two-ice-cream-sundae kind of days."

The boy jumped up. "Yay."

"First you need an apron." She grabbed the smallest they had and dropped it around his neck. The bottom of it brushed his feet.

"Now I scoop." Jimmy stretched toward the scoop but she stopped his hand.

"Now you wash your hands." Janie ushered Jimmy toward the sink and found him a stool. She poured a little soap on his hands and adjusted the water. "Now scrub."

The boy's lips twisted, but he obeyed. "Smells like flowers."

She handed him a towel and he wiped his hands.

He ran back to the ice cream freezer, picked the scoop out of the warm water, and jabbed it into the mint chocolate chip.

Janie added a little weight to get it moving, but he finished it off. "You keep this up and you could have a job here someday."

The bell jingled and she spun to face the door.

Thomas. Her eyes roamed over him. He was okay. Whole. Breathing. He'd abandoned his gear, but his face was still shadowed with ash and darkened by smoke. His floppy hair crisscrossed in several directions on his head. He was a mess. A beautiful mess.

Tears blurred her vision, and she didn't bother pushing them away. "Everything okay?"

His eyes studied her, consumed her. Maybe it had been an eye-opening night for both of them.

He took a hesitant step toward her. His Adam's apple bobbed and he cleared his throat. "Fire's out. All four buildings—gone." The rawness of fighting fires for hours had weakened his voice.

"Four?" The Manor had burned. Hannah would be crushed. "And Luke?"

"In the hospital a few days, but he'll be fine."

"Whoa. You're dirty." Jimmy eyed him from head to foot. "If you want ice cream, she'll make you wash your hands."

Thomas's lips turned up in a smile. "Good to know." He looked back at Janie. "Why didn't you leave when they evacuated the area?"

"We did, but we returned when the all clear was given. I had to close up."

Thomas's brows pinched. "But I could have—"

Janie nodded toward Jimmy.

"Right." He focused on Jimmy. "Ice cream, huh? I could use one of those. How about you scoop me some cookies and cream."

"I'm on it." Jimmy held up the scoop and then stabbed it into the ice cream. "But I bet she'll still make you wash. And dude, it smells like flowers."

Thomas laughed as he stepped toward the kitchen sink. "Good to know."

A few minutes later, Thomas emerged from the kitchen with his face and arms scrubbed pink. His hairline, wet from the scrubbing, twisted in a few unruly cowlicks.

"Ice cream's ready." Jimmy hopped down and carried his bowl over to their booth with pride.

Ten minutes later all three scraped the bottom of their dishes as they told jokes.

The bell above the door jingled again as a middle-aged couple entered. The strain on their faces disappeared as soon as they spotted Jimmy.

"You found me!" Jimmy jumped out of his chair and ran to them, hugging the man around the legs. "I knowed you would."

"You must be Mr. and Mrs. Adams." Janie followed and extended her hand. "Hi, I'm Janie Mathews. I'm so sorry—"

"No, thank you." The woman shook Janie's hand. "We had to go to Grand Rapids and Luke was supposed to have him all day. How is Luke?"

"Stable." Janie ruffled Jimmy's hair. "And this guy was no trouble. It was fun."

"I beat her in UNO."

"I'd expect nothing less." Mrs. Adams hugged Jimmy before turning to Janie. "Do I owe you anything?"

"No, that was too much fun to be work." Janie waved good night as they disappeared out the door.

Thomas stepped over to the cash register to close it out. Not that it would take long after today. "It was fun to see you laugh tonight."

Janie grabbed the change and started counting it out. "That's one awesome kid. Makes me want to adopt him."

"What?" His fingers paused over the adding machine.

The expression on his face was so intense that she fumbled with the quarters. "I mean, he's a great kid who needs parents, and . . . Why are you looking at me like that?"

"No reason." He added the last few receipts and handed her the slip before he turned toward the kitchen. "Why don't you go home? I'll close up. It's not like we'll be open tomorrow anyway."

"I don't mind helping." Janie checked her number against the amount he'd given her. Was he giving her a way out, or did he want her to go? She gathered the ice cream dishes, carried them to the kitchen, and dropped them in the sink where Thomas stood, filling it with hot water.

Her hand brushed his in the water and she yanked it out, sending a cascade of bubbles through the air. "Sorry."

He didn't move. She chanced a peek at him. His eyes were locked on her.

She caught the corner of her lower lip between her teeth and allowed her focus to roam his face. A smudge of soot shadowed his jaw and disappeared behind his ear. "You still have black from the fire behind your ear."

He reached up with bubbles on his hands. "Here?" Suds dripped a trail down his neck and over his collarbone and darkened the neckline of his well-fitting T-shirt.

She sucked in a lungful of air to cool the heat building within her. She reached for a clean rag on the shelf above them and rubbed at the spot. Her hands shook. "Got it."

His gaze shifted to her lips. Time stopped as Janie's lungs refused to work. As if the past year hadn't happened, every cell in her body ached for him, called to him. His hand settled on her waist, and his eyes locked with hers again, something raw and vulnerable swirling in their depths.

His fingers toyed with the skin at her side as his focus dropped back to her mouth. He dipped his head to the side, as he'd always done just before he kissed her.

Her eyelids fluttered closed as she lifted her chin, inviting him home. Finally. "I've missed you so much."

Thomas stiffened and jumped back, setting her off balance as he did. "Janie, I'm . . ."

Janie's eyes popped open as she swallowed down nausea.

He shoved his hands in his pockets as he turned away. "I never . . ."

"Never what? Never should have broken up with me? Or never should have gotten my hopes up?" Janie bit her tongue to keep from saying more. But it wasn't like after closing her eyes and leaning toward him she had anything left to hide.

His eyes landed on her and his intensity consumed her, begged her to understand. Understand what? That he was committed to someone else? Oh, she understood that, but she didn't understand why.

He broke eye contact and took another step back. "I gotta go." He bolted for the kitchen door.

A few seconds later the front door slammed, sending the familiar chime through the diner and a chill through her skin. At least she had little doubt where she stood—rejected by Thomas once again and left to clean up the mess.

eleven

She'd turned out even worse than her mother. Hannah sprayed Otis's brass nose with the blue cleaning solution once more and rubbed it with the rag. Most of the ash had come off his brass body, but would he ever be the same? Would Heritage be the same? The beautiful Manor, gone . . . burned away with the rest.

Hannah returned to her car and tossed the rag and spray bottle through the window into the passenger seat. She'd wanted to make the town beautiful, refreshed. This was a graveyard.

Every hope of restoring that beautiful old building—gone. What was she going to do now? The entire plan for the contest had been centered on the Manor as a key piece.

Hannah wiped at the corners of her eyes. The beautiful canopies of Donny's and the rest of the storefronts all along 2nd Street and Teft Road were a tattering of cobwebs. When the wind had shifted during the fire, it had been all the firemen could do to keep the flames from jumping the street. But the damage was inevitable.

Aunt Lucy and Uncle Donny couldn't afford to fix this. Insurance would cover most of it, but that still left the deductible. She'd have to pay for it out of the project money. The project money that had been meant to fix up the center square of the town. The square that was now empty all the way to Henderson Road, making Luke's place visible from the diner. She'd made a black hole in the center of town that now sucked the life out of her project.

All for what? A stupid potbelly stove that had made it through the fire unharmed anyway. She picked up a pebble from the edge of the charred ground and whipped it at the stove. The metal released a resounding bong. She nudged the remains of the washtub with her toe and coughed against the thick stench of wet soot that wafted up. Only the tub was left—the wringer and legs had burned away.

At least no one had been killed. She leaned against her faded blue Volkswagen, her fingernails digging into her palms. It could've been worse—so much worse.

Bile rose in her throat like it had when Luke emerged from the fire with blood dripping down one hand, her phone clutched in the other. He'd ended up with twelve stitches in his shoulder, not to mention almost losing his life, all because of her carelessness, her stubbornness, and her faithlessness in him.

She'd been by to visit him every day, but he'd always been resting. She didn't wake him because she was terrified of his response. He'd been right and she'd been wrong. So wrong it almost cost him his life. A fresh set of tears filled her eyes. This time she didn't bother to brush them away.

She pulled her new phone from her purse. Her finger hovered over his name. No, some things needed to be done in person.

Hannah followed the sidewalk around the burned land to Luke's house and knocked on his door. After a minute or two, the door opened with its familiar creak.

"Hannah?" Luke's rough voice testified to the smoke damage.

She yanked back the screen door. "I'm so sorry."

He stepped back and widened the door. His curls were wilder than normal and his gray T-shirt was wrinkled.

She followed him to the kitchen and sat at the table but stood up again. Spitz nudged her hand for a rub and she obliged. Anything to keep her hands from shaking.

"Water?" He pulled down a couple of glasses from the cupboard.

She twisted her hands in front of her as a fresh sob broke, choking her. Why was she shaking? She'd come to thank him and say she was sorry, not stand here and blubber. Maybe she needed a deep breath—or two. "You were right about everything. About the houses, about me being too pushy and not listening—"

"Hannah . . ." He leaned his back against the counter.

She had to get this out before she started sobbing again. "I wish I could take it all back. I wish I was a better friend—"

"Hannah." The word came out firm but muted by his raw throat.

"I know you must hate me but—"

"Hannah." Luke crossed the kitchen as he spoke, coming to stop right in front of her, his dark eyes intense. His right hand reached up, his fingers trailing along her jaw as his thumb wiped away a tear that still clung to her cheek. "I promise. I don't hate you."

The pad of his thumb traced its way to her bottom lip as his left hand landed at her waist, offering the slightest tug. Hannah's heart pounded as she let herself be pulled against him. "But I'm difficult and I'm—"

His lips brushed across hers, cutting off her words. His mouth, cool at first and tasting of orange ChapStick, softened and warmed as every cell in her body stood up and sang.

Her breathing quickened as he slid one hand behind her neck. Leaning back an inch, his eyes sent a silent question as if asking if he'd overstepped. She couldn't answer. He'd managed to steal every thought and word from her head. Instead, she gripped the front of his T-shirt and pulled him closer to capture his mouth once more.

Her reaction must have been all the encouragement he needed. He leaned closer and deepened the kiss. His hands slid down her back and then back up to her shoulders. And when he began kissing along her jawline toward her neck, his arms were the only things keeping her upright.

Her skin hummed and her mind clouded. All her memories of their one shared kiss hadn't done him justice. It had been wonderful, but that kiss was with Luke, an uncertain seventeen-year-old boy. This was Luke the man. And this man knew exactly what he wanted.

As if he was thinking the same thing, his fingers began to weave through the back of her hair as he pulled her closer, possessing her lips once again yet leaving enough room for her to push away.

Pushing away was the last thing on her mind. Hannah slid her hands over his shoulders and leaned further into him. When a deep groan emerged from his chest, her fingers instinctively tightened on his shoulders.

"Ahh!" Luke's head pulled back as his face whitened, and Spitz rushed over to lick his hand.

"Your stitches!" Hannah sprang backward. "I'm so sorry. See, I can't do anything right."

His lips curled on one side, showing off the ever-present dimple. "I believe you were doing it very right before that."

Warmth crawled up Hannah's neck and spread across her cheeks. Luke had kissed her. Kissed. Her.

Her heartbreak after their last kiss flashed

through her mind. But things were different now, weren't they? They'd better be, because she wasn't sure she'd ever recover from that kiss.

"Are you all right?" Luke shot her a quick look as he examined his bandage.

"Fine." More than fine. She just needed to take it slow. Yes, slow was good.

He reached across the space between them and snagged one of her fingers, pulling her back to him. His phone vibrated on the counter. "They can wait."

"You should at least see who it is." Hannah ducked under his arm and reached for his phone.

He tugged her around the waist and pulled her closer as he took the phone. His eyes narrowed on the display, his hold loosening. "Chet? He never calls. Hold that thought." Luke landed another brief kiss on her lips before answering the call. "Hello?"

Hannah backed up and reached for the glass of water Luke had poured for her. She needed water. Maybe oxygen.

"Don't move. I'll be right there." Luke ended the call and reached for his keys.

"What happened?"

"Chet fell and thinks he broke his leg. He's too stubborn to call an ambulance, so I'm going to take him to the hospital." He slipped on his shoes and reached for his jacket.

Hannah pushed away from the counter. "Let me

run and grab Thomas's keys from his house. You shouldn't drive with that arm. And that way Chet can lay down in the back seat."

Luke paused and pulled her toward him for a quick kiss. "Thanks, Hannah."

She still wasn't sure what was going on, but something had changed. Fire had a way of doing that. Most of the change she regretted, but this change in Luke—she'd take that.

Luke rubbed his eyes, trying to keep the fatigue away. Chet slept ten feet away with a tangle of tubes and wires connecting him to a variety of monitors, all doing their part to keep him in this world. One minute he was strong and feisty, the next, close to the edge of death. But the steady rhythm of beeps and hums that filled the room offered hope that he fought on.

The fall that had broken his leg had resulted from a stroke. At least the leg had gotten them to the hospital in good time.

Hannah shifted on the couch next to him as she fiddled with her phone. Kissing her hadn't been his plan. But maybe it should've been. The memory of her warm lips shot a fire through him just as it had the moment he'd tasted her. Her mouth was tense at first, but soft and sweet once she let herself give in to it. Those few seconds had knocked any coherent thought out of his head. If it hadn't been for Chet calling, they might be still standing in his kitchen kissing. Or something.

Hannah worried her lip between her teeth.

He didn't want to mess this up again. And by the look on her face, he might be already doing that very thing. "Everything okay?"

She offered an unconvincing nod.

"Let's take a walk." He laced their fingers together and pulled her to her feet. He led her into the hall, stopped at the elevator, and pressed the down button. "What's up?"

"Nothing." Her voice had an unusually high pitch.

Not good enough. Luke gave her hand a gentle tug. "Look at me."

She lifted her head, eyes wide.

"What's wrong?"

"I just have to know why you kissed me." The words tumbled out so fast Luke almost missed them.

Why did he kiss her? Didn't she know? Maybe he'd read the whole situation wrong.

He shifted from one foot to the other and loosened his grip on her hand enough so she could pull away. "Am I wrong to think that you wanted that kiss as much as I did?"

"I did. I do. It's just . . ." Tears gathered in the corners of her eyes.

"What?"

"I don't want to get hurt again." The words came out barely above a whisper and scraped against his heart. "I never really knew why you kissed me last time. Well . . . I thought I knew. But the next day you were . . . done."

Hannah's face that day as she sat on his steps after he'd ended things was one memory he'd done his best to erase. He closed his eyes and pressed her hand to his lips. "Hannah, I'm so sorry for what happened in the past. I was . . . an idiot. But I promise I won't give up on us again."

The elevator arrived and opened empty. They stepped inside, but Luke wasn't ready to end the conversation.

He pressed the button for the first floor and then turned her toward him. "Honest."

"So tomorrow you'll still—"

"Want to kiss you?" A low chuckle vibrated his chest as he pulled her closer. She had no idea. "I'll absolutely want to kiss you tomorrow and every day after that."

Her shoulders seemed to relax.

"Do you trust me?"

She nodded as she reached up and brushed her lips gently across his. She tasted of lemon, and that lavender scent filled his nose and clouded his mind. If only he could kiss her more fully like last time. He might've tried if the chime that they'd arrived at their destination hadn't snapped him back to his senses.

He pulled back just before the doors opened to a family waiting to board. He took Hannah's hand and led her over to the vending machine. "Want anything?"

"No." The doubt still lingered in her eyes.

How could he get her to believe that he wouldn't fail her again? Hannah valued honesty. Maybe it was time to be a little more transparent with her. Even if the idea of opening up made him feel ill, he could do it if it helped Hannah to see things would be different this time.

Luke lifted his Coke from the machine, then led them back toward the elevators. "Chet . . . means a lot to me. He's the closest thing I have to an uncle." Maybe with Hannah, talking about Chet could be freeing, rather than the soul-crushing weight that had always accompanied every attempt to talk.

"Did he ever talk about adopting you?"

Nope. Still soul-crushing.

He stopped at the elevators and pressed the up button. "No, he said I needed a mother. He tried to talk Mrs. Shoemaker into it when they thought I wasn't listening." His mind traveled back to the whispered arguments.

Hannah squeezed his hand.

Luke shrugged and stared unseeing out the nearby window. "She always had a reason why it wouldn't work right then. The last time I remember them talking about it, I was in sixth grade. Chet had gone so far as to drop off the paperwork she needed to start the process. It was the one time I let myself get my hopes up.

But I found the papers the next day in the trash." The memory weighed on him just like that day. "That's when I knew . . ."

Part of him had given up hope that day that his life would ever change. That he'd ever find a forever home. That he'd be part of a family.

The elevator arrived empty—thank goodness.

"Knew what? That you'd never be adopted?"

Luke blinked away the memory and stared down at their hands. "Yeah, that—but more than that . . . I'd never really belong."

The words stripped him bare inside, and it took all his strength not to drop her hand and get off alone on the next floor. Not that he didn't want to share this with Hannah—suddenly he wanted to share everything with her—but every story, every secret, still came with the cost of emptying himself.

Hannah reached up and wrapped her arms around his neck. Her voice softened to a whisper. "You do belong."

Her words smoothed over the rough memory. He wrapped his arms around her and squeezed tighter.

A slight sniff emerged from her as she buried her forehead in his neck. "I wish I could go back and tell you how special you were."

"Your friendship did a lot, Hannah. More than you'll ever know." He brushed a lock of hair behind her ear.

The elevator announced their arrival on the fourth floor. She stepped out of the elevator, pulling him with her.

He'd done it. He'd opened up and survived. Hannah even seemed more affectionate because of it. Why had he been holding back again?

When they stepped in the room Chet was still asleep, so they settled on the couch. Luke picked up her hand and traced the back of it with his thumb.

Her body melted into his side. "It's because you and Chet are so close that he sold you the house at a steal, isn't it? He must want you to stay around here too. I must remember to thank him."

Luke's thumb stopped. He still hadn't told her about the house. But the last thing he wanted right now was to announce that he might have to move. Besides, nothing was certain yet. He'd tell her, just not right now. Maybe after he got word from the council.

"He's been a big part of my life. That's why I've decided it doesn't matter who my mom was. I guess whether she was Ann or Sarah, the fact is, she's not here. I need to spend less of my time searching for things that don't exist and more time enjoying those that do. Like Chet. Jimmy. You."

"You never found anything more on your mom?" Hannah shifted next to him, her eyes darting about the room.

"Nope. I guess I never figured I would. But as I

searched and came across all these names, I kept wondering if I was related to any of them." A familiar ache settled in his gut. "Remember your family reunion you took me to in junior high?"

"I remember."

"I never really understood what I was missing until that day. I know your parents are both gone, but you've got so many aunts, uncles, cousins."

"We're pretty spread out though."

"Spread out or not, I'd love just one." Luke tightened his free hand, tapping his fist on his leg.

Nate's words about adoption and a new heritage floated into his mind. But was it really that easy?

Hannah released his hand and leaned forward next to him, picking at her nails. "That was the summer before my mom left."

"Have you ever heard from her?"

"No. When you leave town with ten thousand dollars of the town's money, you tend to stay where the law, and your daughter, can't find you."

"Ten thousand? I hadn't realized it was that much."

"Give or take. It wasn't all at once. Embezzling a little here, a little there. Since she worked for the town no one questioned her, until one of the receipts the mayor tried to call about belonged to a nonexistent company. She disappeared the next day without a word." Her voice hitched at the end.

He pulled her closer. At least his parents hadn't

had a choice. Her mother had chosen to leave. "Do you have any idea where she went?"

"My guess is that she moved to Italy. She always talked about it." She wiped her hand across her eyes. "Following her dream of being an artist."

Their kiss had been good—amazing, actually—but laying your heart bare before someone else was another level. "Did—"

"Luke?" Chet's husky, slurred voice interrupted his words.

Luke jumped to his feet and stepped to the side of the bed. Chet's deep-set eyes blinked against the light. "Hey, man. You gave us quite a scare."

Chet's wrinkled hand landed on Luke's. "I'm glad you're here. You're the closest thing I ever had to a son."

An unexpected emotion filled Luke's chest, and he swallowed back a lump. "Stop talking in past tense. They expect you to make a full recovery."

Hannah offered Chet a sip of water from his straw, then adjusted his oxygen tube, which had slipped off his ear. She was so gentle with him.

He could trust Hannah, and he'd prove to her that she could trust him as well. He wasn't walking away this time.

Going to Al behind Luke's back had been a mistake—a mistake she needed to fix. Hannah lifted another pile of papers. Where was that blasted card? And why hadn't she saved the number in her phone when she'd called him the last time? She was normally an orderly person, but her apartment was so tiny that one small project consumed every surface. And the boxes of archives that Mrs. Ferguson had dropped off was no small project.

She lifted another stack. Nope.

She hadn't planned to betray Luke. She'd done it because she wanted the best for him. But if he found out she'd hired a private investigator after he'd told her not to, their future might end up like the ash-filled lot at the center of town.

She lifted another box. Bingo! She snatched up Al's card and typed in the number on her phone.

Al's voicemail beeped. "Hey, Al, this is Hannah Thornton. Call me as soon as you get this."

A knock rattled her door and Luke's face appeared in the peephole. Her feet did a little hop. What was she, thirteen? She took a second to compose herself. This was still just Luke. Best friend Luke. Super kisser, so-hot-she-wanted-to-scream Luke.

So much for being composed.

When she opened the door, he greeted her with a light kiss. She could get used to this.

Luke placed a long tube on the table, then pulled a Coke from the fridge. He motioned to the mess. "What's all this?"

Hannah straightened a few of the piles she'd been sorting. "Mayor Jameson mentioned they might have an old storeroom in the town hall that I could turn into a historical room to add to the contest entry. If the town will still let me enter. The room would have a few pictures on the wall and that old stove from the vet house—I still can't believe it survived the fire."

Luke leaned against the counter. "Iron stoves wouldn't work very well if they didn't survive fires."

Too bad she hadn't thought of that before she'd nearly killed Luke. She'd made a lot of mistakes in her life, but so far that one took the prize.

"Any ideas what you'll do with the square yet?"

The few spring rains had compacted the charred mess a bit, but she still didn't know what to do with it.

"Every time I drive by I want to cry." Hannah dropped into a chair at the table. The ache that had taken up residence since the fire pressed in on her chest.

"I like the open look."

"It does give the town a different feel. Unfortunately, not the one I was going for."

He stared at his pop can. "I actually had an idea." He took a gulp of pop. "Remember when you were telling me about that star place—from the *Gabby Girl* show?"

"You mean Stars Hollow from *Gilmore Girls*?"

"Whatever." He set the can on the counter and reached for the tube he'd brought in with him.

"Didn't you say it had a gazebo in the center? Well, it got me thinking." He pulled out a roll of paper from the tube and unfurled it across the table. A sketch of the town with a beautiful open square, complete with fresh grass and a gazebo perched in the center.

Hannah's mouth dropped open. "This is amazing! Where did you get this?"

Luke shifted from one foot to the other. "I drew it."

She studied the design again, running her finger across the fine lines. How had she not known he could design like this? A corner of another sheet of paper peeked from underneath. She folded back the top sheet and looked at the one below. This one contained a more detailed plan of the gazebo with measurements and supply needs. "Why are you a business major if you can do this?"

"Not sure how much call there is for gazebo building."

"If you can do this in a few days, you can do more than design gazebos." Her finger landed on the drawing. "How much are we talking?"

"I think I could get the lumberyard to donate the wood at cost, and if I got a few guys to help me build it, we could do it for around eight thousand dollars."

Hannah pinched her lip with her teeth. Eight thousand. That was cutting it close with the deductibles she'd have to cover for the businesses. "How would we get the field ready? I mean, have you seen it?"

"I've been asking around." He slid into a chair at the table. "We could gather and sell all the scrap metal left behind. A couple of farmers in the area own backhoe loaders, and they could push all the wood and ash into the large root cellar the Manor left behind. It takes care of the hole and takes care of the mess."

"Is that allowed?"

"Because it wasn't the controlled burn it was supposed to be—"

"Thanks for the reminder."

"But because of that it's no longer an institutional demolition project. Now it's just like any house fire and falls under the residential exemption, which means the local fire department decides what happens to the ash. Chief Grandy likes my plan. And as far as the topsoil, I know Kensington has that pile next to his construction on McCain Road."

Her eyes flashed to his. "He'd never give it to us."

"If the whole town was watching, I bet he would. But you'd have to ask nicely. No . . ." He made an explosion motion as he lifted his hands.

She shoved his shoulder. "Do you think they could work around Otis?"

"Probably. I was hoping he'd move by now—"

"I think I killed him." Hannah dropped her head

into her hands. "What if the fire damaged him and he won't move anymore? More than a hundred years of Heritage tradition and I killed him."

He pulled her into a hug. "I can't say for sure because I have no idea how he moves. But brass withstands heat much hotter than an average house fire. He should be fine."

"Then why hasn't he moved?"

"I don't know."

Hannah shook her head and stared down at the plans again. "You really think the lumberyard, the farmers, and Kensington are all going to donate their time and money for this?"

"People love this town, Hannah. Many families have been here for generations. Yes, I think people would do it for the town. But the truth is, no matter what you think their opinion of you is, they respected your father and your grandfather, and many of them would simply agree to help because you asked. You focus so much on how your mother's choices affect the way people see you, but that's only half your history. The Thornton family is respected and loved in this town."

Would people really help if she asked? Her mind drifted to Al. He'd jumped at the chance to help free of charge. Even if it had been a mistake to call him, the gesture warmed something in her. Had she been selling the whole town short?

The clock on the wall chimed. Luke stood and

carried his can to her bottle-return bin. "Think about it."

"I will." Hannah opened the door for him and leaned against it. "You took a class last semester in web design, right?"

All expression faded from his face. "Why?"

"I need to have you help me set up a website for the town." Her phone chimed and she glanced at the display. Alfred Mathis. "I've got to take this. Call me later."

As soon as the door shut behind Luke, Hannah snatched up the phone. "Hey, Al, I'm glad you called. I—"

"I think it's a fake." His chuckle carried over the line.

"Excuse me?"

"Everything you've given me has come up empty. Which means you gave me wrong information or the birth certificate is a fake."

Could she have gotten it wrong? She didn't have a photographic memory, but it was better than average. Hannah swallowed and watched Luke's truck disappear down the road. "Why would someone have a fake birth certificate?"

"Lots of reasons. Hiding from the law. Hiding from people. Illegal immigrants. I need to do some more digging."

"Illegal immigrants?" Hannah's mind spun with ideas.

"Luke was born near the end of the Cold

War, so it is possible his parents defected and settled here illegally. It happened. Or his parents could've been running from the law. I must say, I'm having fun with this case, Hannah."

Hannah wiped her moist palm on her jeans. She needed to tell him to stop. To end the search. But this changed things.

She could ask him, but then she'd have to admit she'd lied. Or at least lied by omission. Trust wasn't something Luke gave easily. Maybe it'd be safer to walk away, but what if this new information led to something? What if Luke's parents *had* defected? What if he had family in another country? Cousins waiting to be known. Isn't that what he'd said he wanted?

"Hannah? Are you there?"

"Yes, of course."

"I could use anything else you might have. And I need to see the birth certificate or at least a photo of it."

Had there been anything else in the folder? Like Luke would turn that over. But he wouldn't have to know if she kept it quiet. After all, she'd only pass on the information to Luke if it turned out good. And if she could present him with a score of Russian cousins, surely he'd forgive her. Right?

"Hannah?"

Hannah cleared her throat and pushed away the twisting of her conscience. "Yes. I'll do my best to get more to you as soon as I can."

twelve

This interview had to go well—moving was no longer an option. Without this job or a house, he might not be able to stay in town. And if ever he had a reason to stay in Heritage, it was now.

Luke rubbed his damp palms down the legs of his ironed black pants and shifted in his seat. Chief Grandy and two longtime volunteers, Burt Mathews and Dan Fair, sat across from him, reading some papers from a manila folder while occasionally asking each other hushed questions. Seemed odd that Chief Wilks was absent.

The first part of the interview had gone well. They'd asked questions he'd felt prepared for and they'd seemed pleased with his answers.

Then they'd pulled out a file and passed it back and forth. What was in the file? The way their mouths had turned down, it couldn't be good. Luke didn't have anything to hide. Not really . . . well, except that D-. Would they care about a bad grade in a web design class?

Dan was the first to look up. He didn't make eye contact. He just drummed his grease-stained fingers on the table. He must have come right from his shop. Although his hair appeared to be freshly washed, so maybe permanently stained fingers were part of the trade.

Chief Grandy ran his hand through his thinning brown hair. He pulled off his glasses and leaned forward on his elbows. "After the recent fire, we interviewed several individuals about the circumstances. Although it all turned out well in the end, we need to make sure nothing like that happens again."

"Agreed." Luke nodded as he held his breath. What was in the file?

"In a testimony by"—the chief slipped on his glasses and glanced at the file again—"Thomas Thornton, he said that before the fire, you'd come to the conclusion that the houses were too close to burn safely. Is this true?"

Luke gripped the arms of the chair a little tighter. "Yes, sir."

The chief pulled off his glasses once more and tapped the earpiece against his chin. "How did you come to this conclusion?"

"I measured them, sir."

"And what did you find?" Dan made an additional note in the file.

"According to my measurements, they were under an inch too close." The arms of the chair squeaked in protest to his tightening grip. He relaxed his hands and folded them in his lap.

Dan added another note without looking up. "Did you record your exact measurements?"

"Yes, sir."

"Would you take a look at this?" He handed

238

Luke a paper. "So are you saying that these are falsified measurements?"

Luke scanned the paper. It was the official measurements that Derek and Ted had made. Measurements in a report with Chief Wilks's signature. Falsified? That was a serious charge.

Luke cleared his throat. "I was not there when Ted or Derek measured the houses. I can only tell you what I found. I don't have the measurements memorized, but no, these don't look correct."

Chief Grandy rubbed his eyes.

Luke wasn't there to throw those guys under the bus. Ted could be lazy but he wasn't a criminal. Derek? He was a jerk, but again, a criminal? How had they gotten Chief Wilks to sign off on the report? The guy was by the book. "I will say, though, the houses weren't exactly square. They were closer in the back by several inches. I measured at the closest point, but Derek and Ted may have just measured along 2nd Street."

Chief Grandy's shoulders relaxed a little. It was one thing to have a disciplinary hearing for negligence. It was another thing to bring up criminal charges against two—maybe three—sons of Heritage.

"Do you still have your records?" Burt clicked and unclicked his pen.

"Yes."

"We'd like to see those." The chief leaned his elbows on the table in front of him. "Did you ever bring this to anyone's attention?"

Luke shifted in his seat. "I told Hannah Thornton."

"But not your chief." The man pinned him with a glare. "Didn't you think it was important for me to know?"

Luke scrubbed a hand over his face and sighed. Why was he suddenly the bad guy here? Wasn't this supposed to be a job interview? Why had he been called to the stand? "In retrospect, I should have gone to you first."

"We agree." Dan leaned back, crossing his arms over his chest. "And that's what makes this interview difficult. You're a fine man, Luke, and you've proven yourself a capable firefighter repeatedly. However, your greatest weakness is that you're not always a team player. You often try to tackle problems on your own, and that quality may not be the best fit for this job."

"I understand, sir." What else was there to say? He did understand. Firefighting required team support. So why hadn't he gone to Chief Grandy? Because he didn't believe that they'd take his word over Ted and Derek's. But maybe Luke was doing exactly what he'd accused Hannah of the other day—selling the town short. "Would it have made a difference if I'd come to you?"

"We'll never know, will we?" Chief Grandy stood and rounded the table, extending his hand to Luke. "We haven't made a final decision yet, but thank you for applying. We will let you know."

Luke nodded and stood, shaking each man's hand before he turned toward the door.

Maybe they would've believed him. Maybe not. But now he'd never know, and his lone-wolf attitude may have cost him the job and his future in this town. And it may have cost him Hannah.

Thomas knocked on Madison's door and waited. Ten o'clock emergency again? Not likely. But he hadn't spent any time with her since—well, since he'd almost kissed Janie. Guilt was an uncomfortable roommate. What had he been thinking? Had her words not jarred him back to reality, he would've kissed her. He was the lowest of the low.

Madison opened the door. Dressed in pajama pants and a tank top, she was modest in the loosest sense of the word. All key parts were, in fact, still covered, but the way she leaned toward him used the sleepwear to its fullest advantage. "You going to come in or just stand there?"

Thomas focused on her face as she pulled him inside. Candles flickered from the coffee table and the wood mantel as a slow country song crooned on about love from the iPod dock in the kitchen.

"I can't decide which I like better, the turquoise dresses or the pacific blue."

"This is the emergency?" He dropped on the tan overstuffed recliner.

"It's important." Madison picked up one of the magazines strewn across the couch with a bride on the cover, then slid onto his lap, her perfume wrapping around him. She pointed at a page, then ran her fingers through his hair just above his ear. "Which one?"

Two smiling models wearing what seemed like identical dresses stood at the water's edge of some beach. Was there a right answer to a question like this?

His gaze traveled off the page. And there was her cleavage. A lot of cleavage. Thomas swallowed and closed his eyes. She had no idea what she was doing to him.

He opened his eyes and forced himself to look only at her face. Her lips turned up at the corners as she licked their edges.

So she did know. Thomas jerked to his feet, forcing her off his lap. He dragged a hand through his hair and drew in a ragged breath. "I need to go. It's late."

A pout formed on her lips as she dipped her chin and pressed herself to his side. "Stay."

"No." He turned toward the door but she blocked his path.

Her fingers played at the edge of his collar. "Don't be like that."

Thomas backed away from her touch. "Why are you doing this?"

"Doing what?" She closed the distance again. "Being sexy?"

Thomas moved away and put a chair between them. "This is seductive, not sexy. You're trying to get me to compromise my values. Why?"

She crossed her arms over her chest, her bright pink nails making indents in the skin. "Aren't I one of your values?"

Thomas softened his voice and gripped the back of the chair. "Yes. But I was clear when we started dating that I wanted to wait for . . . this."

"Why?" Her hands flew into the air. "It's not like you're religious or anything."

The words stabbed Thomas. Maybe he wasn't on speaking terms with God at the moment, but it didn't mean he'd thrown out his faith completely. He was just . . . mad. Downright mad.

But it wasn't just that. He wasn't about to throw something like this away out of anger. Especially something that he and Janie had been so careful about. Maybe it was really about Janie. Maybe it was about God. How had his life gotten so tangled?

"I used to be. And . . . I think I want that again."

Madison's lip curled into a sneer. "You want to be religious?"

Hannah was right. There was so much they hadn't talked about.

"Not religious. A person who follows what the Bible says. Do you believe anything?"

A look of uncertainty crossed Madison's face as she wrapped her arms around her waist. "If I say no, are you going to dump me?"

Thomas dropped back into the recliner, cradling his head in his hands as he tried to sort through the words and thoughts. He looked up at Madison. "Why do you want to marry me?"

"I love you. And I thought you loved me." She spoke the words through clenched teeth.

"What do you love about me?"

She played with the ends of her hair as her eyes traveled from his head to his feet. Her smile seemed a little lost. "You're good-looking, and you're tall—"

"I'm tall?" Thomas gripped the arms of the chair. It was worse than he'd feared. "You want to marry me because I'm *tall?*"

"I wasn't done. You're strong, brave, and I can trust you to . . ." Her gaze lost focus for a few seconds before locking back on him. "I can trust you."

He tilted his head. "You can trust me to what? Not hit you? Get you out of town?"

Madison's eyes brightened with unshed tears. Her shoulders sagged as she looked at him, then dropped her gaze. "Is that so bad? No one ever

244

has stood up for me like you have. No one has ever treated me like I was something special to them. But you're willing to sell your house and leave with me just because I asked. Why would I not want that?"

Her words sliced through him. That hurting girl was back. The one he'd seen that night outside the club, who'd tried to keep her dad from driving home drunk. He'd stepped in and taken the punch that was meant for her. The look she'd given him that night had made him feel like someone again—like he could be a hero to someone.

Marrying Madison made him feel needed, but how long before he wasn't enough for her? She needed healing and a grace he couldn't offer. He'd allowed her to make him her savior, and he'd enjoyed it.

"You're special, Madison. I know not enough people have told you that in life, but you are."

One tear escaped down her cheek before she brushed it away.

"I'm sorry."

"For what?"

"I almost kissed Janie." Oh man. Why had he said that?

The frown eased from her face as she drew a deep breath and stood, gathering magazines off the coffee table and straightening them. "So, all of this is just a confessional because you feel guilty? Well, you're forgiven. Don't let it happen again."

Was she serious? "It doesn't bother you?"

Madison paused sorting the magazines. "I don't like it, but it isn't like you slept with her. You didn't even kiss her. Now it's out of your system, and we'll move on. As soon as we get out of this godforsaken town you won't have to see her again."

"It's not, you know."

"What? Out of your system?" Her hand wrinkled the edges of the magazines.

"No." Well, maybe, but that wasn't what he meant. "The town. It's not godforsaken. In fact, He seems to be doing a lot of work here."

"Luckily, He's left me alone." She massaged her temple, then stared at him, all emotion dropping away. "You don't want to marry me, do you?"

Thomas rubbed his hand against the arm of the chair. "Deep down, I don't think you ever wanted to marry me. Just the idea of me."

"I'm not sure I even know what love is." Another tear slid down her cheek as she dropped the magazines on the table. "I can't stay in this town anymore."

"Where will you go?"

Madison shrugged. "Doesn't matter—away from my dad, away from everything."

"You don't need me or anyone else to make a

new life for you. You're stronger than you think."

"After knowing you, I actually believe that."

Thomas stood. "I gotta go."

Madison slid the ring he'd given her off her finger and held it out to him. "I'm going to really miss . . . this ring."

Thomas laughed and slid it into his pocket. A lot of her superficial side was all an act with Madison, but she'd really perfected it over the years.

"Goodbye, Madison." Thomas wrapped her in his arms and pressed a kiss to the top of her head. "May you find what you're looking for."

Luke shaded his eyes against the midday sun as he scanned the smooth, even field of fresh dirt. All evidence of the fire had been erased by many hands and generous farmers. Ground leveled. Even a layer of topsoil and fresh seed. He'd try to keep his damage to a minimum. But if he was going to build a gazebo he'd need to walk somewhere.

The breeze was a little cool, but May was definitely finding its way to Michigan.

Luke stepped on the concrete foundation that they'd poured. Hannah had hired that out, wanting to be confident it was done right. It'd make it easier to get the gazebo placed dead center. And once he added the four steps to lift it off the ground, the gazebo would really have a dynamic presence in the square. The two electrical outlets that stuck out of the ground by the cement would have to be incorporated into the design, but having them there was good planning.

Once he'd shown her those drawings, Hannah had run with it. Even sat down with Kensington and had a civil meeting about the dirt. Seeing her joy and pride as they'd settled on the details of the gazebo had made it worth it. Even if he'd had to miss the last meeting at the firehouse.

If only he could be so helpful with the Heritage webpage. Why hadn't he just fessed up about failing the class? But he'd let his pride get in the way, and now he was stuck trying once again to figure out HTML.

"I brought lemonade," Hannah said from behind him.

Luke reached for the thermos she held out to him, then pointed to the southeast corner. "They were able to work around Otis."

"He still hasn't moved." Hannah stared at the hippo, a frown forming a crease between her eyes. She wore an old pair of jeans and her gray T-shirt that featured a Beatles album cover. She turned back to him with a half smile. "I wish I could help you here, but this is the only time Janie said she could work on the historical room."

"No problem." A wisp of her hair lifted in the breeze, and he tucked it behind her ear. "I asked Nate to help me. He should be here soon. Somehow I think he might be more help than you."

"Hey." She shoved his shoulder but only managed to set herself off balance instead. He grabbed her and dropped a kiss on her lips.

She cleared her throat and stepped back. "Is there anything else you need?"

"Well, now that you mention it . . ." He kissed her along her jaw, drinking in the familiar lavender scent.

"Luke." The warning held a teasing note. "We are standing literally in the center of town."

"I was going to say music." He backed up and held up his hands. "What were you thinking?"

"I've got just the thing." She jogged toward Thomas's house, leaving Luke to study the plans.

A few minutes later she returned, carrying a boom box in her hand circa 1985. "How about this?"

"Wow, did you take your DeLorean to go get that?"

She held it up higher. "It was in the garage at Thomas's. I think it was my dad's."

"It plays cassette tapes. Don't you believe in streaming music and mini speakers?"

"This is classic. It's very John Cusack from *Say Anything* . . ." Hannah lifted it above her head but started to wobble.

"Whoa, Rocky." Luke grabbed the stereo. Her

backside would match her muddy shoes if she wasn't careful.

"Not Rocky. Lloyd." Hannah stared at him like that should mean something. "From *Say Anything* . . ."

He shook his head, lifting his hands. "You lost me at chick flick."

"Lloyd stands in front of his girlfriend's— actually, his ex-girlfriend's—house, holding up a radio playing their song. I forget it now, but I'd know it if I heard it. Anyway, it's not a chick flick. It's an epic cinematic moment."

Luke stared at her. "So, the girl hears the song, comes out, and they live happily ever after?"

"No." Hannah sighed. "She rolls over and ignores him, leaving him out there alone."

"So this guy is standing out there laying his heart out in front of the entire town, and she just leaves him there looking like an idiot? That makes a great classic scene?"

"Yes. He's showing how much he loves her."

"Maybe he should've written her a note."

Hannah laughed, lifting the radio again. "This is so much better."

"*Say Anything* . . . , right?" Nate walked up and dropped his tool belt on the concrete slab.

Luke shook his head. "You watch chick flicks?"

"Hey, watch it. That's John Cusack. He's in a category of his own."

"Thank you." Hannah set the radio on the

250

cement. "The radio works and probably the tape deck. Maybe if you're lucky there's a mixtape in there. I'm off to meet Janie, but call me if you need anything."

"I'll just stand outside the building with the radio and hope you come to the window," Luke said.

"That would be awesome." Hannah made her way back to the car. "I'll be waiting."

"You two seem to be getting along pretty well." Nate made his way to the lumber pile and began separating the boards.

Luke picked up the plans they'd finalized and studied them. "We're dating now, I guess. I mean, we haven't actually had a date yet, but—"

"But you've kissed her."

Heat crawled up Luke's neck. "Yeah, something like that. We need to start with a couple two-by-fours."

"Hey, no judgment here, brother. But be careful." Nate lifted the wood and carried it to the cement foundation. "How long do we need these?"

"Six feet." Luke dropped the paper and found the tape measure. "You think I'm going to hurt her?"

"No. Just make sure it's not only the fun stuff. You know, take her out. Romance her. Talk about the important stuff." Nate measured out six feet and marked the spot with his pencil. "Our culture today equates how close two people are with physical intimacy, but a relationship based on that is like an empty piñata."

"An empty piñata?"

"Yup. It sure looks good from the outside, but when the kids bust it open and nothing is inside, it isn't good." Nate jammed his hands on his hips. "Did you know the piñatas at the store are empty?"

"I never thought about it."

"Me neither. Until I threw a Cinco de Mayo party at the shelter. Talk about a roomful of disappointed kids." He pointed the pencil at Luke. "Don't make your relationship an empty piñata. Get to know each other. Share. Make her feel special. Be romantic."

"Like standing outside her place with a radio." The thought made his skin feel too tight.

Nate chuckled and passed the wood to Luke. "Yes, but no. I mean, *Say Anything* . . . isn't really a good example of healthy dating. Pick stuff that's meaningful to both of you."

Luke carried the board to the miter saw he'd set up on the concrete slab. He knelt next to it, squeezed the trigger, and eased the sharp blade through the wood. "You seem to know a lot about relationships for being single. I mean, you can't be much older than I am."

Nate paused his work but didn't look up. "Experience is a painful teacher, but you can choose to learn from it."

Wasn't that the truth.

Nate marked another board and held it out. "Hey, I'm starting a new Bible study on Thursday nights. Interested?"

"Maybe." Luke grabbed the next board.

They worked in silence for a while, but Luke couldn't help tumbling the conversation through his mind. If he had a new start with Hannah, he wanted to do it right. It was time to plan a date she wouldn't forget.

thirteen

She couldn't believe she was doing this. Hannah retrieved Luke's hide-a-key again and let herself in. Sure, she'd done it before, but last time she hadn't set out to do something Luke wouldn't approve of. But the more she'd debated the idea in her head, the more she'd determined she couldn't let it go.

Spitz came trotting up and nuzzled against her leg. "He's not here, boy. He's playing basketball." She checked her watch. "At least for a few more minutes. I thought he might have taken you."

With any luck, Spitz would at least give her fair warning if Luke arrived home early. Hannah crossed to the stairs and took them two at a time. She made a beeline for his room and then straight to the desk. *Please be there.*

The dog barked and released a small whine. She turned and scratched his ears again. "I know he wouldn't want me to do this, but he could have a family somewhere. How cool would it be to have family in Russia, Romania, or Latvia? Where's Latvia anyway?"

Hannah opened the drawer and froze. It was empty. Great. Now what?

Spitz stood and pawed at her, then barked again.

Hannah scanned the room. Nothing. Spitz jumped up, barked again, and licked her hand.

She laughed and pushed him down. So Spitz wasn't on her side. "Okay, fine."

Hannah took a step toward the door and stopped. On the dresser by the door, under a few books, a familiar manila folder peeked out.

She slid it out with a shaky hand. This was it. Laying it open on the desk, she spread out the papers and pulled out her phone. Pressure built in her chest. Was she doing the right thing? It had been a long time since she'd really prayed about anything and waited for the answer, and she had a feeling this should be one of those times. But she didn't have time to wait.

The dog barked and ran from the room as the front door slammed.

Hannah jumped. Speaking of running out of time. What was he doing home so early? She snapped a photo of the birth certificate, one of the internet searches, and the photo of Luke and his father, then scrambled to get the papers back in the file before shoving it back where she'd found it. Her fingers shook, unease settling through her. *Thief.* The word was stuck on repeat in her mind.

She ran across the hall to the bathroom and shut the door without much of a sound.

"Hello?" Luke called up.

Hannah ran cool water over her hands and dried them before opening the door. "I was in the bathroom. The one downstairs is still under construction."

It wasn't a lie, right?

"Well, someone has me working on other things."

She made her way down the stairs. Why was he dressed up? Not that she was complaining. "I thought you were playing basketball."

"Chet was released, so I helped him settle into the rehab center. They're expecting a full recovery." He slid out of his jacket and then paused. "If you thought I was playing ball, why are you here?"

Shoot. *Think, Hannah.* "I was having a nice conversation with the dog." Okay, she couldn't keep up these not-quite-a-lie excuses for long.

Spitz barked twice. No doubt trying to rat her out.

"I know he seems to prefer you, but I haven't given up on him being my dog." Her voice came out a bit too chipper, but Luke didn't seem to notice.

He dropped a kiss on her forehead. "Feel free to visit him as much as you want."

Mission Redirect, success. Then why did she feel like she'd been punched in the gut? "Maybe I will."

The dog pawed at Luke's leg and barked. Tattletale.

Luke pushed open the back door. "He always does that when he needs to go out."

Duh. The dog wasn't debating with her—he

257

was telling her he had to pee. Maybe her guilt was pricking at her for a reason. She should delete those photos and tell Al to let it go.

Luke eyed her as if weighing his words. Did he suspect? "The final bill came in for the wood for the gazebo. It's just over nine thousand."

"Nine thousand?" Hannah dropped into a chair at the table. "I can't afford nine thousand. That will put me almost fifteen hundred over budget."

"I know." Luke rested his hand on her shoulder as he took the seat next to her. "I already talked to the mayor. They are so thrilled with what you've done so far that they wish they could extend the budget, but the funds just aren't there. But they put a collection jar in the diner, and the first day it had over five hundred dollars."

"That still leaves a thousand dollars—"

"Give them time. The town is behind this. Trust them."

What choice did she have? "So, you took care of all this?"

Luke leaned toward her and picked up her hand. "I didn't want you to stress about it. I know you have a lot on your plate right now, even with the housing market slowing down."

"I think everyone is waiting to see what happens with the square."

Luke reached up and tucked a strand of hair behind her ear. "They're probably hoping it'll raise their home value."

"Because no doubt with the fire I lowered it. I am the worst Realtor ever."

"No you aren't. You need to relax. And if you give me a minute to change, we can hang out. Watch a movie maybe." The stairs creaked as he hurried up them.

The bathroom door slammed, and Hannah rested her head against the chair. Luke had taken care of it all because he knew it would cause her stress. Wasn't that what she was trying to do for him? Of course, he'd specifically said to leave it alone, but just like he'd known how to help with the budget issue, she knew how to help him find his past.

Hannah ignored the churning in her gut as she slid her phone out of her pocket. In the end, he'd see she was right, especially if she could present him with a *sem'ya*—she'd already looked up the Russian word for *family*. And if it led nowhere or was bad news, she'd burn it like it never happened.

She ignored the warning in her heart and tapped at the screen, emailing the photos to Al.

"Ready?" Luke appeared at the bottom of the stairs in jeans and his standard gray T-shirt.

"Yup." Her head snapped up and she slid her phone in her pocket.

Luke shoved his hands in his pockets and then pulled them back out. "Go out with me Saturday?"

"Sure. What did you have in mind?" She followed him into the living room, dropped onto his sofa, and reached for the remote.

"I don't know. Dinner, movie, typical first date things." He settled into the seat next to her and pulled her into his side.

Oh, like a date. A real date. Hannah's pulse hammered. But why not? Shouldn't she expect him to ask her out?

Her mind flashed back to high school. Prom was supposed to have been their first date. And, well . . . that never happened. But things would be different this time. He'd promised they would be.

She forced a casual tone. "Sounds like fun."

Her phone buzzed, and she pulled it out to glance at the display as Luke claimed the remote. A text from Al.

> Everything came through great. I'll get right on this.

Her teeth pinched the inside of her cheek as a lump settled in her throat. This was the point of no return. But she was doing this because she cared about Luke. He'd see that in the end. He had to.

He'd been waiting for this day for more years than he cared to count, and the weather couldn't be any better. Without a cloud in the sky, they were going to have a great picnic. Luke scanned the blue sky as he slid out of his truck and took the stairs to Hannah's second-floor apartment.

Hannah had the door open before he reached the top step. Her smile faded as she looked him up and down. "I dressed up too much, didn't I?"

"What?" Luke glanced down at his jeans and T-shirt and then back at her pink dress that ended just above the knees. Her brown hair was swept up in that ponytail/knotty bun thing she did a lot, with a few strands falling around her face.

"You look good." He dropped a quick kiss on her nose. "Real good."

"Thanks." Her cheeks reddened as she tugged at her lip with her teeth.

When they got to his truck, he held her door. A large cloud was now visible in the west. They were still good. What could one cloud do?

About ten minutes out of town, he slipped his hand in hers across the truck bench seat. "How does a picnic at the lighthouse sound?"

"Perfect. I can't think of a—"

Her words were cut off as the truck jerked and coughed.

Luke released her hand and shifted into a lower gear before steering the truck to the side of the road. It sputtered a few times before it died. Perfect. Of all days.

"Did we run out of gas?"

"No." Luke leaned down and popped the hood. "I filled it up yesterday."

"Are you positive it's filled up?"

Luke stared at her. Was she serious? Did she think he was sixteen with a new license? He shook his head and hopped out of the truck, trying not to slam the door. Didn't work.

That single cloud had turned into a handful. And more were rolling in. Nothing like Michigan weather to turn on a dime.

Her door popped open, and she came to stand next to him. "I'm serious, Luke. I've had the nozzle flip off before it was full. Especially at Highway Oil on the third pump—"

"I know how to fill my truck with gas, Hannah." He bit his tongue to keep from saying more.

"I'm just saying—"

"No." He pushed off the truck and resisted the urge to kick the thing. "You're trying to fix things. It's my truck. I'll handle it."

Luke peered back under the hood but didn't know what he hoped for. A neon sign saying "Here's the problem," maybe.

Construction—piece of cake. Mechanic stuff—never quite his bag. He slid his phone out of his pocket just before it began to ring. Cindy's name flashed across the screen, and Hannah stiffened next to him.

"I'll leave you to your call." She marched around the truck and slid in the passenger seat, slamming the door.

He tapped Ignore and called Dan's Garage for

a tow before sliding back in the cab. "It will be about fifteen minutes."

She stared out the side window.

"I never called Cindy."

"I didn't ask."

He tossed the phone on the dash. "Yeah, well, you're not asking pretty loud."

"Why is she programmed in your phone?"

"I programmed her number so I wouldn't answer when she called. I was hoping if I didn't answer she'd get the hint."

"How's that working for you?"

Luke gripped the steering wheel, whitening his knuckles. "I'm serious, Hannah. I haven't talked to her once."

Silence.

Luke rubbed his hands over his face.

"I'm sorry." Her voice came out small, defeated. "It just brought a lot back. Being dumped for Cindy once was quite enough."

"I never dated Cindy."

"Yes you did." She jabbed her finger in his shoulder. "You ended things with me, and then you were all over each other at that bonfire. Then you left together, and her car was at your house all night. All night, Luke."

Luke winced and turned to face her, putting some distance between his shoulder and her bony finger. "First of all, we weren't all over each other. She flirted with me the whole night, but I never encouraged her. She was my ride and she was drunk, so I wasn't going to leave her there or let her drive home. Yes, I did leave with her, but I dropped her off at her house and returned her car the next day." He rubbed the back of his neck as his shoulders tensed at the memory.

"Why did you end things with us?"

He turned forward and leaned his elbow on the window's edge. "I didn't fit in your world."

Her hands flew in the air. "That sounds as crazy now as it did then."

"Do you remember the day after we kissed?" He lowered his voice but kept his gaze out the windshield.

"Yes." Her voice cracked. "Having you say it stunk hours later was a real morale booster."

"I never said it stunk." He scratched at the velvety upholstery between them.

"No, you said, 'It was a mistake.' Translated as, 'Why did I ever think I wanted to kiss you?' "

"I did want to kiss you. More than that, I wanted you to be my girlfriend more than anything I'd ever wanted in my life. It was you . . . who didn't want me."

Hannah fisted her hands. "You ended things. Not me."

"Before that day, I never thought you saw me the way others did. You didn't even seem to notice or care that I was poor."

"Who cares about that?" Her hands flew into

the air again. He seemed to have a knack for getting her to do that.

He leaned back. "I couldn't afford a tux, and you offered to pay for it so you wouldn't be embarrassed—"

"That's not why I offered to pay for it." She laid her hand on his arm. "I offered because prom was my thing, not yours. You were trying to save money, and I didn't think it was fair to make you pay for something you'd rather skip."

"I would've spent that money on you, Hannah. I may not have been the best-dressed one there, but I wouldn't have embarrassed you. But hearing you tell your friends that I'd be in a tux if you had to pay for it yourself made me feel . . . small. Worthless."

"Why didn't you talk to me? I'd have skipped prom if it meant having you."

"I tried to, but you interrupted and offered to pay to fix the tires on my car. That's when I realized I wouldn't be enough for you. You were determined to step in and fix all the little things that weren't quite right about me."

She turned to face him, her lip curling. "That's not fair. I offered to pay for the tires because I hated that Cindy kept giving you rides home from work. Do you think I couldn't see the way she looked at you? I wanted you with me, not her."

Luke turned away, watching the first drops of the spring shower darken the asphalt. "I didn't need you fighting my battles. And I didn't need you trying to fix my life—fix me."

"So you gave up?" The pain in her voice pierced through his defenses.

Luke dropped his head back against the seat. "Yes, and I've always wondered if that was the biggest mistake of my life. But Hannah, what guy wants to be his girlfriend's project? I wanted to be someone you'd be proud to date, not someone you had to help."

"I *was* proud to date you." She massaged her temple with her finger. "Why make up a story about Cindy?"

"I didn't. The rumor mill did. I just didn't set the record straight."

"So you let me think you were moving on to dating someone new as if what we'd had meant nothing." The vulnerability in her voice matched the raw emotion in her eyes.

Luke pressed his lips together, his fingers whitening on the steering wheel again. "You accepted a date to prom the next day."

She shook her head. "I didn't go to prom. The tags are still on the dress."

"You told Jon some family friend had asked you to his prom."

"Oh." Some of the fight seemed to drain out of her. She turned back to the windshield. "He did ask, but I didn't go. I knew Jon would tell you, and I didn't want you to know I was sitting at home on prom night, crying my eyes out."

Drips filled the windshield, clouding Luke's view. "You sat at home on prom night?"

"Eating a half gallon of chocolate ice cream. Shocked?"

"No." He cringed as the image settled in. "Do you really have your dress with the tags still on?"

"Hey, I loved that dress. But every time I looked at it, I thought of you. So I used it to remind myself why I should never let myself fall in love with you again. But here I am back in love with you, and our first date is a disaster."

Luke stared at her. Did she say . . . ? "You love me?"

Hannah's eyes widened as she opened and shut her mouth a few times. She twisted her fingers in her lap. "I said . . . I mean . . . I guess I thought . . . maybe it's too soon—"

"I love you too." Luke grabbed her hand across the span of the cab to pull her closer.

She came an inch then let out a squeak. "Seat belt."

Luke started fumbling with the buckle when a yellow light flashed through the window. He released a groan. "We'll finish this later."

Gideon Mathews knocked on his window, then pointed at the tow truck. "I'll start hooking it up then?"

Luke nodded and turned back to Hannah. "I'll tell you what. Gideon can give us a ride back to town. You put on that prom dress, and our first date can be the prom we never had."

"That sounds . . . cheesy."

He poked her gently in the side. "How often are you going to get me to volunteer to dress up? I still don't have a tux, but I have a black suit."

"Okay."

Luke reached for the door handle but turned back. "There's one problem. Can I borrow your car?"

Her best friend had to have lost her mind, but Janie showed up with her makeup kit nevertheless, because even crazy people needed friends. Janie knocked several times on the large oak door and swallowed her unease. Why did Hannah want to meet at Thomas's house anyway?

Hannah opened the door in her bathrobe, wearing a green face mask and curlers. "Thank goodness." She grabbed Janie's hand and yanked her inside.

Janie dropped her purse by the door and followed Hannah up the stairs to her friend's old bedroom. The infamous prom dress that hadn't moved from its hanger in seven years was draped across the bed.

The girl had finally snapped. There was no other explanation. So many years of trying to control the uncontrollable, and it had pushed her right over the edge.

"It still fits. I can't believe it since I'm not exactly the same size I was in high school. But the fabric and cut are very forgiving. So what do you think, makeup or dress first?"

Janie sat on the edge of the bed and patted the spot next to her. "Why don't you sit down?"

"I don't have time to sit. He'll be here in ten minutes." Hannah dug through an old shoebox and then lifted a faux ruby-and-bead earring. "Here's one. Now where's the other?"

"I'll look. You wash your face." Janie took the box from Hannah and started digging through it. "Who's coming?"

Hannah hurried over to the bathroom but left the door open. "Luke," she yelled between splashes. "We haven't really talked since the fire, have we?"

"No." Janie's mind filled with all she'd yet to tell Hannah. She located the missing earring and grabbed it. A red velvet case caught her attention. Janie flipped it open and pulled out a beautiful strand of antique pearls. "Forget the beads—you should wear this."

Hannah stepped back into the room, drying her face, and froze, her gaze fixed on the necklace. Then she seemed to shake herself out of it. Taking the pearls from Janie, she dropped them back in the box and snapped it shut. "I'll stick with the red jewelry."

She claimed the other earring as if that weird exchange hadn't just happened. "So after the fire, I went over to apologize to Luke and he kissed me. Then today he took me out on a date and it was going terrible. We fought because we do that a lot, but it was good fighting because we talked about the past. He said he regretted not taking me to the prom so he would tonight, and he'll be here in ten"—she glanced at the clock—"make that five minutes. So, dress or makeup first?"

Janie's mind spun. "Luke kissed you?"

Hannah grabbed the dress. "I'll go with the dress."

She slipped the gown over her head and turned her back to Janie.

Janie worked the zipper as her vision blurred. "Thomas almost kissed me."

Hannah whirled to face her. "What? How almost?"

Janie's mind flashed back to the moment he'd leaned toward her. "Very almost."

"What happened?" Hannah reached up and started undoing a few of the curlers. "Are you two—"

"No." Janie lay back on the bed and rested her arm across her face. "He fled. Ran out the door, and we haven't said more than a polite hello at work since. I feel terrible. Terrible for doing that to Madison and terrible because I wanted to kiss him so much. Standing with him in the diner . . . nothing had ever felt more right. I wanted it to be our diner . . . our life."

The bed shook as Hannah plopped onto it. "I

can stay home if you want. We can watch old movies and eat ice cream all night."

Janie laughed and wiped away a tear. "And ruin your second chance at a senior prom? No way. Where are you really going anyway?"

"I have no idea. He's planning it all." Hannah smoothed her hands across the velvet dress as her face grew serious. "Is this a mistake? I mean, I'm not sure a fancy date will fix the past hurts even if I do understand him better now."

"Of course it won't fix them." Janie sat up, pulled out one of the heels from a shoebox, and handed it to Hannah. "Luke can't fix the fact he hurt you, but you can forgive him, and you guys can take what was broken and make something beautiful and new out of it."

"When did you become so wise?" She slipped the shoe on and reached for the other.

"I've had a lot of lonely evenings to reflect." Janie stepped over to Hannah's old desk and lifted a framed photo from a few years ago. It was a snapshot of their college group down by the beach. Janie was snug against Thomas's side with her head on his shoulder. "You're going to have to clean all this stuff out if you sell the house."

"Don't remind me." Hannah stepped closer and glanced at the photo. "You two looked so happy."

Janie set the photo back down with a thud. "*Looked* is the key word."

"Photos don't lie. Wait. That's it." Hannah

darted over to a shelf, pulled an old photo album off, and started flipping the pages.

What was that girl up to now? "Is that us in junior high?"

"Yup." Hannah paused on a page, grabbed her phone, and snapped a photo.

A knock at the front door echoed through the house, and Hannah's hands flew to the remaining curlers in the front of her hair. "I'm not ready."

"I'll get it." Janie hurried down the steps and opened the front door.

Madison. Her smile died on her face as her lips pressed into a line. "It was only a matter of time."

Janie held up her hand. "It's not what—"

"Not my problem anymore." Madison held out a box and pointed to her car. The little red Honda was packed to the roof. "I'm on my way out of town and found a few things I thought he'd want back."

"You're leaving? Does Thomas know?"

Madison ignored her question and made her way down the steps but paused by her car door to look back. "Take care of him. He's a great guy." Without anything more, she climbed in, slammed the door, and peeled away from the curb.

"Was that Luke?" Hannah stood halfway down the stairs.

"Madison." Janie motioned to the box. "She's leaving and wanted to give Thomas back some stuff."

Hannah rushed down the remaining steps. "Do you think they actually broke up?"

Janie shrugged as her mind somersaulted with possibilities.

"Maybe that near-kiss was a wake-up call for him after all." Hannah squeezed her arm and slammed the door.

The blue plates above their heads rattled, and they held their breath before they burst out laughing.

"We still have your eye makeup to do." Janie turned Hannah toward the stairs and they hurried up.

Another knock came five minutes later and they both squealed.

Janie shut her makeup bag. "I'll answer that. You have to make a grand entrance."

The knock came again, and she rushed down to open it. Luke stood in a black suit, hair tamed back, and smooth shaven. If she wasn't so in love with Thomas, she might've swooned.

"Is Hannah—" His words halted as his gaze fixed on Hannah descending the stairs.

The black velvet suited Hannah, and the ruby jewelry she'd chosen drew attention to her large hazel eyes. The dress may have been almost a decade old, but the cut and style were timeless. Her hair fell in beach curls around her bare shoulders.

"Wow. Now I really regret not taking you seven

years ago." Luke took her hand and leaned down to brush a kiss across her lips, then paused and glanced at Janie. "Hi."

"Hi." Janie finger waved. "You two have fun tonight."

"Oh, we will." Luke pulled Hannah toward the car.

She sent a smile back to Janie. "Thank you."

Janie nodded and closed the door behind them. That was a happy ending. The way life should be.

She caught sight of the box she'd set on the coffee table. Had Thomas and Madison really broken up? She plopped on the second step. It was almost too good to believe. Maybe her happy ending was just around the corner too.

The jingle of keys and creaking of the door made Janie jump. She stood as Thomas opened the door and stared at her with a blank expression. "Why are you in my house?"

His house. Right. This must look stalkerish. "I was helping Hannah."

Thomas glanced around. "Where is she?"

Janie closed her eyes as her neck and ears grew impossibly hot. Just bury her now. "She left."

"But you stayed?" He hung his keys on a hook by the door but didn't come closer.

"She went on a date with Luke. They just left. I was leaving too. Now." Janie stepped to the door and then motioned to the box. "Madison stopped by while we were here and left that box for you."

Thomas's expression didn't change. "What did she say?"

Janie forced her face to remain calm as she shrugged. "Not much."

Madison hadn't said very many words. But she sure had hinted a lot.

Tell me, Thomas. Please. Let's put this whole terrible year behind us.

He held the door for her to go. "Okay, I'll see you at work tomorrow."

Janie's heart dropped to her toes. "Sure thing."

She snatched her purse as she hurried out the door. Her makeup bag was still upstairs, but she'd make Hannah get it for her. She had no desire to stay a minute longer where she wasn't wanted.

fourteen

She hadn't thought that Luke had planned for anything more than a fancy dinner. But when he pulled up in front of the Amway Grand in downtown Grand Rapids, Hannah about passed out.

Luke jumped out of the car and came around to open her door. He extended his hand with that charming dimple in his left cheek. "Ready to go to the prom?"

His warm hand engulfed hers as he tucked it into the crook of his arm and gave the keys to the valet.

"So, what're we really doing here?" she asked.

A stretch limo pulled up to the curb where her car had been a moment before. Laughter spilled out when the driver opened the door, and one by one, four couples emerged. Sequins, taffeta, tuxes, and only one or two old enough to vote.

Luke led her through the main doors where a sign welcomed Riverwest High School.

Hannah was really at a high school prom for the first time at age twenty-five. A laugh bubbled up inside her.

Her steps faltered as they neared the line where they were expected to hand over tickets. "Luke, we can't go in there. We don't even know where Riverwest High is."

"It's west of a river." He gave her hand a squeeze and pulled past the line, aiming for the door. "Just smile."

A round woman's lips thinned as they approached. She marched toward them, sprouts of hair escaping from what was probably once a nice hairdo. "You there."

They were going to get kicked out of the prom before they even got in.

The woman bore down on them, sweat beading at her temples. "Glad you two are finally here. I can't do everything. Cover the dance floor. I've got to keep these yahoos from bringing more of this junk in here." She held up a flask and eyed it with longing.

"Sorry we're late." Luke's voice was calm, confident.

She snapped her focus back to him. "Just keep them from getting indecent on the dance floor, would ya?"

"Nothing indecent. Got it." Luke pulled Hannah toward the archway of balloons that led to the main hall.

The area was dim, but different-colored lights angled around. "I thought you just came up with this idea," Hannah said. "Did you volunteer us to—"

"No, but since it's May and this is one of the most popular places to hold a prom, I took a chance that there would be one tonight and they'd be shorthanded on chaperones." He entwined their fingers and led her through a clump of teenagers. "Looks like I was right."

Hannah shook her head. "What would you have done if you were wrong?"

"Toured this beautiful building with you. Maybe taken a walk by the river. Danced by the car. I don't know." He took both of her hands in his. "We don't have to stay if you don't want to."

"Are you kidding?" Hannah pointed to the banner. "The theme is Reel Romances. I love movie romances. Let's go look."

She yanked Luke to the side, where a row of six-foot line drawings on plywood stood up like paper dolls. All unforgettable cinematic moments. "There's Audrey Hepburn from *Breakfast at Tiffany's*, and there's Baby and Johnny's final dance from *Dirty Dancing*, and of course, the flying scene on the bow from *Titanic*."

Luke stared at her. "I'm glad you're having fun."

Wrapping her arms around his neck, she dropped a quick kiss on his dimple. "I am. Thank you."

A cutout of a boom box peeked over Luke's shoulder, and she spun him around and pointed. "Lloyd."

"Lloyd? The radio dude?"

"John Cusack in *Say Anything . . .*" She tugged him over to the cutout and handed her phone to him. "You have to take a picture of me."

"You and your Lloyd." He snapped it and shook his head.

"Don't worry. I think I like you better."

"You think?" Luke grabbed her hand and pulled her to him, wrapping her in his arms.

"Okay, I know. Let's get a picture of us too." She took her phone back and tapped on the screen so they could take a selfie.

"Dance with me?" He tugged her close, his gaze intense.

Hannah melted a little before her pulse started to climb. Somehow their fun, joking banter of the evening had turned serious. The smoky-eyes kind of serious. She swallowed and drew a breath. She'd forgotten to do that for a minute.

She followed Luke out on the dance floor and leaned into him. They might fail as chaperones since she couldn't make herself pay any attention to what was going on beyond the set of wide shoulders where her head rested.

After three dances, a Beyoncé tune picked up the tempo, and the teens around them began to move in ways that didn't look much like dancing to Hannah. Had she really been out of high school that long? Luke led her to the side, where they found an empty table.

Hannah snapped a few photos of the room and then scanned through the ones she'd taken so far. She stopped at the one she'd snapped from her photo album. It captured Luke and Mrs.

Shoemaker at their eighth grade graduation. Him with his goofy grin and Mrs. Shoemaker with her ever-present gray bun and dressed in her Sunday best. She was smiling as wide as any proud parent.

"Remember when you said at the hospital that you were never wanted?"

He tensed and nodded.

"I think you're wrong. Mrs. Shoemaker may have had her own issues, but she loved you and wanted you. Just look at her face." Hannah passed over her phone.

He studied it a minute and handed the phone back. "Trying to fix my issues again?"

"No, I—"

"Relax." He reached over and claimed her hand. "I was just teasing. Maybe you're right. Either way, I appreciate that you care."

Maybe he'd feel the same way about Al. Or maybe not.

"Would you send that to me? Along with the photos of us." Luke stood and motioned toward the refreshment table. "Want me to get you some punch?"

"Yeah, but you better make sure it isn't spiked."

As Luke disappeared into the crowd she texted him the photos, then sent a few to Janie. Wait until she found out Luke and Hannah were really at a prom.

"You're too beautiful to leave alone." A voice that had changed maybe six months ago did its best to sound older than the person it belonged to. "Want to dance?"

"She's with me." Luke's voice came from behind her.

The boy paled and backed up. "Sorry, mister."

Luke's suit emphasized his wide shoulders. Yes, he could be intimidating. Unless it was Hannah looking at him, then his appearance made her insides go warm.

"He's right, though, you are too beautiful to leave alone." His gaze darted back to the stage. "Want to dance?"

"Where's the punch?"

"I'll get it in a minute." Luke captured her hand and pulled her toward the dance floor.

"We have a special request from someone tonight." The DJ spoke into the mic with a smooth tenor. "It dates back a bit, but considering the theme, I thought it fit right in. And he gave me fifty bucks."

Luke shifted from one foot to the other, waiting for the song to start. Strange. He wrapped his arms around her, but his hold was stiffer than before.

The first few notes traveled through the room, and she leaned back and stared at Luke. "This is that song from *Say Anything* . . . I was telling you about. 'In Your Eyes' by Peter something."

"Peter Gabriel." He seemed to be holding his breath.

"Wait, you requested this?"

"Too cheesy?" One eyebrow lifted, his back still ramrod straight.

Hannah reached up and brushed her lips across his. "No. I love it."

He released a breath and pulled her to him, cradling her head against his shoulder. "I'm glad, because I'm not up to doing the whole boom-box-in-the-road thing."

Hannah laughed and sank into the smell of Luke. It couldn't get more perfect than this. She leaned her head back and met his gaze. "Have I changed your mind about selling your house?"

He leaned down and pressed his lips next to her ear, sending a chill down her side. "Let's get out of here."

He pulled her through the crowd. Good thing. She wasn't sure she could have navigated it at the time. Her brain had started misfiring the second his breath traveled along her neck. This would definitely be a night she wouldn't forget.

It had been two weeks since Madison left, and he still hadn't gotten the guts to bring it up to Janie. Thomas added up the last of the receipts from the day and tried not to look at her. Didn't work. She wiped the counter down from the last customer before her eyes darted to him and then away. No doubt she was waiting for him to spill his big secret. No, she was waiting for him to say they still had a chance, but he couldn't do that. Whether he was engaged or not, the real problem hadn't changed.

Gideon, Janie and Olivia's eighteen-year-old brother, poked his head in the front door and shook the remains of the rain from his shaggy blond hair. "Ready, Olivia?"

"I thought I was taking you home." Janie stood up straight and folded the rag in her hand.

"Gideon offered, so I'll go with him." Olivia gave her sister a pointed look and nodded in Thomas's direction before walking out the door.

That was subtle. There was no more avoiding it. "Janie, I need to tell you . . ."

"Yes?" Janie twisted the rag in her hands.

Thomas swallowed against his tight throat. "I'm sorry I almost kissed you. That was out of line."

The color drained from Janie's face. "I see." She scrubbed at a spot on the counter, this time with a little more vengeance than the coffee smudge required. The patter of the rain on the roof filled the silence.

He punched a few numbers on the cash register and the drawer popped open. "Why don't you go home before the rain gets too bad? I'll finish up here."

She stared at him for a beat, then tossed her rag in the bucket and marched toward the kitchen. She must have parked in the alley. The back door rattled as it slammed.

That hadn't gone well, but then what had he expected? How would they survive working together much longer?

The bell above the door jingled as Hannah pushed in and fought to put down her umbrella. "It's starting to really come down out there. Where's Janie?"

"Just left." Lifting the twenties out of the cash drawer, he started counting. "Jar's over there."

Hannah retrieved the jar before returning to the counter where he was working. "Have you told her yet?"

"I told her that I was out of line for nearly kissing her." He stared at the money in his hand. Shoot, he'd lost count.

Hannah dropped her purse on the counter with a thud. "I got a call on your house today. Are you still selling?"

His hands paused on the money. "Yes."

"That's really what you want?" Her tone punched out each word.

He pulled a velvet box from his pocket and set it in front of her. "It's really what I want. Here, you and Luke might need it someday."

Hannah flipped it open and shook her head as she slid it back toward him. "Grandma Hazel left it to you. For *your* wife."

"What wife?" Thomas pushed the box back to her. He scratched the amount of the twenties into the right column of his ledger and reached for the tens. "At this point, it doesn't seem as if I'll ever have one."

"You'd have one if you'd be honest." She slammed the box on his ledger.

"We've gone over this. Besides, the ring needs to be passed down. Face it, I won't have anyone to pass it down to. I can't have kids, remember?" His voice rose to a near shout as he slammed the box down in front of her.

Hannah's eyes widened. "Janie—"

"Janie wants a big family. I can't give her that." Thomas dropped the tens back in the drawer and pushed it shut. He'd count it later.

Her lips tightened. "Stop—"

"No, *you* stop." He was tired of this. Wasn't his sister supposed to be on his side? "Don't you know how hard this is for me? Why can't you support me?"

"Janie's behind you." The words came out rapid-fire.

Janie stood about ten feet behind him, her hand clutching the pass-through door to the kitchen. Her face ghostly pale. "I forgot my sweater." She lifted it from the hook, her eyes not focusing on anything. Her hair, damp from the rain, clung to the side of her face, and goose bumps covered her arms. "Did you really break up with me because you found out that you can't have children?"

"And that's my cue to go." Hannah grabbed the jar of money and her keys, shouldered her purse, and pushed through the front door into the rain.

Thanks a lot, little sister.

"Did you?"

She wasn't supposed to find out like this. Or ever.

The ticking of the clock echoed in the room. The storm outside even paused for his answer.

"Answer me." Her face was still pale. Her hands clutching the sweater shook.

Thomas took a hesitant step toward her, then stopped. "I found out last summer. Because of my treatment for cancer I had as a kid, I can't have kids. I know you want a big family—"

"So you dumped me?" Tears gathered at the corners of her eyes.

"I did it for you, Janie. Can't you see that?"

"For me?" She marched toward him. "Oh, please, do explain."

Thomas stood up straighter. "I know how much you want to be a mother. Don't you know how much I wanted to give that to you? But I can't. You deserve to be with someone who can."

"You think I wanted that more than I wanted you?" She shoved her arms into her sweater with such force he feared she might rip it.

"My mom never wanted kids, and she'd always dreamed of spending her life traveling the world."

"And . . ."

He leaned against the counter, gripping the edge. "Don't you see? My dad knew that, but he married her even though his life was here. Then two kids later she finds herself strapped to a town and a life she never wanted. How fair was that? Who could blame her for leaving?"

She crossed her arms over her chest. "It wasn't your dad's fault that your mom left, Thomas. She left because she was selfish."

She didn't get it. But how would she, coming from her perfect *Leave It to Beaver* family?

Thomas stared at the floor, then pushed away from the counter. "Yeah, well, my dad knew what she wanted when he married her. But he trapped her here just the same."

"Trapped her? Did she marry him against her will? Was she unaware that your dad's job was here when she married him? She chose the marriage as much as your dad." A crack of thunder rattled the front window.

"That's my point. He convinced her she wanted it. Kids were never in her plan." He raised his voice to be heard above the rain.

"Life doesn't always turn out the way we expect, but it doesn't mean we throw in the towel. Yes, that's what your mom did, but it doesn't mean that's what I'd do." Janie dug her fingers into her hair. "Don't you get it? I was ready to commit 'til death do us part."

"But I didn't want you to have to give up your dream." His voice echoed in the room as the rain quieted.

She marched over and jabbed her finger in his chest. "No, you didn't want to take the chance that I'd turn out like your mom. But instead of giving me the chance, instead of trusting me, you decided for me."

Thomas captured her hand as his voice quieted. "You say that, but I know how much having a big family means to you. Passing your heritage on and all that."

"Heritage isn't bound to the genetic code, Thomas." She yanked her hand from his grasp and took a few steps back. "It's what we give the next generation, whether by birth, adoption, being an aunt or uncle, or mentoring a kid in the community. It's investing in others, and that investment is a choice."

Crossing his arms over his chest, he shook his head. "You think it wouldn't bother you to never have kids?"

The wind picked up, whipping the tattered awning back and forth against the front window.

"That's a dumb question. Of course it would. It's something I've always wanted, but it's out of my control. No matter who I marry, it's out of my control. What if *I'm* infertile? What if I carry a rare genetic disorder that affects my kids? People like to pretend they're in control of the whole children thing, but they're not." She pressed her lips together and stared at him. "If I never have kids I'm sure I'll grieve that dream, but that won't be the end. God will give me a new dream."

The growing rumble of thunder indicated the worst of the storm hadn't even passed.

"God would've given us a new dream *together*. Don't you see? I wanted to walk through this *with* you. Cry *with* you and find answers *with* you." The tears spilled down her cheeks and she wiped them away with the sleeve of her sweater. "You never gave me a chance. You just shut me out. That's not love."

Thomas took a hesitant step toward her. "You'd have regrets."

She backed up to the kitchen door. "No. The only regret I have is trusting you with my heart in the first place. You obviously don't believe in me." Shaking her head, she wiped away another tear. "I wonder if you ever did."

Lightning flashed again, followed quickly by a crack of thunder. The lights flickered but stayed on.

"So thank you for dumping me. Because I'd hate to marry someone who thought so little of my character."

The words were like a sucker punch. How could she think that? "That's not—"

"True? Fair? Kinda stinks having others tell you how you feel, doesn't it?" Janie marched through the kitchen, and a moment later the back door slammed again.

A crack of thunder shook the diner again, then the lights went out and stayed out.

Luke added the numbers in his checkbook for a second time. Unfortunately, his math had been right. Fixing the truck had nearly emptied him out. If he hadn't still been paying on it, he'd have scrapped it and bought a new one. His and Hannah's date this weekend would have to be a night in. A rented movie and frozen pizza. He could afford that. Maybe.

Sweat dripped down the side of his face, and he rubbed his cheek against his shoulder. Ugh. Summer warmth had decided to arrive in spades. He flipped the latch on the window above the sink and cranked it open, letting the afternoon breeze flow through the house.

His goal had been to save enough each month so he could stop living paycheck to paycheck. But between the money he'd put into updating the house and his truck, he'd landed himself back at the bottom.

He cringed as he mentally added up how much he'd invested in this house already. If Kensington bought the house, it would be a total loss. After all, Luke had no right to the property. Maybe he could return the windows he'd yet to install. But they were all custom sized.

He'd take on more hours at work, but the gazebo was eating up all his extra time. Then there was the website he hadn't even started yet. He poured himself a glass of water and dropped into his computer chair. Luckily, Hannah's tastes in websites ran simple. He could do simple. Probably.

He slid the SD card out of her camera into the port of his laptop and dragged the folder icon to his desktop. The icon transformed into a spinning hourglass and Luke rolled his head around, waiting as the photos transferred. One. At. A. Time.

What he wouldn't give for a new computer. And something stronger than this water or he'd never stay awake.

He pushed out of his chair. Please let there be a Coke left.

He was halfway to the fridge when a loud crash halted his steps. Twisting around, he caught sight of Spitz crashing through the room as he chased a squirrel that ran along the porch railing outside the window. "Spitz, no!"

Too late.

The dog crashed into the side of his computer desk, toppling the glass of water all over the laptop. The screen blinked twice before going black. No. No. This wasn't happening.

He raced back to the computer, his fingers fumbling as they pulled out the SD card and shoved it into the camera. *ERR* flashed on the display. His pulse pounded an ache into his temples.

Shoot.

He held up the computer by one corner as the water dripped off while he yanked out the power cord and disconnected the battery. He pulled a towel from the drawer, laid it out, and did his best to towel off the laptop. Rice supposedly helped, but he didn't have that much on hand.

Thomas was a techie. Luke reached for his phone.

"Hey, Luke, what's up?"

Luke ran through the scenario of what happened. "Any hope for the card?"

"With only an error message it's hard to say."

Luke flipped the camera on again and hit Display as if it might miraculously start working. Nope.

"Sometimes the data can be recovered. I know a few guys in Grand Rapids. It's not cheap, though, and no guarantees."

His bank balance flashed through his mind, and he rubbed his eyes with his hand. He bit back a few unpleasant words.

The phone beeped in his ear. He glanced at the screen. Hannah was trying to call. The phone nearly slipped out of his sweat-slicked palm. Shoot. He'd call her back. The last thing he wanted to have to tell her was that he'd lost the photos. "Know anyone who does work on the side, in town?"

"There is someone local who could probably

help, and he might not charge you because he's not hurting for money, but . . ."

Not hurting for money? That could only be one person. "Who?"

"Derek. He had a computer minor in college."

Of course. Luke's gut tightened. "I'll figure something out."

He threw his phone aside. Maybe he could take the SD card in after payday and Hannah would never be the wiser. He might be able to distract her for a few days.

His voicemail chirped. He picked up the phone and tapped the screen. "Hey, Luke, I just wanted to know if you've gotten the photos yet for the website. I really was hoping to get the site up and running before Friday. Call me."

Okay, waiting until Friday wasn't an option. Luke reached for the phone book. Derek was going to be able to save the day for Hannah once again.

Thirty minutes later, he pulled into the Kensington estate, following the long drive up to the pillared house. Mansion. He hadn't been here since Jon had left for Europe. He slid out of the car and headed toward the door, but Derek had it open before he got there.

"Derek."

"Luke."

Okay, he needed to sound a bit friendlier. Derek was saving his hide, after all. A fact

Derek wouldn't soon let him forget, no doubt.

"Thanks for doing this." There, that sounded . . . pleasant. He could be nice.

"Does Hannah know you jacked up her card?" Not so pleasant.

Luke pressed his lips together to keep from saying something he'd regret. "Can we get on with this?"

Derek stepped back inside, leaving the door open. Luke followed him through the house to the office. Neither spoke as Derek dropped into a plush leather chair and held out his hand.

Luke passed over the card. He had no desire for chitchat.

Derek slid the card into the computer and punched a few keys until a progress bar appeared. One percent done. This could take a while.

"So, I hear you're losing your house." Derek tapped a pen against the desk as the bar moved to two percent.

Luke crossed his arms in front of him. "The town council hasn't voted yet."

Derek offered a half laugh and rocked back in the chair. "Formality. My dad can pay more than it's worth. We Kensingtons tend to get what we want."

"Hannah," Luke coughed into his hand.

The muscle in Derek's jaw twitched. "You think this little fling you two have going will last? Come on. You know she wants to stay in town, and if you lose that house . . . There isn't much for sale right now in town, but you could always look at the housing in Muskegon."

"I'll remember that." Luke leaned against the wall behind him. "I heard you fudged the numbers on the survey. Guess things aren't looking so great for the assistant fireman's job. Too bad Ted signed off on it too."

Derek's eyes hardened. "Well, at least I didn't break protocol and run into the burning building without equipment, costing personnel and resources to save me."

The bar on the screen crawled a little farther. Four percent done. Really?

Derek must have read his thoughts. "I can drop it off."

"Today?"

Derek stared at him. "Sure."

Luke made his way to the front door, doing his best not to slam it on the way out. Derek would drop off the photos and Hannah would never have to know. He just had to keep Hannah distracted until then.

fifteen

Agreeing to watch her six-year-old sister today could be categorized as pure brilliance. Janie was not ready to be alone with Thomas. She jabbed the floor with the mop to erase a black scuff, then dropped the mop back in the bucket. Thomas stood at the cash register, punching numbers into the calculator. Dark circles under his eyes testified that he hadn't been sleeping well either. He blinked and slammed the money drawer shut. When he looked up they locked eyes. He opened his mouth as if to say something.

"I think they should have made her dress pink," Trinity announced from a nearby booth as she colored in her book.

It broke the spell. Thomas blinked and turned away. He lifted Trinity to stand on the seat of the booth and turned his back to her. "Want to help me start the soup?"

She jumped on his back and the two disappeared into the kitchen. Thomas had always been so good with Trin—he'd been good with all of Janie's siblings, for that matter.

Trinity's laughter floated over from the kitchen. Janie had to get out of here, but it wasn't like she could leave. The door that led to the adjoining storefront snagged her attention. It wasn't as far away as she wanted, but maybe it was far enough.

"I'm going next door." Janie wheeled the bucket to the door and undid the old latch. Stale air filled her lungs, and she coughed and blinked against the dim light. The old glass display counter, tin ceiling, and wrought-iron chairs with matching tables gave the place character, dirty or not. Too bad the little candy shop hadn't made it. It would make a perfect bakery. If only she had the money.

Dust disturbed by her entrance swirled in a beam of sunlight that peeked from a tear in the butcher paper covering the front windows, and she sneezed. She unlocked the ornate wooden double doors that opened onto the street and stepped into the fresh spring air. A definite improvement.

She closed her eyes and lifted her face to the sun. June offered a welcome change.

"Nice day, isn't it?"

She gave a small scream and jerked her head back down.

Nate stood on the sidewalk in a T-shirt, his hands in the pockets of his jeans as if he had all the time in the world. "Sorry, I didn't mean to scare you."

"No, I'm sorry. I don't usually startle that easy."

He shrugged, dismissing the apology. "I was actually looking for you. Would you consider leading a Bible study? I have a small group of junior high girls interested but can't lead that myself."

"Me?" She rubbed her dirty hands against her apron. Her words to Thomas filled her mind. *Heritage isn't bound to the genetic code. It's what we give the next generation, whether by birth, adoption, or mentoring a kid in the community. It's investing in others, and that investment is a choice.*

Was this what she should do? "Truth is, I don't know how long I'll be here."

"Do any of us?"

"I don't mean like dying." A laugh bubbled up as she leaned against the door frame. "I don't know if I'll even be in Heritage by the end of the summer."

His brows arched. "You're moving?"

"I don't want to, but I need a job."

"A job?" Nate clutched at his chest. "Please tell me you aren't going to stop making your pie. I think I've become addicted."

"This is a temporary job to help out Don and Lucy. But when they're back I doubt they can afford another full-time employee."

"Make this a bakery." Nate motioned to the dirty old shop behind her.

"Tempting. But that would be taking a big chance. I mean, the candy shop went bankrupt. And I'm not sure that Heritage eats enough cakes and pies to support a bakery either."

"You'd just have to make a presence. I bet people would drive for many miles to get some of that pie." He patted his stomach. "My stomach thinks it's a great idea. But seriously, if it is really something you want, pray about it. Maybe God will start opening doors."

Pray about it? Janie plopped down on the concrete step. "I'm not sure I trust my ability to hear God's answer. Have you ever been so sure you knew what God had planned for you, only to be completely wrong? I prayed about . . . something. And I believed I knew what His plan was, yet it all fell apart."

Nate eased down next to her, dropping his elbows on his knees. "I'm not sure if it's always the end goal God has in mind as much as our willingness to follow Him on the journey no matter what happens."

"Well, I did, and now I'm left with nothing." She picked up a pebble and tossed it at the curb.

Nate leaned back and gazed across the field. "That's a good place to be."

She blinked at him. He had to be kidding.

He focused back on her and shrugged. "When you've got nothing left, that's when you see how real your faith is. Faith with everything you want is easy. But faith when everything goes wrong? That's when God alone has to be enough."

Her head dropped in her hands. A year ago she'd thought she had everything she wanted, and now look at her. Job's story from the Bible came to mind. "Kind of like Job. Except he had it worse."

Nate clapped his hands together. "That's it. Job. Good one. That's a solid GP."

"Grace point. You've mentioned that at church."

He relaxed back on his hands again. "I'm not saying the Bible is a vending machine for life's problems. But chances are if you're in a tight spot, you're not the first person to have that struggle or one much like it."

Nate was quite different from their last pastor. "If Job is my GP, does that mean I get everything back better in the end?"

"Wouldn't that be nice? But like I said, the Bible isn't a quick-fix problem solver. You have to look at the bigger truths being told. Truths about the problems of humanity and truths about the unchanging God. In Job's story, we see that God wasn't afraid of what the enemy brought. He was with Job through it all. And after it was over, Job learned that God alone had to be enough."

Janie stared across the field to Thomas's house. Was God alone enough for her? Her Sunday school–saturated brain said yes. But would she be okay with never being married, never being a mother, never being a pastry chef?

The idea made it hard to breathe. But if she had to choose those dreams or God, she'd choose God 100 percent of the time. Because no matter how much she thought she knew what she wanted, only God knew what was best for her, and she still believed He had a plan.

Janie picked up a jagged chunk of cement that had broken off the step and tried to fit it back where it belonged. It refused to stay. "Do you think someone else could mess up God's plan for my life?" She tossed the broken corner to the ground and dusted off her hands.

" 'Mess up' isn't the right word." Nate pointed to the new field across the street. "That field wasn't Hannah's plan. I heard some grumblings about how Hannah had messed up. After all, the center of town was a pile of ash. But what do you see now?"

"It's beautiful."

"Exactly. The enemy is out to steal, kill, and destroy anything God has for us. But I also know that nothing surprises God. I know He hasn't forgotten you. And I know that if you continue to make Him your first love, He'll honor that. He has a way of making beautiful things out of piles of ash."

No matter what Thomas did or didn't do, God hadn't forgotten her.

Nate picked up a small white rock and scratched a forty-five-degree angle across the concrete at the corner of the step. Then he handed the white rock to her and pointed to her broken corner. "We may never know what could have been. But let's see what can be."

Janie scratched a rough forty-five to match his, eliminating the broken corner and adding an attractive angle to the ends of the step.

"Pastor Nate! You're here." Trinity ran through the door. Her blonde pigtails swayed as she dropped her arms around Nate's neck.

"Is that a bad thing?" He grabbed her hands and stood, pulled her onto his back, and started turning in circles. Trinity had every eligible bachelor in town wrapped around her little finger.

"No. I like you. You're fun." Trin giggled as she spun and then staggered when he set her down. "You should come to my house to visit. I think Olivia likes you."

His face reddened as he laughed and rubbed the back of his neck, revealing another tattoo on his forearm.

"Trinity Rose." Janie shot her sister a look. Nate and Olivia's relationship, or lack thereof, seemed to be as mysterious as it was sensitive to both of them.

He pulled his keys from his pocket. "Think about the Bible study. And I'll be praying that you open a bakery." He patted his stomach again. "Uh . . . I mean, I'll pray God gives you wisdom if you should open one."

Janie laughed and offered a wave as he jogged across the street to his car. Maybe she'd pray that whatever was up with him and Olivia would work out too. She could get used to him as a brother-in-law.

Could she really open a bakery? She turned to survey the entire front. It would be so much work. And take so much money. She could lose everything.

Having nothing is a good place to be. Then God alone has to be enough.

Was God alone enough?

Turning to Trinity, she lifted the girl's pudgy hand. "Let's get this place cleaned and see what it can be. What do you say?"

It had to be here. There was no other option. Hannah dug deeper into her purse, pushing aside her wallet and sunglasses. How could she have lost it? It wasn't like that much money could hide behind her tube of lipstick. It wasn't there. A chill ran down her body as she upended the entire purse, scattering the contents across the passenger seat.

Eighteen hundred forty-two dollars and seventy-six cents. She'd counted it that morning—twice. Aligned the bills in sequential order. Rolled the coins. She couldn't have lost it.

Think. Where had she been?

She'd stopped by Luke's, but he'd been at work so she'd gone to the diner for lunch. Then she'd driven straight here to the town hall to drop off the money. But it was gone. Just gone.

"Hey, Hannah darlin'." The mayor's voice boomed from outside the open car window. She jumped and spun to face him. "I heard the collection was a success."

Hannah swallowed. "Yup."

"Great. When you get it all counted, just drop it off to Marcy at the front desk."

Should she tell him? No, she couldn't tell him. "Sure thing."

She offered a quick wave and threw her car into Reverse. The money had to turn up before anyone knew it was missing. How could almost two thousand dollars disappear? It might not be as much as the ten thousand her mom had taken, but it wouldn't be long before everyone in town started connecting the dots. And when they did, they'd draw an arrow pointed directly at her.

She pulled in front of the diner and slid into the last open spot. Gathering the remains of her purse, she lifted her chin and walked toward the diner. *Must appear casual.*

Pushing through the door, Hannah halted as she took in the family filling up the booth where she'd eaten lunch. She could see from where she stood that there was no large blue envelope under the table. Great. She turned to Olivia walking by. "Did anyone turn in anything . . . lost?"

Olivia topped off a glass of water at the closest table before looking at Hannah. "Can you be more specific?"

"A blue envelope."

Olivia filled the other two glasses at the booth. "Not that I know of, but I'll ask around."

Hannah leaned against an empty barstool. What

would she do if she couldn't find the money? She didn't have two thousand dollars in her account to cover it.

Maybe Luke would know what to do.

Derek slid onto the stool next to her, draping his arm on the table behind her. "Hey, pretty lady. Mind if I join you?"

Hannah leaned away from him. "Actually—"

He held out a thumb drive and SD card in the palm of his hand. "Here are the photos Luke erased from your camera. I couldn't get them all, though, only the stuff from the past five weeks."

"Luke erased my photos?" Her hand tightened on the handle of her purse as she calculated what had been on that card. That meant all pre-fire pictures of the veteran houses were gone. Her stomach tightened. Those would be a bit hard to replace. She took them from his hand. "I can't believe he didn't tell me."

It wasn't like she'd have been mad. Okay, a little mad, but things happen. She stepped away from the stool, but the knit of her skirt snagged on a screw.

"Don't take it so hard. He has a lot on his mind, with losing his house and all."

Hannah tugged at her skirt, trying to free it. "What're you talking about?"

Derek leaned back, crossing his arms in front of him. "Didn't you hear? It turns out Old Lady Shoemaker's will turned up in some box in a

306

wall. It says that the house he was trying to buy was supposed to go to the town."

Hannah's movement stopped as every nerve went numb, then she slowly turned back to Derek. A box in a wall? The box she'd found? "But they can't just take it from him."

"My dad can offer a higher bid than Luke ever could. He's anxious to get a few more businesses on the properties that line the square. He likes what you've done, even if you didn't crash and burn like he hoped."

"Crash and burn?"

"I mean, when he suggested the fire he figured you'd fail. I think he figured he'd come in and save the day with his big project." He ran his finger along her arm. "But I knew you could pull it off."

She jerked her arm back. "He suggested the fire? You promised you wouldn't even talk to your dad about our meetings."

Derek blinked. No doubt trying to come up with a quick lie.

She held up her hand. "You know what? I don't care."

"You've got it all wrong. I was—am on your side. But you impressed my dad and that isn't easy to do. He now hopes to buy all the houses on Henderson Road." He pointed out the window. The air cooled as thick clouds drifted over the sun, dimming the diner.

Did he not realize he was also talking about her childhood home? The guy was clueless. At least Thomas still had control of his house for the time being. But if Kensington bought Luke's . . . She might be sick. "When did Luke find this out about the will?"

The last few days had been a blur and she hadn't seen him much. Why had she let herself get so busy? Maybe she had a missed call. She checked her phone but only the black screen stared back. Dead battery again. Why could she never remember to charge her phone?

"My dad mentioned it a couple months ago, I guess."

Hannah shook her skirt again until the ripping of the threads set it free. "A couple months ago?" Her voice climbed to an all-time high.

His lips lifted in a smirk. "Luke'll figure something out. I think he's said something about looking at houses in Muskegon."

He wouldn't leave without telling her first, would he? Flashbacks of her mother's abrupt disappearance assaulted her mind. She'd been laughing with her mom in the kitchen one day, and the next day when she got home from school there had been nothing but a note saying goodbye.

Derek leaned a little closer. "You want to go out this Friday?"

Hannah squeezed the two small devices in her palm. "You're a real jerk."

Olivia appeared as Hannah approached the door. "No one has seen anything like that, Hannah. But we'll let you know if something gets turned in."

Right, the money. "Thanks."

What in the world was she going to do? She needed to have a little talk with Luke, that's what.

A blast of summer wind whipped her hair past her shoulders as she pushed from the diner. Why hadn't he told her?

He'd known about the house for at least a couple months and hadn't said a word. That was a long time. Long enough to be looking into moving. Long enough that many replayed conversations in her head seemed a lot more like lies. How long had her mom planned her escape before she ran? Her vision blurred as she stared at the devices in her hand.

He'd told her things would be different this time. She'd been a fool to believe him.

It had been two days and Luke still hadn't heard anything from Derek. He'd left the guy three voicemails and dropped by his house. Nothing. Luke stretched his neck, wrapped his gloved hands around the edges of a sheet of three-quarter-inch plywood, and slid it into the bed of the pickup. It had been a long day and he'd clocked out twenty minutes ago, but when Mrs. Jameson had come in looking frustrated and lost, he couldn't tell her no. He wiped the sleeve of his shirt across his forehead and reached for another sheet.

"Oh, thank you, Luke. Harold's got some fancy project to do with his brother this weekend. I think Hannah Thornton has the whole town spiffing up. He never cared about the worn-out porch before." Mrs. Jameson pulled her purse from the cart. "I can't believe he asked me to pick this up. But I can tell you this, he'll be the one to get it out."

Luke slid the last one into the bed and closed the tailgate. "No problem, Mrs. Jameson. If he needs any help, have him give me a call."

She waved at him as she slid into the truck.

As he drove through town, it looked like Mrs. Jameson had been right. The Mackerses seemed to have taken extra care with their front lawn, and the Fairs had hung a new sign at the mechanic shop. Hannah had lit a fire under the town—literally.

Luke pulled into his driveway and paused. A gray Tundra was parked in front of his house, and Alfred Mathis sat waiting on his porch. Why was the old police chief visiting him?

Luke took the steps two at a time and extended his hand. "Hey, Al. What can I do for you?"

The older gentleman stood, leaning on his cane, and motioned to the house with the briefcase he was holding. "Mind if we go and sit down?"

An unease settled in his joints. "Sure thing." He unlocked the door and blocked Spitz from overwhelming their guest, then nudged the dog toward the back door. "I'll be just a minute. He needs to go out."

"I see you're doing some updating." Al followed him into the kitchen. "Mrs. Shoemaker lived here a very long time. I'm not sure she updated much."

Was Al here about the will? Luke pulled two bottles of water from the fridge and held one out. "Thirsty?"

"No, thank you." Al set his briefcase on the table and popped it open. "I'm here because Hannah asked me to find out about your family."

Luke's bottle of water paused halfway to his mouth. "My family?" The bottle shook in his hand, and he set it on the counter. Hannah had gone behind his back? She just had to fix the situation. Fix him. He would never be enough for her as he was. Luke leaned forward and gripped the table with his hands.

"I called Hannah but it went straight to voice-mail. And after what I found, I didn't want to delay getting this information to you any longer." Al pulled a file from his case and stared at it. "I was on the police force then. I should've put it together. But my wife's death was the month before and I wasn't on top of my game." The man's voice cracked.

His wife's death? What did this have to do with Luke's family?

"When you and your father moved into town . . . I never made the connection. The Chicago PD had his picture everywhere. But the paperwork your dad had was good. Real good. And he'd shaved his beard, which can change a man's looks, you know?" Al gazed at the file and shook his head.

What was he talking about? Did he say Chicago PD? "Are you saying my dad was wanted by the police?"

Al held out the file. "Maybe it would be best if you read the report. I did my best to be thorough."

Luke had always wanted to know something about his father, but this? A criminal with an APB out on him? It didn't get much worse than that. His lifelong hope of finding out about his history now seemed like a cruel joke.

Al stood, leaning heavily on his cane. "I'll leave this file on the table for when you're ready. If you have questions, call me. I'll need to contact Chicago so they can close this case, but I can give you a few days before I do."

Luke had been staring at the closed file unseeing for who knew how long when Hannah stormed in, her hazel eyes shooting fire. She was mad? Really? She had no idea what mad was.

She dropped a thumb drive and an SD card on the table. "Want to tell me about this? Or about the fact you're losing your home? Or house shopping in Muskegon?"

He slammed his hand down on the table where the file still rested. "Why don't you tell me why you hired a PI when I told you not to?"

Hannah's face paled. "He gave the file to you? What does it say?"

She reached for it but he didn't move his hand. "My dad was a criminal, wanted in Chicago. How's that for news?"

Her eyes widened as she reached a hand to his arm. "Oh, Luke—"

"I don't want your pity." If he'd thought he wasn't good enough before, looking at her face at this moment sealed the deal.

Hannah's eyes hardened. "Is that why you didn't tell me about your house? You don't want my pity? It's not pity, it's concern. It may be hard for you to believe, but people in this town care what happens, Luke. I care what happens to you."

"No, you want to rescue me like you rescued Spitz, like you're trying to rescue this town."

She flinched at his words but held her ground. "Don't push me away. You said it would be different this time."

Luke grabbed the file and waved it in the air. "Yeah, well, I thought I could trust you."

Her eyes filled with tears. "If you trusted me you wouldn't be hiding stuff from me."

Him? She was blaming this on him?

"Like hiring a PI wasn't hiding stuff from me?" Luke flung the file across the counter, spilling the contents a bit. A print of the photo of him and his dad peeked out. How had Al gotten—unless . . .

Hannah's ashen face proclaimed her guilt. She had gone through his stuff when he wasn't home.

Her hand shook as she held it up. "I'm sorry, Luke. But Al had said—"

"Don't." Luke's harsh word sliced through the room, causing her to jump. His hands gripped the back of the chair with enough force his palms ached.

She drew a breath as if drawing courage. "What else did he find out?"

If she'd been unsure of him when she hadn't known his history, the details of his father's criminal past didn't matter.

"You said you wouldn't give up on us this time." She laid her hand on his arm.

Him give up? She'd shattered what they had, didn't she see that?

He stepped away from her touch. "I think you need to go."

Hannah reached down and grabbed the SD card and thumb drive from the table. "I'll go now so you can calm down, but this isn't over." With the slam of the door, she was gone.

But it *was* over.

Luke didn't move until his phone rang. "Hello?"

"Hey, Luke, this is Chief Grandy."

Luke stiffened. "Afternoon, sir."

"This wasn't an easy decision. We consider you a valuable part of the community and hope we can still count on your volunteer service. But we've decided to hire someone else."

Luke's stomach tightened. So that was that. "May I ask who?"

"We hired Nate Williams. The new pastor."

Everything in Luke went numb. Nate? Not that Nate wasn't a great guy—he was. But he had lived in Heritage less than a year. He had come in and managed to achieve something in a year that Luke hadn't accomplished in the twenty years he'd lived here. Acceptance.

Luke nodded and struggled to find his voice. "Good choice, sir." He ended the call and tossed his phone aside.

Hannah.

The house.

The job.

No reason left to stay.

Luke pushed out the side door. Thomas stood by his house with a rake in hand. "I was working on the yard."

"So you heard everything?"

Thomas didn't answer.

"And you know they hired Nate?"

Thomas nodded once.

"Can you watch Spitz for me? I need to . . . go."

"Where?" Thomas set the yard tools down and leaned on the rail.

The gazebo still sat unfinished, but Nate could finish that. "Away from Heritage. I need to clear my head."

"Are you sure?"

"If something comes up, I'll have my cell. But I won't be answering it for the most part." Luke headed back toward his house. "Tell Nate congrats for me. I mean it. He'll do a great job."

Luke marched directly to his room and started filling his duffel bag. Was he sure? Was he sure there was nothing left for him in Heritage?

Yeah, he was pretty sure.

sixteen

Luke had been driving for over two hours without a destination in mind, just following the highways that hugged the edge of Lake Michigan. The lush green foliage whipped by in a blur as his stomach rumbled in protest to his missed lunch. Was it really four o'clock already? He'd passed South Haven a few minutes back. There had to be beach access around here somewhere. The sign for Van Buren State Park grew closer. That'd do.

Luke pulled off the exit and made his way to a parking lot that overlooked the beach. Lifting the lid of the cooler, he found the sandwich he'd made. Wasn't much. He'd have to grocery shop soon.

He grabbed a Coke, slid out of the truck, and kicked off his tennis shoes. The warm, soft sand slid between his toes as he made his way down the beach. A cool breeze blew over the lake, which was absent of swimmers. The water was no doubt still at skin-numbing temperatures.

He plopped down about twenty feet back from the waves and started in on his sandwich. His appetite was lacking, but his growling stomach demanded attention.

A dog's barking stole a bit more of his appetite. It wasn't like he wouldn't have loved to bring

Spitz, but since he didn't even know where he was staying, it didn't really make sense to bring the dog. And Spitz was technically Hannah's, with her name on the paperwork.

A black Lab ran to catch a Frisbee that landed a few feet from Luke. He covered the top of his Coke just before the dog arrived, paws kicking sand everywhere.

"Barney, no!" a feminine voice shouted.

Luke glanced up at the blonde running toward him. Her long legs and flat stomach held a tan that couldn't have been acquired in the sun this early in the season. He looked back at the dog, which stood staring at the sand-covered sandwich. Might as well give it to him now. Luke tossed it toward the dog and he caught it in the air.

"Bad dog, Barney." The blonde knelt down, scratching the dog's ears. She slid a wisp of hair behind her ear. "I'm really sorry about that."

"It's all right. I have a dog, or did have one. I guess it's my girlfriend's—ex-girlfriend's—now. Anyway, no biggie." He tipped back his Coke for a drink. At least he'd saved that.

"My name is Christina." She dropped in the sand next to him, stretching out her long tan legs. "You from around here?"

Luke shifted his gaze to the waves licking at the shore and shaded his eyes against the sun. He hadn't meant the ex-girlfriend comment as an invitation. After all, they'd only broken up, what, two hours ago? "No, I'm from . . . uh . . ." Could he still claim Heritage, or was he now homeless?

"Just passing through?" She dug her toes into the sand and scratched at the dog's ears.

She was beautiful. There was no denying that fact, but she had one big flaw. She wasn't Hannah. No matter how angry he was at Hannah right now, she still owned his heart. Who knew how long it would take to get it back, or if he ever could?

Then again, maybe he didn't want to get over Hannah. He had a lot more thinking to do, and sitting here talking to "Barbie" wasn't going to help.

"It's been nice meeting you." Luke stood, brushed the sand off his shorts, and marched toward his truck. *Lord, what do I do?*

The file still lay on the floor of the truck where he'd tossed it. He'd been so consumed with Hannah's betrayal that he'd put the folder out of his mind. Besides, who wanted to read about a criminal father? A father wanted by the Chicago PD. Hardly the heritage he'd always wanted. Nate's words came back. *You've been adopted by Christ. You have a new heritage.* That was probably easier to say when reality wasn't sucker punching you in the gut.

Luke grabbed the file from the floor and laid it open across his lap. On top was a black-and-white flyer with a photo of him as a child, a photo of his father, and bold letters asking, "Have you seen me?"

Luke's stomach lurched as bitter acid filled his mouth. Kidnapped? He couldn't breathe as sickening pain traveled through his limbs.

He flipped the page to the police report, reading as fast as his eyes could travel across the page. His father had been wanted for kidnapping. Kidnapping him.

Reaching out a trembling hand, he flipped the paper aside. A copy of a family photo stared back. There were four faces. The boy, age two or three, had to be him. Same hair, same dimple, same smile. He looked so happy. A girl, a few years older, sat next to him with blonde pigtails. A sister?

He let out a series of short, unsteady breaths.

The man in the photo wasn't his father. Or at least not the person he'd called Father. His finger traced the face of the woman. His mother. His breath stopped as he rested his forehead on the steering wheel.

He leaned back and lifted the report again, poring over the details. Ann. His mother's name was Ann. She was still alive. All the years he'd spent yearning for a mother, she'd been alive all along.

The man he remembered had, in fact, been his own father. But his name wasn't Joseph Johnson. It was Brian Taylor. He'd kidnapped Luke after a custody dispute. He'd then acquired fake documentation, including the birth certificate listing Sarah Johnson as Luke's mother, and settled in the small town of Heritage before the fatal accident.

Luke's head dropped back against the seat as tears burned at the corners of his eyes. Kidnapped. Not orphaned. It took every ounce of strength not to punch his fist into the dashboard. His family had been stolen from him by the one man he'd trusted most.

Flipping another page, he devoured the information, trying to absorb how the world was changing with every word. His mom was still alive and lived in Lynwood, Illinois. Where was that?

He yanked out his phone and typed the address. Not too far from Chicago, and only two hours from where he now sat. His hand tightened on the phone. His mother, his family, two hours away.

His mind traveled back to Hannah. Maybe he had made a mistake in leaving without a word. After all, it was her nosiness that had uncovered all this. Glancing behind him, he threw his truck in Reverse, peeled out of the parking lot, and turned back to the highway.

Two hours south, his family. Two hours north, Hannah.

Hannah's face flashed in his mind. But did the end justify the means? How could he ever trust her again?

Luke came to the on-ramp and stopped. North to Hannah or south to his family?

He flipped on his blinker and turned south, the choice made. He pulled into traffic and put the pedal to the floor.

Still no luck finding that money and still no luck waiting for Luke. But one of these things was getting settled now, because like it or not, Luke might be the only one who could help. Hannah pulled into the driveway. His truck was gone. No matter, she'd play with Spitz and wait him out.

Hannah slid out of her car and took the porch steps two at a time. She lifted the pot and reached for the hide-a-key. Nothing. That was odd. Cupping her hands around her eyes, she peered through the window. No dog.

"He's gone." Thomas's voice carried from his porch a few yards away.

Hannah stepped to the edge of the railing, the word echoing in her head. "What do you mean, 'gone'?"

Thomas turned to his door, glancing back at her before opening it. Spitz nosed his way out, licking Thomas's hand before sprinting to the grass.

Her throat went dry. "How long does he plan to be gone?"

Thomas shifted his weight from one foot to the other. "He called off work. Didn't give them a return date."

"Why didn't you call me?" Hannah marched across the driveway and stood at the bottom of his steps, hands on her hips.

Thomas shrugged. "It wouldn't have changed anything. He has things he needs to sort out."

"We can sort them out together." Hannah withdrew her phone and tapped Luke's name.

Thomas cast her a glance and sighed. "He won't answer."

He'd answer. They needed to talk this out. Her stomach tightened as the phone rang on. Shoving it back in her pocket, she marched up the steps. "Then give me your phone. He'll answer for you."

"No. He's done, Hannah. You can't fix this." Thomas whistled for the dog and walked into the house, letting the door shut on her.

Oh yes she could. Hannah stormed after him and slammed the door with more force than she ever had in her life. "Thomas James, give me—"

Her words cut off at the sight of his horror-stricken eyes focused just above her. The plates. Her breath halted as if it could stop time, but it was too late. She covered her face as the shattering of glass pierced the air. Then silence.

Hannah lowered her hands. Shards of blue everywhere. No, no, no. She swallowed the bile that rose in her throat.

"Don't move." Thomas grabbed Spitz and led him away from the glass and out the back door.

Hannah squatted down and picked up two pieces, trying to fit them back together. "Do you have any g-glue?"

"Hannah, stop."

She reached for another piece, her hands shaking. "It will take time, but if we can find all the pieces . . ."

Thomas stepped toward her, the glass crunching under his shoes. "You can't fix this."

Her fingers trembled. "But if I—ahh!" The blue razor edge sliced through the tip of her finger.

He pulled her to her feet, took the pieces out of her hand with slow, gentle movements, and examined the cut as a crimson ribbon appeared. "Wait here."

He marched to the kitchen, and Janie's words floated back into her memory. *When we hold the broken pieces of our lives too close, they'll cut us up inside.*

Thomas held out a rag and wrapped it around her finger. "You can't fix Mom's plates with a little superglue. You can't fix your relationship with Luke with a phone call." He stared out the window to the field as he wrapped her in his arms. "And you can't fix Mom's leaving by winning this contest."

Something broke inside her as she sank into her brother's hug. A sob welled up in her throat and poured out. So much she'd locked away over the years: when her mother left, when Luke had broken her heart in high school, and now her regret for breaking Luke's trust.

When the tears finally slowed, she eased back from her brother and toed a few pieces of glass. "I've ruined everything."

Thomas gazed around at the shards surrounding them. "It'll clean up."

Hannah bent over and, with more care, picked up a piece of glass and examined the sharp edge. Maybe she was holding her past too tightly, but then she wasn't sure she was ready to let go either. "I want to keep the glass."

"Why?" Thomas squatted next to her and gathered a few large pieces.

"I don't know."

He stared at her as if he'd argue but shook his head and went and found a box. Together they worked in silence to collect any pieces large enough to save, then swept up the rest.

Hannah tucked the box under her arm and stepped out on the porch. "I'm sorry about the plates."

"I'm not. It's time for us to stop living with Mom's and Dad's mistakes hanging over our heads."

Hannah set the box of glass down and sank onto the third step. "How did we become so dysfunctional at relationships?"

Thomas sat next to her and rested his elbows on his knees. "Mom abandoned us for a new life, leaving Dad bitter at God. That's not the best recipe for raising emotionally healthy children. Still, we did all right. I've kept Donny's from going under while Aunt Lucy and Uncle Don are gone, and you're turning this town around."

Hannah rubbed her eyes. "Luke lost the photos and I lost the collection money."

"How much?"

"Just over eighteen hundred dollars in cash." She wiped under her eyes with her sleeve, turning it black. She must look a mess.

"What did the mayor say?"

"I haven't told anyone. And with Luke gone, there's no way I can get the gazebo done in time." The half-built gazebo in the distance made her heart hurt. "It may be time to throw in the towel. I don't even know if I care anymore."

"You can't be serious."

She shrugged and cleared her throat. "Kensington is ready to bulldoze Luke's house. He'll be after this house next. I don't even know why I'm trying to stop it. He always gets his way. Did you know the fire was even his idea? Why do you think Wilks had a full report ready to go? How did I not see it?"

"His idea or not, that square is great because of you."

"The townspeople have helped some, but as soon as they find out I've lost their money they'll turn on me."

Thomas pulled her to his shoulder. "You're wrong. People are excited about what you've done already—"

"Done already? I burned down the most beautiful building in town." She pointed to where the Manor had stood.

Thomas offered a soft chuckle. "I'm pretty sure you're the only person in town who saw it that way."

"But with enough money—"

"I'm sure you'd have made it beautiful again. I mean, just look what you did to the square after the fire. But sometimes we're meant to fix things and sometimes we have to let go. Like the Manor . . . Like Mom."

Hannah ran her finger along the well-worn grooves of the wood step. "I'm going before the board on Monday, and I'll have to admit that I'm no better than Mom."

Thomas turned her toward him. "Mom stole the money—you lost it. There's a big difference."

Hannah wiped at the corners of her eyes. "Different in intentions, but the same on paper."

"Have you ever stopped and asked God for help in all this?" Thomas stretched his legs out in front of him.

"God? You think He cares about a contest?" She let out a huff.

Thomas leaned back on his elbows. "He cares about you. He cares about what you're going through." His shoulders lifted in a shrug. "Maybe God's the one who gave you a passion to help the town. If so, maybe all you need to do is let Him lead."

She lifted an eyebrow and studied him. "Since when do you give advice about God?"

"I've been going to a Bible study with Pastor Nate. Luke went a few times too before he left."

Hannah turned and gazed across the fresh green field. Trust God? With the gazebo? With Luke? Sounded like a fairy tale. Life had taught her that if she wanted something done, she had to do it herself. "It all just seems so impossible."

"The Bible is full of stories of God asking people to do impossible things." He sat up again, talking with animated hands. "He once asked this weenie dude to destroy a whole army with three hundred men. For Gideon alone it was impossible. But with God, no problem. Nate said that God specializes in using our weakness to show off His strength."

Hearing her brother talk like this warmed something deep inside her that she'd let grow cold for some time. "Do you trust God to get Janie back?" she asked. Advice and application were two different things.

He drew a deep breath. "Get her back? I'm still not sure that would be best. I'm just praying He'll show me what to do next. Maybe the next step is all we're supposed to know."

A longing rose in her heart. Once upon a time she'd prayed every day and believed God would answer. She really didn't know when she'd decided to go it on her own. A slow decision over time. "Maybe you're right." She stood, picked up the box, and headed to her car.

"What're you going to do now?" He stood as well, shoved his hands in his pockets, and leaned against the rail.

She opened the car door and slid the box in the back. "I don't know. Maybe pray. Then again, maybe I should have started praying about all this from the start."

"It's never too late."

She shut the door and leaned her back against it. "You sure?"

"I hope not. For your sake and mine."

Three days he'd come here and sat, and three days he'd chickened out and returned to his room at the nearby motel. Luke's confidence evaporated once again as he studied the white two-story house that had been pulled from a storybook. A couple of oak trees shadowed the wide yard and stirred a strange foggy memory, but nothing solid.

He grabbed the file that he'd practically memorized. Pulling out the photo, he stared at the mom for what seemed like the hundredth time. Nothing.

No matter how many times he looked at it, the

woman didn't stir the slightest memory. Not the long blonde hair, not the warm blue eyes, not even the dimple in her left cheek that was a perfect match to his. Shouldn't he know his own mother?

If he'd forgotten her, what if she'd forgotten him? She'd probably moved on. Maybe he should too. After all, that would be easier than trying to fit into a family that already had their shared stories, inside jokes, and established traditions. He might share genetics with them, but the fact remained that they were strangers.

Every day he'd left with no intention of coming back, but every day he'd returned, expecting it to be easier. It wasn't. But the time Al had given him had run out, so unless he wanted his mother to hear the news from the police, it was today or never. Luke reached for the handle, stepped out of the truck, and walked up to the white house.

Moisture gathered on his brow as his finger pressed the doorbell. After what seemed like an eternity, the door swung open, revealing a version of his own face five years back, but with blue eyes instead of dark brown. If he'd had any doubt that he was in the wrong place, it vanished.

The guy blinked at him, looking confused. Join the club. Then again, Luke had had three days of mental prep work.

Luke cleared his throat, shoved his hands in his pockets, and then pulled them back out. "Hi, I'm Luke, and I think . . . I'm your brother."

The guy stared at him.

Maybe he'd try a different approach. "Do Len and Ann Kingsley live here?"

"Sorry, come in." The guy blinked a few times, then stepped aside for Luke to enter. "Uh . . . Dad?"

A man with salt-and-pepper hair and black-rimmed glasses glanced up from his paper and froze, all expression melting away.

Luke cringed. What had he expected, showing up out of the blue?

"I've got the popcorn." A door swung open and a woman floated into the room. "Libby's grabbing the pop. Could you help her, Liam?"

Her hair was cut short now and fully gray, but the warm eyes were the same and so was the dimple. Her gaze traveled from the guy next to him to Luke, then back to the guy, then back to Luke. She dropped the bowl, sending popcorn across the wood floor as her hands flew to her face.

Luke shifted from one foot to the other, then back. This wasn't going well. He stared at his feet, anxious to get away from the three sets of eyes. He drew a breath and lifted his head. Make that five sets. Great, now the whole family was here. He glanced back at the door. "Maybe I should go and—"

"No!" The collective shout filled the room.

Luke swallowed and stepped a foot closer to

the door. He wanted to stay, sort of. He wanted a family, at least. But this was a ready-made family. Complete without him.

"Luke?" The older man stood and stepped toward him. He was much taller than Luke would have guessed. He took another step and extended his hand. "I'm Len Kingsley. Your stepfather. This is my wife, Ann, your mother."

Ann took a hesitant step toward him. Her shaky hand touched a curl at the side of his head. "You're so beautiful."

She wrapped her arms around his shoulders and he offered a clumsy hug in return and stepped back. Everything felt off. He didn't even know this woman.

The man continued with the introductions. "Luke, you already sort of met Liam at the door, and that's his fraternal twin, Logan. They're your half brothers."

Logan shook his hand. "You look more like Liam than I do, and we're twins."

"You look like your father, Logan. They both look like my father," Ann said in a shaky voice. She turned to Luke. "Only Liam got his father's blue eyes, and Luke got *his* father's."

Tension rose in Luke's shoulders, but he offered a half smile and nodded.

"That's Libby. She's a few years older than you and was my sister's daughter. She came to live with us when you were just a baby."

Libby must have been the girl with pigtails in the photo. She still had the long blonde hair. And her eyes were blue just like everyone else's—everyone but him.

"We adopted her shortly after Len and I married. So she's biologically your cousin and your half sister by adoption." Ann sat down, her hands clutched in her lap. "Would you like a seat?"

Luke chose the chair closest to the door. "Do you know why my father took me?"

Len sat next to Ann, slid his hand into hers, and gave her an encouraging nod.

"I don't know what he told you," Ann said, "but I do know your father loved you. We married young and were divorced before our second anniversary. You were less than a year. I had primary custody, but your father had every other weekend and a lot of holidays. I know he wanted full custody but seemed content with the arrangement until I started dating Len, who was military at the time and was considering a transfer to San Diego. When your father found out, he went crazy. But I never guessed he'd do what he did."

Luke closed his eyes, trying to make sense of all the pieces. "How did you know it was him?"

"It was my fault." Libby's voice tumbled out as big tears pooled in her eyes. "I'm sorry. It was my fault. I—"

"No. Libby, you can't think that." Ann reached out and placed a hand on her arm.

"I was seven and you were almost four, and we were playing tag in the yard." Libby stared at him and then back to the floor. "Your dad pulled up and said he'd come to take you for the weekend. I remember it seemed odd. He was in a hurry and you usually took a bag with you. But he insisted it was fine."

Ann closed her eyes as if returning to that day. "At first we weren't sure if it was a surprise trip. He did that occasionally. He'd stop by to take you to Dairy Queen or the like. By the time I contacted the police, you'd been gone several hours." She opened her eyes and drew a deep breath. "After it became clear we wouldn't find you, I waited for him to change his mind. Waited for him to contact me. Waited for something. Did he not tell you any of this?"

Luke rubbed his hand over the back of his neck. "Maybe he planned to. But I was only five when he died."

As soon as the words were out, he winced. He hadn't meant to break that news quite so abruptly. When he lifted his head, his mother's face had gone ashen.

"Who raised you?" Liam voiced the question written on all their faces.

Luke glanced at Ann and swallowed. What mother wanted to hear that her baby had grown up in the foster care system? It was one thing to believe the child's loving father raised him, but to know he never knew the love of a parent . . .

He cleared his throat. Why was it so hard to swallow all of a sudden? "I bounced around a few foster homes before settling with Mrs. Shoemaker in the second grade."

Ann crumpled into Len's shoulder, her hands shaking.

Len pulled his wife closer and rubbed her back. "Did she adopt you?"

"No." Pressure built in his chest. "She was a very kind foster mother, though."

"I should've looked harder." Ann's voice had dropped to a whisper.

Len took her by the shoulders and made her look him in the eye. "Ann, stop. You put yourself in the hospital searching for him."

"She really was kind." Luke swallowed his own emotions. "You want to see a photo of her?" Lifting his phone from his pocket, he pulled up the photo of him from eighth grade that Hannah had sent him after the prom and passed it to Ann.

She looked at the photo a minute before her eyes closed. "I missed so much."

"She reminds me of Grandma." Logan peered over his mother's shoulder.

Ann blinked and wiped away a few more tears. "Do you have other photos of growing up? How old were you here?"

Luke shrugged. "Eighth grade. I think I have a few at home."

Liam picked up the phone and flipped back a photo. It was another one Hannah had sent from the night at the prom. "Is this your girlfriend?"

"No." His chest squeezed, but he'd kept his voice light.

Liam studied the photo. "Want to introduce me? She's hot."

"No." Okay, not so light that time.

Everyone stared at him as he reached for his phone. Not awkward at all.

Ann pressed her palms to her cheeks, then stood to her feet. "I need to make some more popcorn. Would you care to help me, Luke?"

He didn't know much about making popcorn unless it involved a microwave, but one inquisition was easier than five. He stood and followed Ann into the kitchen. "Sure thing."

"We do it the old-fashioned way. Put a quarter cup of this in that pot there." She handed him oil before turning to measure the kernels. "I have so many questions, but I'll do my best not to overwhelm you. Where do you live now?"

Luke filled the cup in his hand and poured the oil in the pot. "North of Grand Rapids—or I did until a few days ago. I don't know if I'll go back."

She measured the popcorn, set it aside, and then dropped just two kernels in the heating oil. "Why not?"

Luke shoved his hands in his pockets. He

wasn't ready for all aspects of family yet. "Aren't you going to pour the rest of the popcorn in?"

She studied him a moment, then turned back to the stove. "You have to wait for the oil to be at the right temperature. When those two kernels pop, that tells us it's time. Some things can't be rushed."

Was she talking about the popcorn or this whole situation? Probably both.

She glanced up at him. "Where are you staying now?"

"In a motel down the way."

"Then stay here while you get things figured out. We have room. Please."

Stay here? Sure, she was his mother, but it seemed weird. Still, he was almost out of money, so what choice did he really have? It was either that or return to Heritage. "That'd be great. I won't impose for more than a week. By then I should know what I'm doing. Thank you, Ann."

She winced at the sound of her given name and turned back to the stove once more. His stomach sank as she wiped the back of her hand across her eyes. He didn't want to hurt her more, but he couldn't make the word "Mom" pass his lips. Maybe it was a mistake staying here. After all, what did he know about being part of a family?

A small pop echoed in the pot. Then another. Ann poured in the rest of the kernels, covered the pot, then shook it from side to side. The kernels exploded at a machine-gun pace, each one offering the smallest amount of hope that with time he could find a place to belong here with his family.

seventeen

Almost three months ago, she'd sat here confident she could fix this town, and now she didn't even think she could fix her own life. Hannah glanced at her watch—thirty minutes. She flipped through her note cards a few times before dropping them in her purse. What was the point? How eloquent do you need to be to stand in front of the town council and say, "I failed"?

Thomas's words floated back. *You can't fix Mom's leaving by winning this contest.* Was that what she'd been trying to do?

She'd prayed a lot the past week, and every time she listened, all she knew was that she had to come to this meeting. Guess it was time to face the music. Maybe another prayer wouldn't hurt.

A nearby chair squeaked as Mayor Jameson settled into it. The button on his coat stretched as far as the material would allow, and his smile puffed his cheeks and added another chin. "After-noon, Hannah darlin'."

He might smile at her now, but wait until he heard what she had to say. "Afternoon, Mayor."

He tapped out an irregular rhythm on the chair between them. "It's too bad about young Luke Johnson's house. Just a shame."

Hannah nodded, not trusting her voice.

"I wish there was more I could do. But as mayor, I have to be impartial. You understand?"

Hannah nodded again. Great, now she was a bobblehead.

He leaned back and stroked his mustache. "However, if a petition were formed by the town to, say, name a row of houses historic, then that would be something."

Hannah shuffled the papers in her lap. "I checked into the national registry for historic homes, but that can take months."

"Not a national registry. Oh, no." His finger tapped at his chin. "A town has the right to zone areas how they want. And historic houses can't be torn down willy-nilly."

"Okay." Where was he going with this?

"Did you know any resident can make a petition? It's true. And with 250 signatures it would go to a vote. If the council saw that it was the will of the people to have a historic district in this town . . ." He shrugged. "Might change some things."

Hannah bit the corner of her lip as she leaned a bit closer. "Are you saying—"

"I'm not saying anything. I must stay impartial, you understand. I'm just observing that it's too bad a petition like that didn't exist." His gaze traveled the room before landing back on her. "Looks like I'm needed up front. Sure to be an exciting day."

Aunt Lucy slid into the chair next to Hannah

and wrapped her in a hug. "How's my sweet girl been?"

Tears pressed at the back of Hannah's eyes as she hugged her aunt. "You're back! Everything has fallen apart since you left. I've failed. The contest. Luke—"

"Hush now. Thomas told me everything. It'll all turn out. Just you wait and see." Aunt Lucy dropped a kiss on her head and patted her knee.

How could she say that? And what had Thomas told her, anyway?

Fifteen minutes later the mayor banged the gavel to start the meeting, with every seat full and even the standing room packed.

"We now call to order the business of the *Reader's Weekly* contest. Hannah Thornton, would you please step forward."

Her hands shook as she fumbled through her notes. "Thank you, Mayor and the rest of the town council. I'm sorry to—"

"We've got a lot on the agenda today, Miss Thornton. We're just going to ask a few questions." The mayor cut her off with a smile. "At your last meeting, you were granted money and permission for the controlled burn and granted ten thousand dollars to beautify the center of town. First, let me address the fire. Did it clear away the condemned houses? Yes or no?"

It had done that and more. "Yes, but—"

"A simple yes will do." He dismissed her with

a wave and looked down at the paper. "After the removal of the Manor, the plans for the park were extended to the entire property with the addition of a gazebo. The wood for the gazebo has been purchased and the construction is in process, and after the donations of generous town members, you've stayed in your budget. Yes or no?"

"No."

A murmur traveled through the room.

Hannah closed her eyes and drew a slow breath. "I've lost the donated funds."

Everyone stared—no doubt seeing not her but her mother. A repeat of history.

"And I think I killed Otis." Hannah dropped her note cards and pushed through the crowd out the back door. She collapsed on the nearby bench and buried her face in her hands as the tears refused to stop. Ultimate humiliation and she couldn't even drive off. She'd left her keys in the room with her purse.

The bench creaked next to her. She wiped at her face and turned to Aunt Lucy. "I've ruined everything."

Her aunt held out a book. *The Art of Glass Fusing.* "Thomas told me about some broken glass you have. He seemed to think you needed to throw it away. I think you were right to keep the pieces."

Had her aunt lost her mind? Didn't she see what had happened?

"Broken pieces are only dangerous if you leave

them broken and sharp. The key is to not let them remain broken." Aunt Lucy focused her eyes on her as if to communicate something profound, but Hannah just didn't follow.

"I already tried to fix them—"

"Not fix them." She laid her wrinkled hand on Hannah's arm. "You can never really fix something shattered. But you can take the pieces and make something even better. Don't leave the painful parts of your life in a box on the shelf. Figure out how to make something beautiful out of them."

"I seem to have broken a lot of things since you left. I'm not sure anything beautiful can be made of them anymore."

"Are you talking about the money? Sweetie, things like that happen. Things get misplaced or stolen—who knows. If you're talking about the town, then I'm not sure you did mess up. Look at this town. I almost didn't recognize the place when Don and I rolled in. If you're talking about Luke—"

Hannah stiffened. "What did Thomas tell you?"

"Enough to know you did mess up there. But it seems so did he. Secrets don't make for a good relationship."

"I know."

"Then why? Did you need him to have a family?"

"No. I just thought if he had a family then—"

"He'd be happier? You know, I think he just wanted you. That boy always knew you were enough for him. But I'm not sure he was ever convinced he was enough for you."

Hannah closed her eyes against the stream of tears. Luke had always been enough. Why hadn't she told him that?

Aunt Lucy patted her knee. "You need to get back in there. The meeting isn't over."

Hannah pulled the book to her chest and pushed to her feet. Time to face her execution.

The room grew quiet as Hannah and her aunt stepped back in. She walked back to the table where she'd left all her stuff and froze. A cup stuffed with cash sat on top of a folder. A lot of cash. She swallowed hard and reached for the unfamiliar bulging folder and opened it up. Pictures. Lots of pictures.

She lifted the first few. The houses. The fire. Even photos of a few of the bachelors. As many photos as she'd lost and more. But these weren't hers. She turned one over. *Property of Danielle Fair.* She reached for another. *Bo Mackers.* Had the town been taking photos too?

"And what's that, Miss Thornton?" A knowing smile played at the corners of the mayor's lips.

"Photos." Her voice squeaked as she continued to flip through what must be over fifty photos. Many were rough shots from cell phones, but some were good. Very good.

344

"Well, they'll be a great addition to the website for the contest, don't you think?"

Under the last photo was a sign-up sheet for the coming Saturday. One list of people agreeing to help work on the gazebo, another list of people willing to help plan the fair. They weren't here to bury her. They were here to help her succeed. How could she have thought the worth of the town was in the buildings and history?

"Hannah." The mayor's voice softened. "We appreciate all you've done. Your vision and heart have renewed something in us all. Even if things haven't gone as smoothly as you'd hoped, we're standing with you. So what do you say—are you ready to win this contest?"

The room erupted in applause. If only Luke were here to see this. A lump lodged in her throat. Luke. What had the mayor said about a petition?

Hannah cleared her throat. "Thank you, but I'd like to add one more thing. I'd like to propose that we make all the buildings touching the new town square a historic district and unable to be demolished."

Dale Kensington sat up straighter on the bench. "You can't do that."

"I can propose anything I want, and if I have 250 signatures on it then you have to vote on it." Hannah lifted her chin and stared him down.

He narrowed his eyes. "And do you have 250 signatures?"

"No." Hannah glanced at the mayor, who offered a slight nod of encouragement. "But I ask the council for time and request that you not make any decisions regarding the property of Luke Johnson until the next meeting."

"Done. That discussion is tabled until next month." The mayor smacked the gavel, bringing a scowl from Kensington.

God had brought the miracle she'd asked for through the great people of Heritage, and just maybe He had more planned.

Sometimes stepping out in faith felt a lot like bungee jumping. Or so she imagined. Janie had never been bungee jumping, but if she got this loan for the bakery, she might go try it. Maybe she'd even drag Hannah along.

Her ever-reliable friend sat in the next chair. She hadn't been sure she could do this on her own, even if the loan manager was just Eddie Fry, who'd picked his nose in the fifth grade. In his defense, he had shown up to the meeting in a suit and he did keep a box of Kleenex on his desk. But his eyebrows still formed that woolly V when he'd scowled at her as she laid out her loan request. And they'd stayed that way as he left the room to talk to a supervisor.

Janie rubbed her moist palms across her navy pencil skirt, smoothed her hair, and wedged her hands under her legs to keep from fidgeting.

"Can you really afford this?" Hannah tapped at a bobblehead dog at the edge of the desk.

Janie picked up the file again and scanned the numbers. "It will be tight. That's why I won't let my parents cosign. They offered but I refused. Bankrupting myself would be bad enough. Bankrupting my family would be a tragedy. But I know your lease is up in a month, and if you wanted to move in we could share rent."

Hannah's teeth tugged at her lip. She cleared her throat. "Maybe Thomas—"

"No, Hannah. Don't." Tears pressed in at the corners of Janie's eyes, but she forced them back. "Thomas is part of my past. I'm learning to be content with God alone."

"You sure you want to close that door?" Hannah studied her before turning to stare out the window. "People make mistakes, you know."

Was Hannah talking about Thomas's mistakes or her own? "I can't be with someone who doesn't believe in me."

Hannah opened her mouth but shut it as Eddie stepped back into the room with a file in hand, the woolly V still on his forehead. "The thing is, Miss Mathews, you don't have the credit or assets needed for this size of a loan."

Miss Mathews? He'd whined like a baby when she'd turned him down for the homecoming dance in the tenth grade, but now she was Miss Mathews?

He pushed up his thick-rimmed glasses and his brow relaxed for the first time. "Now, if you had a cosigner with some equity, that would be another story."

"I don't."

"I see." He examined the file in front of him. "The crazy thing is . . . I do."

"What?" Go into business with Eddie Fry? Her nose twisted before she forced the expression from her face. No reason to insult the guy.

"We had a visitor today who wishes to remain anonymous and *is,* in fact, willing to cosign. A silent investor, so to speak. He has good credit and equity, and, well . . . his father was a close friend of the bank owner. So, if you agree, then we'll process this." He slid a paper across the desk to her. "With a few signatures, I can get the paperwork started."

Hannah spoke up. "An anonymous cosigner? I've never heard of such a thing."

"It isn't our usual practice, but we like to keep things small-town around here. And like I said, he's a solid member of the community, and Mr. Mackers insisted." He held out a pen to Janie and tapped the paper where she should sign.

Janie studied him. She wouldn't sign if it were her father, but who else could it be? He was a close friend of Bo Mackers, the bank owner. Then again, who wasn't? "Who is it?"

"Would you like me to look up the definition of

anonymous for you?" Eddie rolled his eyes and tapped the paper again.

"Tell her, Eddie." Hannah leaned forward, placing her hands on the desk.

"No." He leaned back and scanned the paper in front of him, the woolly V back in place. "He'd kick my . . . tail."

There went the idea of it being her father.

Hannah lunged across the desk and snatched the paper from his hand.

"Ouch." Eddie stuck his finger in his mouth. "You gave me a paper cut. Take it. It's your crazy brother, anyway. I told him it was a stupid idea."

Janie's heart stopped. "Thomas?"

"I'll give you two a minute." Eddie left, his finger still stuck in his mouth. "I'm going to find a Band-Aid."

Janie grabbed the paper from Hannah. Thomas was putting up his house as equity. His signature was scrawled across the bottom.

Hannah read the paper from over her shoulder. "He did call me this morning and tell me to take the house off the market."

Janie's hand began to shake. "Why would he do this?"

"Because he loves you. Because he does believe in you. Because even if he can't have you, more than anything in life he just wants you to be happy."

"He told you this?"

"No." Tears filled Hannah's eyes. "But I'd do the same for Luke in a heartbeat."

Janie's gaze returned to Thomas's signature scrawled at the bottom under his printed name. Her name was printed out with the line waiting for her signature a few spaces over. Seeing his name next to hers did strange things to her heart.

Hannah laid a gentle hand on her arm. "Remember a few months ago in my apartment you told me not to leave things left unsaid with Luke? Now I'll throw it back at you. Are you sure you aren't leaving things left unsaid with Thomas?"

Eddie returned with a sizable bandage on his finger. "What's the verdict, ladies?"

Janie shook her head and stood with the paper in hand. "I'm sorry, I can't do this right now. I need to go."

With that, she fled to her car. She needed to think, to pray.

She placed the paper carefully on the seat next to her and started the car. *Why, Lord? I was content for it to be just You and me. Why this? Why now?*

Once upon a time he'd thought Janie would wear this ring. Thomas pulled the ring from the velvet box, slid it halfway to his knuckle, and inspected the princess-cut diamond in the antique setting. Maybe if Hannah didn't want it, it was time to sell.

Had he pushed Janie away because he was afraid she'd be like his mom and leave? Maybe. Guilt pricked at his conscience. Okay, definitely. But at the time, he'd really convinced himself he was doing it for her.

He'd told Hannah he'd been praying about it, and that was true. If only the answer would arrive in writing, like an email from God. That'd be awesome.

The chime of his doorbell interrupted his thoughts. He dropped the ring in his shirt pocket as he pulled open the door. "Hey, Nate, what's up?"

"I think this is yours. 'Greg Thornton'?" Nate held up the familiar leather Bible. "I think you left it at Bible study."

"That was my dad's." Thomas reached for it. "Thanks."

Nate spun his keys on his finger and then caught them. "What do you think of the Bible study?"

"It's good. I just . . ." Thomas shifted from one foot to the other. "I don't know if I have a—whatever you called it—grace thingy."

"Grace point? It's not a requirement—just a way of looking at the Bible. Don't get hung up on this concept. If you're seeking God, He'll show you how your life and problem intersect with the gospel."

"Who said I have a problem?" Why did he say

that? Of course he had a problem. More than one.

Nate didn't react, he just tucked his keys in his pocket. "Most of us do. Some are big and affect the course of our lives. Others are just the problem of the week. But that's the thing—God wants to offer answers not just for the big ones but for the small ones too."

"Yeah, I remember you saying that." Why was he so defensive? Hadn't he just been telling Hannah some of this same stuff? Well, it was easier when he was looking at someone else's faults rather than his own.

"Busy now?"

He didn't really want to talk about it. Then again, he'd been praying for answers, and he couldn't really lecture Hannah if he wasn't ready to listen to the advice himself.

Ten minutes later Nate was sitting on Thomas's couch with a cup of coffee in his hand, listening to the drawn-out saga of him and Janie. Thomas had planned on just sharing the bare bones, but he found it was good to tell someone who wasn't going to turn around and yell at him for being an idiot. At least he hoped pastors didn't do that.

"Abraham." Nate lifted his coffee mug and took a long drink.

Thomas wrinkled his brow. "It was his wife who couldn't have kids, not him."

"Abraham's problem wasn't that his wife couldn't have kids." Nate paused and stared at

352

him. "His problem was he didn't trust God to handle it and took the matter into his own hands."

A weight pressed against his chest. That was exactly what he'd done. He hadn't trusted God with his problem but became angry and set off to do what looked right. He'd lectured Hannah about trying to fix everything her way. Maybe it ran in the family. Or maybe it just ran in human nature.

Nate leaned forward, placing his elbows on his knees. "I'll tell you this. God's not done with you. Maybe by a physical miracle like He did with Abraham, or maybe the miracle will come a different way."

"A different way—like adoption?"

"That's a decision between you and God. But remember, just because kids come through adoption, foster care, or mentoring at the community center, it never means they're God's second best for you. They're His first choice for you. Maybe there are kids being created or born right now who will be handpicked for you to raise, to love. God will knit them together with you in mind as their father, not the biological dude. You, Thomas."

Thomas stared at the floor as a strange sensation settled in his chest. He could have a son out there waiting for him right now. Jimmy's face flashed through his mind. A baby girl could be born this minute—someone he'd raise, he'd love, who would call him Daddy, and who

God was making perfect right now just for him.

He struggled to swallow. Not raising someone else's kids. Raising children meant for him, picked by God for him.

Nate downed the rest of his coffee and stood. "I've given you a lot to think about and I have a meeting, so I'll let myself out. But call me anytime. Okay?"

Thomas nodded and sat back and stared at the ceiling. The latch clicked in the distance and he closed his eyes. Could he really trust God with all this?

A knock at the door echoed through the room. Nate must have forgotten something.

He rushed to the door. "Did—"

Not Nate. Janie.

She held up the document he'd signed at the bank. "What's this?"

Thomas winced, then dipped his head. "I'm going to kill him."

"Leave Eddie out of this." Janie whipped the screen door open and pushed past him. "He didn't rat you out. Hannah was with me and, well . . . you know Hannah."

He knew Hannah all right. "Want a seat?"

She dropped into the recliner and then jumped to her feet. "No." She paced a few feet and whirled to face him again. "Is it a guilt offering? 'Hey, I won't marry you, but have a bakery instead.'"

Thomas shoved his hands in his pockets. "It's not a ploy and it's not out of guilt."

"Then what? And how did you even know I was applying for the loan?" She turned to pace the other way.

"It's a small town. People talk. As far as why . . . does it matter?"

"Yes." Pausing midstep, she held his gaze.

Had she shown up before Nate, he might have come up with some lame excuse and sent her on her way, but he had to stop trying to protect her. He had to be honest. He still didn't have the answers, but it was time to trust God and Janie with what he did have.

"Because . . . I love you. Because if I could go back, I would've asked you to marry me that day we went to the beach like I planned, instead of breaking up with you." There, he'd said it.

Her face paled as she swallowed and drew a shaky breath. At least he wasn't the only one having problems breathing here. "We can't go back."

"Believe me, I know." Thomas turned away before he did something crazy like kiss her and beg her to take him back.

"I'm sorry." Her voice was weaker now. "But if you don't trust me—"

"I do." He whipped around and cupped her shoulders with his hands. "I'm sorry for letting my issues with my mom get in the way. But you,

Janie Abigail Mathews, you I trust. The one I lost faith in was God." He stared at his father's Bible sitting by the door. "But He and I have been having a lot of heart-to-heart talks lately. I'm still a work in progress, but the point is that I'm getting things worked out. I understand if it is too late for us, Janie. But I do trust you."

"What are you doing to me?" Janie sank into the recliner with a thud. "You love me. You leave me. How can I ever believe a word you say again?"

"I don't know. But if you do"—Thomas stepped closer and squatted by her feet—"I promise to spend the rest of my life being honest with you about my struggles."

The rest of his life? Where had that come from? He didn't know, but now that it was out it sounded so good to him. He wanted her next to him, pursuing God's best with him, working through the hard parts of life with him. He wanted it to start right now.

"You still want to marry me?" Her voice came out breathy.

Thomas reached into his pocket, pulled out the ring, and held it out to her. "More than anything."

Janie's eyes widened. She reached out a hesitant finger and touched the stone. "That's beautiful."

"It was my Grandma Hazel's." His voice caught and he cleared his throat.

"I heard you tell Hannah you wanted it to stay

in the family. What if we can't have kids?"

"We'll have kids, Janie. Naturally or hand-picked by God for us. Either way, I believe God will give us a son to pass it on to. Or a daughter." His eyes filled with moisture and he blinked it away. "God might just be creating a little girl right now for us to love. How awesome is that?"

"Pretty awesome." Tears filled her eyes.

"So what do you say? Marry me, Janie."

Janie wrapped her arms around his neck, bringing her mouth to his.

Her lips were as soft as he remembered and tasted of lip balm. He released a groan as a year of absence washed over him. He pulled her to her feet and crushed her against him. She fit right here—how could he ever have thought differently? He kissed the soft skin along her jaw and then found her lips again. He'd missed every inch of her.

Janie leaned back a fraction, seeming to catch her breath. "I love you."

Thomas brushed her hair away from her face. "Is that a yes?"

"Yes. I'll marry you." She brushed her lips against his. "But I won't let you cosign."

"But—"

Her hand covered his lips. "Because if we're getting married, then we're both taking out this loan. After all, you need a diner if you're going to be a cook."

"Buy both?"

"Why not?"

He captured her lips again, deepening the kiss. For months he'd been begrudging his future. Now he couldn't wait. Because no matter what came their way, they'd be in it together.

eighteen

Hannah grabbed the glass cutter and scored the piece of broken plate in her hand, applied gentle pressure on both sides until the crack filled the silence, then added it to the other arranged pieces on the stone slab. She pressed her hands to the small of her back, stretched against the ache, and drew in a deep breath. She coughed, forcing the musty air from her nose. Thomas's basement held the typical damp and stale odor, but it made the most sense to work near her mother's kiln. And Spitz curled up in the corner sleeping erased the creep factor.

Hannah cut another piece of the plate and studied the growing starry sky. It was so clear in her head, but something wasn't coming together right. She moved a few stars. Nope. Maybe the answer would be in the next piece of glass.

Janie had been right that day in the vet houses. Hannah had given up her love of art out of anger at her mom. She'd kept her art bottled up for so long, now that she'd started doing it again she didn't know if she could stop.

She reached for another broken piece and visualized where would be the best cut.

The door to the upstairs creaked open. "Hello?"

Spitz barked and rushed up the steps to greet the new arrival.

"Janie? Did you get my message? Come on down. Thomas is out so you don't have to worry."

Janie rubbed the back of Spitz's neck with her right hand and held up her left hand. Grandma Haze's ring.

Hannah gave a little scream then covered her mouth. "He did it? You said yes? You guys are—"

"Breathe, Hannah." Janie took a deep breath to demonstrate and coughed. "Ugh. How do you work down here?"

"I can't believe we're going to be sisters." Hannah reached out and hugged her friend. "I guess this means you don't need a roommate anymore."

"I still will for a few months. I'm so sorry." Janie's sweet tone was nearly Hannah's undoing.

"For what? Getting the happily ever after you deserve? It's not like it was either you and Thomas or Luke and me. I'm happy for you two. Beyond happy. Tell me every detail."

"I will. But since I only have about thirty seconds before Thomas walks down those stairs to claim me, that will have to wait." Janie turned to face the table. "So, what are you doing here? Are those your mom's plates?"

"The blue ones are. I bought the white glass. I'm trying to create a starry sky. But I can't figure out what's missing."

"Missing? Hannah, this is amazing. The blues

are so vibrant." Janie picked up a broken piece of glass, twisting it in the light.

"Careful, they're sharp." Hannah rearranged a few pieces. The balance was right. Was it the varied shades of blue?

"I think it's amazing. I'm so proud of you." Janie set down the piece in her hand by the edge of the mosaic.

The mild blue made a bold contrast to the piece next to it. That was it. Hannah started rearranging the shapes as fast as her fingers would go. "There." She stepped back and placed her hands on her hips.

"Wow. I didn't think you could improve on what you had, but you're right. That's stunning." Janie studied her ring in the light, then wiped at a tear. "Isn't that so much like life? All the pieces are there, but it takes the Master to arrange them in the right way."

The steps creaked as Thomas clomped down them. He scowled, trying to look mad. "You aren't allowed to make my fiancée cry."

Janie swatted him on the arm and he laughed. "What do you say, little sis? Do we have your blessing?"

"Of course." Hannah wrapped her arms around his neck. "I'm so happy for you two."

He stepped back and glanced at the table. "Whoa. Are those Mom's plates? That's cool. But how are you going to get them to stay together?"

Hannah pointed at the kiln. "It's called glass

fusing. First I'll melt them together. Then I'll put them in that mold to make it like a bowl. I'm hoping to make it a cover for a ceiling light."

"So maybe you *were* right to keep them."

"What was that?" She nudged his shoulder.

"You were right." He flicked a glance at Janie. "About many things."

"Don't forget it."

"Like you'll let me." He squeezed her shoulder and turned back toward the steps. "Ready, love?"

"Sure," Janie said. "We got a movie if you want to join us. That's okay, isn't it, Thomas?"

"Of course." As soon as Janie faced Hannah again, Thomas's eyes widened as he shook his head at his sister.

Who could blame the guy, though? "Actually, I want to finish this tonight so I can fire it tomorrow."

"We understand." Thomas winked at her and tugged on Janie's hand. "Come on."

Janie pulled her hand away as she dropped a kiss on his cheek. "I'll be right there. Go ahead and start it. I hate previews anyway."

He stared at her for a moment before disappearing up the stairs, Spitz following at his heels.

"I don't think he's anxious for the movie, Janie." Hannah offered a pointed look.

Janie laughed as red crawled up her neck. "Probably true. But I want to make sure my best friend is really okay before I go."

"I am. I'm learning not to hold the broken pieces too tight." Hannah tapped at the box. "Learning that beauty can come from the broken. Does that about cover all your advice? Oh, and make sure God is enough."

Janie just stared at her.

"Okay, all joking aside, I appreciate all your advice, and whether I wanted to hear it or not at the time, you've taught me a lot. I consider myself fortunate to be your sister."

Janie wrapped her in a hug. "One more word of advice?"

"Sure, why not?"

Janie tapped the glass with her finger. "Sometimes all the pieces are there, but they haven't fallen into the right place yet. When they do, you'll know without a doubt."

She disappeared up the stairs, leaving Hannah staring at her creation.

Although she couldn't see it now, she had to trust that God had a beautiful picture in mind for her life. Even if Luke's absence made it feel like some of the biggest pieces were still missing.

He'd been here for a week and everything still felt off. Luke dropped onto the bench on the back porch, watching a robin build a nest where the roofline met the house. For as long as he could remember he'd believed that if he had a family, then he'd have a place where he really belonged.

A real home. But maybe it wasn't that simple.

Everything he connected with home was two hundred miles north of here. Jimmy wandering down the road and asking to play ball with Spitz. Thomas stepping out his front door ready for a pickup game in the driveway. A certain brunette stopping by to discuss the next big problem she had to solve.

Without Hannah, everything felt wrong. As if his very skin was too tight.

Len reclined in the seat next to him, pulled a cloth from his pocket, and started cleaning his glasses. "A frown like that usually means a girl."

Luke lifted an eyebrow. "You can tell by my frown?"

He shrugged. "Well, that or your mom may have mentioned that the girl in the photo was a sensitive subject. It was a guess."

Luke chuckled and leaned back. "Good guess."

"Why didn't it work out?"

Luke rubbed his eyes with his fingers. "She didn't love me, I guess. Not really."

"Why do you say that?"

Luke was getting better at this opening up thing, but he still wasn't an open book. His gaze traveled the area as he searched for the words and found the bird still at work. "I don't think she saw me as anything more than a project to be fixed."

"She wanted to change you?" A hearty chuckle

364

escaped from Len. "You got a lot to learn about women, boy. They only try to change the ones they love. If a woman ignores you, that's when you need to worry."

He stared at Len. "You're saying any girl I love is going to change me?"

"I hope so."

Luke blinked at him.

"No one's perfect. We've got a lot of rough edges, and God uses those closest to us to knock off some of those rough edges, just as He'll use us to knock off a few of theirs. Tell me you never gave Hannah advice. Tell me you never told her how to do something better. Were you trying to fix her? We can either stay rough or let people speak truth into our lives and grow."

Luke shook his head. "I can't handle feeling like a failure in front of her."

"Has she ever called you a failure?"

"Of course not."

The robin carried another twig to the roofline and jabbed it in the growing nest. The whole mass of twigs shifted, causing the bird to flutter back, but it just picked up another piece and jabbed again. It didn't look much like a nest at this stage, but the bird refused to give up.

Len's face sobered. "Perhaps it isn't Hannah. Perhaps deep down you believe you're a failure."

Luke pressed his lips together. Nothing like a direct hit.

"Do you believe in God, Luke?"

"Yeah."

"Do you believe what the Bible says about Him? About you?"

Luke shrugged. "I'd just started taking my faith seriously again. But this . . ." He nodded to the house. "This has sent my beliefs spinning again. I mean, how could a good God—a God who supposedly loves me, loves Ann—put us through this?"

Maybe God claimed to adopt him, but how could he trust a God who had orphaned him in the first place?

"The whys can drive you crazy if you let them. But don't quit seeking Him. You may never fully understand, but you will get a larger view of God." Len patted Luke's shoulder. "We know you said a week, but your mom wanted me to tell you that you're welcome as long as you want."

"How is Ann taking all this?"

"I'm handling it." Luke's head snapped up as Ann stepped on the porch. "Some days my 'handling it' looks a lot like tears and yelling at God, but I'm confident He's big enough for that."

"But you still believe in Him? Believe He's good?"

"Yes. But that doesn't mean this has been an easy road to walk. I just keep repeating, 'What they intended for evil, God will use for good.' It's from the story of Joseph. I may never know what that good was—or will be—but I have to believe that God has used it in your life, maybe even in Mrs. Shoemaker's, maybe in others', and He'll continue to do so."

Chet's words came back. *You were good for her, whether you saw it or not.*

"Don't give up on your faith." She settled in the chair next to his. "If there was anything I could give you, it would be a solid faith in God. But unfortunately, you have to find that on your own."

"I'm working on it."

She leaned closer and laid a hand on his cheek. "Not a day went by that I didn't pray for you to return to me. And here you are. But more than your return, I prayed that your faith would grow strong. Keep working on it. God can still move in a heart that's open."

Could he still be open? It had been hard enough to believe when he'd simply been orphaned. But kidnapped? Foster care when he already had a family? That just blew his GP out of the water. He wasn't sure he was up to following a God who'd allow all that.

Letting his familiar whistle fill the air, he walked to the edge of the porch. The bird still worked at its nest, and the thing was finally taking shape. Was making a home that easy?

"Hey, Mom." Libby stepped out the back door. "Wow."

Luke turned around to Ann, Len, and Libby staring at him. "What?"

"That tune, that song." Ann smiled and wiped at the corners of her eyes with her sleeve. "I made it up when you were sad one day. After that, if you were upset, you always made me sing the 'Happy Song,' as you called it.

"There are days you may be down,
Life might make you sad.
But make a smile out of that frown,
And turn your grumpy mood to glad.
Because Mommy will always love you,
Mommy always cares,
Mommy is always thinking of you.
You're always in her prayers."

Ann's voice caught at the end as tears trickled down her face.

Luke's heart swelled, and he drew a breath against the ache. He did have a good memory of his mother. It might not be a memory of her face or her voice, but he'd remembered her love in the form of a song, and that had carried him through some of the darkest times of his life.

He stepped toward his mother and wrapped his arms around her. "Thank you."

A lump lodged in his throat as tears welled in his eyes. He'd never had someone hug him with such love and abandon. The moment poured like salve over a deep wound that he'd carried as long as he could remember. So this was what a mother's love felt like. He'd never have guessed it could be this sweet. His shoulders shook as emotion welled in him.

"I'd like to stay a little longer . . . *Mom*."

They had two and a half weeks to pull this fair together, and today she'd find out who was with her—and who was not. Hannah printed *Fair Games* in black marker across a piece of paper and added it to one of the table groups Aunt Lucy had helped her arrange in the diner that morning. She picked up the last piece of paper and scanned her list. What was left? She'd already made a sign for the website, historical room, and bachelor auction. Right. The gazebo. Her fingers felt heavy as she wrote out the block letters. Luke should be here.

She should call him again. She pulled her phone from her pocket, pulled up her contacts, and stared at his name.

It was time, but any conversation with Luke would take more than the five minutes she had. She'd call him as soon as the meeting was over. At least to tell him how everything was going. And she wouldn't chicken out this time. She typed "Call Luke" in her reminders and then slid the phone back in her pocket. Now she had to call him, because there was nothing worse than an unfinished to-do list.

Hannah handed Janie a clipboard. "I have you heading up the bachelor auction." She turned and handed another to Thomas. "And I have you taking charge of the website. Do you think you two can handle being separated for a little while?"

"Funny." Thomas bumped her in the shoulder as he moved to his table.

Aunt Lucy walked by and patted Hannah on the back. "Good news about Otis moving, eh?"

Hannah rushed to the front window and stared out. Sure enough, Otis had moved from the southeast corner to the southwest corner. She hadn't killed him after all. Was it strange that she had the sudden urge to hug a statue?

The bell at the front door rang and then rang again as volunteer after volunteer arrived. Today would be a good day.

"Here are the signatures." Chet's gravelly voice filled the room as he stepped closer.

"What?"

"You needed 250 signatures for Luke's house, right? Well, here they are. Actually, 249. I thought you'd like to be the one to finish it off."

Hannah accepted the clipboard and scanned the names. Would Luke really come home if they saved his house? She bent over and added her signature across the final line. Then she stood and wrapped her arms around Chet's neck. "Thank you, Chet."

When she pulled back, the man's face had gone three shades redder. "H-happy to do so."

The room grew stuffy as more and more people arrived. She'd never expected this many.

"Slide those booths over," Aunt Lucy shouted over the crowd. "I've been meaning to clean back there anyway."

"Look at this." Olivia bent over and lifted a blue envelope. "Hannah, is this what you lost?"

"The money!" Hannah ran over and pulled it from Olivia's hand. It was still sealed. She ripped it open and fingered the bills, doing a quick count. It was all here. She marched over to the mayor and held it out to him. "I told you I didn't take it."

His brow pinched as he glanced from the money to her. "No one ever thought you did." After wrapping her in a giant bear hug, he stepped back. "We trust you, Hannah darlin'. Time for you to start trusting us." He offered her a wink before moving on.

He hadn't even taken the money. They trusted her. Hannah surveyed the roomful of people. Every one of them believed in what she was doing. Believed in her. It was time she started believing in them.

"Hey, quiet, Luke's on TV," Uncle Donny shouted over the noise.

Hannah spun to face the plasma TV over the bar. Sure enough, there was Luke, her Luke, on TV. What was he doing on TV?

Uncle Donny wiped his hands on a towel slung over his shoulder, then upped the volume. A newswoman shoved a microphone in Luke's face as the camera zoomed in. Luke seemed to avoid looking directly at it. Being the center of attention was never his thing, but he looked good. So many things she should have said—still should say.

Luke shifted his weight as his gaze moved between the reporter and the cameraman. "It was a shock, but it's amazing. I don't even know how to describe it."

The screen flashed back to the reporter. Her perfectly lined lips highlighted her airbrushed complexion. "Those were Luke Johnson's words after discovering the family he never knew about. Kidnapped by his father, who falsified documents and lived on the run. Orphaned, or so everyone thought, in a car accident. A young man who grew up in the foster system, despite having a mother, stepfather, and three siblings only a few hours away. Although he had a relatively happy childhood, Luke admits he's always longed to have a family of his own, and now he does. This is Robyn Turner, and I'm happy to report that after over twenty years, this tragedy has a happy ending."

Luke had a family. That was what was in the file.

He couldn't hate her. After all, she'd found his family for him. So why hadn't he called her? It was everything she'd hoped for and more for him.

But not.

Her palms grew slick as a cool sensation washed over her. He had a family. Which meant . . . he wouldn't be coming back. And if he hadn't called, then . . .

He didn't need her anymore.

The news flipped to another story and the room erupted with voices. Janie and Aunt Lucy stared at Hannah, but she didn't have a response.

"Did you have any idea?" Thomas finally asked.

"No." Her voice wavered. "Not at all."

She gripped the clipboard in her hand a bit tighter. Whether they saved his house or not, he wouldn't live in it. Why would he? He'd just gotten everything he wanted.

Hannah rubbed her chest where a deep ache had formed. Trusting God didn't mean she'd get everything she wanted. But she'd hoped. She'd let herself hope that God would bring Luke home.

He had. God had led Luke to his real home—his family.

She smiled against the pain. A happy ending. Without her. But a happy ending for Luke.

Hannah pulled out her phone and opened the

reminders. She swiped the words "Call Luke" to the left and then pressed Delete. In its place, she made a note to remove Luke from the bachelor auction.

Luke had the family he'd always wanted. And she . . . she didn't have Luke.

Who knew it was possible to be so happy and so miserable at the same time.

nineteen

He'd answered every question Chet had at least twice, but the guy still seemed reluctant to hang up. Luke shifted the phone to the other ear and leaned on the wood railing of his mom's back porch, the one quiet place he'd found to talk. The Sunday afternoon spring breeze still held the sweet scent of the grass that he'd mowed an hour earlier. His mom had refused to take money, but until he found a job to get a place of his own, he refused to be a loafer.

"When are you coming home?" Chet's gruff voice carried over the line.

Luke's heart tripped at the question. That was why Chet didn't want to hang up. "I just told you. My real home is here."

"That's hogwash. Your home is here. You have a family here. People here need you." His voice hitched at the end.

Luke drew a deep breath and ran a hand through his hair. Chet's words floated back. *You're the closest thing I ever had to a son.* Why couldn't life be simple?

"I'll come visit you, Chet. I promise."

"I'm not talking about me." He cleared his throat. "Not just me. What about that Thornton girl? She needs you."

"Hannah?" She didn't need anything. Luke shook his head even though Chet couldn't see him. "I wasn't even supposed to be in that town. I was supposed to be here. This is where I belong."

"I don't agree with what your daddy did, boy. But you ending up here was no mistake. Lottie needed you something bad. You may have never seen it, but you healed something in her. I never thought I'd see her smile again after Timmy. But you came along and brought life to that house again. And what about Hannah?"

Luke pinched his eyes shut as images of Hannah's smile filled his mind. Would the memory ever not be painful? "What about her?"

"Her daddy once told me he was pretty sure you were the only thing that kept her from shrinking away after her mama skipped town."

Luke had found her crying in the treehouse the first day of summer after seventh grade. He hadn't known what to say or do, but he'd known what it felt like to be lonely. So he sat with her and painted the treehouse ceiling for her. They'd ended up spending the whole summer together fishing, biking, and playing games in the tree-house.

"If I hadn't been there, God would have used someone else." His words lacked conviction.

"But He didn't. Don't you see? God chose you. He used your bad situation for good things." Chet drew a deep breath. "Just like that Joseph in the

Bible. The one sent to Egypt as a slave. What his brothers did was bad, but God used it for good."

Joseph again? And since when did Chet even talk about God? Sure, the guy had had a permanent spot in the third pew from the back ever since Luke could remember, but he'd never once in all their conversations brought up faith.

Luke must have paused too long.

Chet cleared his throat again. "Didn't know I knew any Bible, did you? I like that Pastor Nate. He told me that God cares more about my heart than whether I smoke a pipe. But he also said if I didn't want another stroke I should quit."

"Nate's a smart guy."

"He was talking about that Joseph on Sunday. And as soon as you told me about your dad, the story came back to mind."

Luke turned against the railing and eyed the robin in its nest, which was now complete. "Even if I did believe that God used me there in the past, I'm not needed there now."

"If you believe that, then you aren't nearly as smart as I thought you were." His voice had turned gruff again. "The town still needs you, Luke. Hannah still needs you. She puts on a good face, but she's walking around like she lost her best friend. You should have seen her face when your mug popped up on the news."

Luke cringed. He hated that story. He'd said a lot more, but they'd picked the one sound bite that made him sound like an idiot. Or at least as if life in Heritage had meant nothing to him. All his words about how great the town and people were had been edited out. But that's the news for you.

He shifted the phone to the other ear. What did Chet expect of him? Didn't he know how much he loved Hannah, how much it killed him to leave half of his heart behind? "I don't even have a house there anymore."

"The council . . . postponed making the decision."

That was vague. "Why?"

Chet didn't speak for a long time. "I never agreed with Lottie when she decided not to adopt you. I don't want you to make the same mistake she did."

"How do you figure?"

"Lottie refused to see the gift she was being offered instead of focusing on what had been taken from her. A lot was taken from you, Luke. I won't question that. But a lot was given to you as well. Don't let that slide through your fingers."

"You mean Hannah? Or Heritage?"

"Come home, son. It's time."

Luke's chest tightened as he sank into the wooden patio chair and dropped his head in his hands. "I'll think about it."

He ended the call and stared at the blank screen. *Lord, what am I going to do?*

He tapped the app to open his photos and

flipped to the one Hannah had sent of him and Mrs. Shoemaker. She did really smile at him as if she were proud. For the most part, she'd treated him like a son and he'd treated her like his mother. But even after the little time he'd spent here, he could see that she'd held back. Held back on fully loving him. Held back on accepting what she'd been given.

I don't want you to make the same mistake she did. Chet's words echoed in his head. How could he say that? Then again, how long had Luke resisted relationships in Heritage? How long had he resisted closeness with Hannah? He'd had a lot taken from him, but God had also blessed him. He couldn't deny that Hannah had been one of those gifts. Maybe it was time to stop slapping God's hand away.

But did Hannah still want him? Chet said she missed him, but she hadn't called since the day he left. Thomas had been mowing his lawn and checking his mail, but he never mentioned Hannah in any of his texts.

He pulled out his phone and stared at it. He couldn't very well text her out of the blue: *I miss you. Do you miss me?*

Yeah . . . no.

He tapped Thomas's number instead and typed out a text.

How's Spitz?

A reply came back a few seconds later.

On a walk with Hannah.

Maybe she didn't need him. Maybe Spitz and Hannah were just fine without him.

You still up for the auction?

The auction? Surely Hannah would have taken him out. He'd been gone almost a month, after all.

Luke pulled up the internet on his phone and typed in *Heritage*. A new home page flashed on the screen. The gazebo. His gazebo. Complete. It looked even better than he had imagined. He clicked the festival link and breathed a sigh when the image disappeared. Just the glimpse had made him homesick.

Sure enough, he was still listed on the auction. Was she hoping he'd still come back for it? Her words from the treehouse echoed in his mind. *I need to have someone to bid on.*

But so much had changed since then. Hadn't it?

He closed his eyes and tilted his head back. What did he want?

Hannah. More than anything, he wanted Hannah. Yet he'd given up on them just like he'd promised he wouldn't. She might never forgive him.

His mom poked her head out the door. "Luke, dinner's ready."

Maybe he should talk to his mom about it. She'd asked about Hannah once—she had even said she'd like to meet her before Luke redirected the conversation. Shutting even his mom out like he did with everyone. Maybe it was time to stop shutting out those he loved.

Hannah might never give him another chance, but he had to try to prove she could count on him. He'd start by introducing his mom to her.

He lifted his phone and pulled up the text from Thomas.

I'll be there. And I'm bringing someone with me.

She had to keep Hannah from seeing these. Janie slid the box of programs under the booth where they'd be hidden by the table skirt. The auction was set to start in an hour, and everything had gone smoothly so far. But this might push Hannah over the edge. Janie rolled her neck around and reached for her thermal mug. Coffee was a must. She had been up baking pies half the night.

"There's my favorite baker." Thomas joined her behind the booth, holding a giant elephant ear. "Please tell me you didn't put all those pies up for sale."

"I did." Her stomach growled as the sweet smell

wafted toward her. She reached forward and tore off a piece of the pastry. "And you've got some explaining to do."

"What?" He took a bite.

Janie reached under the table and pulled out a program, shoving it in his face. "You told Hannah you'd remove Luke from the auction."

"No, when she asked me to, I told her I'd take care of it. And I did." He shoved the last bit in his mouth and dusted the sugar from his hands.

She dropped her hands on her hips. "Thomas James, what did you do?"

He tugged at her arms to pull her closer. "I texted Luke and asked him if he'd be here for the auction."

Janie gave a little hop as she clapped her hands together. "He said yes?"

"Yes." Thomas held up a finger. "But . . ."

"But what?" She clutched the front of his shirt. "Why are you making that face?"

"He also said he was bringing someone with him."

An uncomfortable wave settled in her stomach. "Like one of his long-lost relatives or a date?"

"He didn't say."

"Didn't you *ask?*" She smacked his arm.

Thomas shrugged. "I figured if he wanted me to know, he'd have told me."

"You're such a guy."

"I thought you appreciated that fact." He leaned

down and brushed a kiss across her lips. His tasted of cinnamon and sugar. He made it so hard to stay mad.

"So, the rumors are true."

"Caroline!" Janie screamed and wrapped her childhood friend in a giant hug. "You're here!"

"We wouldn't miss it." Caroline's husband, Grant, turned to survey the new center of town. "I mean, look at this place."

"I know, right? It was all Hannah. Well, and Luke."

"Oh my goodness." Caroline clasped her hands in front of her. "I can't wait to see them. Where are they?"

"Hannah is around here somewhere. But Luke's not here."

"Yet. I have faith in my boy." Thomas leaned on the table as he offered her a wink. She wished she had his confidence.

"What do you mean, not here?" Caroline stepped closer to Janie and picked up the program.

Janie didn't want to gossip, but she'd also hated having to tell everyone herself when she and Thomas had broken up. "Hannah and Luke had a fight about a month ago, and he hasn't been back since."

"But he's coming back today?" She flipped through the program. "This says he'll be here."

"Hannah hasn't seen that." Janie sent a pointed look at Thomas. "Thomas was supposed to take him out. But he texted Luke and asked him to be here. And he's bringing someone with him."

"Who?" Caroline's eyes widened.

"Thomas failed to get that detail." She shot another look at him.

"Seriously." Caroline smacked Thomas's arm with the program. "And Hannah doesn't know any of this? This could be interesting."

"Hey, look who's back in town. I thought you forgot your way here." Nate walked up and offered his cousin a hug. Then he turned to Grant. "Now that you married into my family you'd think I'd see you more, not less."

Grant gave Nate a quick man-hug. "The ranch has been very time consuming, but we're looking at opening this fall."

"Really?" Nate offered a nod. "Maybe I need to make a visit that way. See what the fuss is about."

"Yes." Caroline clapped her hands. "We love visitors. Bring Olivia so I won't get bored when you two are off doing guy things."

Everyone got quiet.

She spun and looked at Nate. "You two still haven't gotten that worked out?"

"I'll try to come visit this fall." Nate's face reddened slightly but he ignored the question. "See you at the auction. I am bachelor number five if you want to take pity on me, dear cousin." He tapped at the button on his shirt and disappeared into the crowd.

Caroline turned to Thomas and held up the program. "How'd you get out of this?"

Grant pulled the program from her fingers and started flipping through it. "Engaged." He pointed at Janie's finger.

"But that just happened." Caroline's brow wrinkled. "The auction has been advertised for some time."

"He was engaged to someone else then." Hannah laughed as she stepped into the circle and offered Caroline a big hug.

Hannah. Janie's pulse spiked as she scanned the table. Where had the program wandered to? She shot Thomas a questioning look, but he just shrugged.

Hannah turned to look at them. "Have you two set a date yet?"

"We're thinking in the spring." Janie smiled and glanced from person to person, doing her best not to seem obvious.

There. Grant had it.

"I don't know how you two can wait so long." Hannah stepped toward the booth, shaking her head. She looked back at the gazebo.

As soon as Hannah's back was to them, Janie jumped at the opportunity. She motioned for Grant to hide the program, but he just looked confused.

Thomas stepped between Hannah and her view of Grant. "Janie wants to save up for a nice wedding. I want her to have that."

Caroline's eyes widened as she caught on to Janie's message.

Hannah turned back toward them and they all froze. Her eyebrow lifted, then she seemed to shake that thought away. "When I say yes, I think I want to have the shortest engagement possible. Maybe even marry the same day."

"You can't be serious." Caroline shook her head as she slid her arm around Grant, forcing his hand holding the program to slide to her back. "We pulled off a wedding in three months and that felt overwhelming. And you never do things simple."

Bless her. Grant stared at his wife with a confused look on his face.

"I am learning simple is better. But I won't have to worry about that for some time." Hannah shifted her gaze around. "Maybe I'll get lucky and snag a guy at the auction today. Did the programs arrive?"

"No," Thomas and Janie said at once with a bit more force than was called for.

"But isn't—" Grant's words were cut off with an "uff" as Caroline's elbow connected with his stomach.

Hannah looked from one to the other. "Let me know when they do. I have to go check on a few other booths. I'll be back." Then she was gone.

Janie turned and smacked Thomas on the arm. "If Hannah gets her heart broken again today, you're in trouble."

"Luke loves her, Janie. Take it from someone who tried to stay away from the woman he loves for almost a year—the guy is miserable. He'll be here."

She shook her head and scanned the crowd. "Yeah, we know he'll be here—he said that in his text. But will it be with or without a date?"

Everything was turning out perfect—well, almost perfect. Hannah stood at the top of the steps of the gazebo and scanned the crowd of out-of-towners and locals. Her heart sank, and she mentally chastised herself for even looking for him. He wasn't coming and she was okay with that. Besides Luke's absence, everything was picturesque.

Luke's gazebo design fit perfectly. He'd even incorporated the look of the turret from the Manor in the roof design. She still hated to have lost that building, but maybe Thomas was right. Sometimes you have to say goodbye to parts of the past. Because as much as she loved the Manor, this open square provided a space for the town to do what they did best—community.

One corner of the square hosted quilts, afghans, and a variety of other quality handmade crafts. Another corner had been designated for food. Jams, jellies, pies, and concession food. Janie had sold out of her pies an hour ago after they'd put out some samples. Very promising for the future of the bakery.

All ages traveled from booth to booth, eyeing and buying as patriotic music flowed from the speakers. The people of the town had poured themselves into the entire production. It had paid off too. Not just today but for the contest.

Hannah rubbed her cheeks against the pain from smiling so much. The letter had come only last week, but she could already recite it by heart. Semifinals. The little-known town of Heritage had made it into the semifinals. She didn't know what the next stage involved, but she'd do all she could to be ready. Win or lose, this contest had turned Heritage around.

"I knew you could do something amazing with the glass, Hannah. But I never expected this." Aunt Lucy stepped up to join her in the gazebo decked out in red, white, and blue. She stared up at the blue and white glass hanging above their heads. "I was surprised you donated it to the town, though."

The twenty-four-inch starry sky served as a centerpiece in the dome and a shade to the central light. The project had taken hours of time and all her emotional energy.

"I needed to make that." Hannah swallowed back the emotion that was clogging her throat. "But I needed to let it go too. And this is a way for my mom to give back to the town. It's not worth ten thousand dollars, but it's something."

"It's perfect." Her aunt embraced her. "I always

knew you had it in you. Now I have to get back to my booth."

"Hannah Thornton?" A middle-aged gentleman with a fedora shading his eyes and the nicest Canon she'd ever seen hanging around his neck entered the gazebo.

"Yes, how can I help you? Nice camera, by the way."

"Thank you. A perk with the job." He extended his hand to her. "My name is Miles Cape. I'm a photographer from *Reader's Weekly*."

"I didn't know we should expect you." Hannah mentally listed all the things she should have planned for the guest. A tour guide at least, and where was he staying? Did he even know they didn't have a hotel in town?

His thick mustache lifted as a smile filled his round face. "Yeah, we like to show up as a surprise at this stage."

Surprise? Why did everyone think surprises were a good thing? She forced her smile to stay in place. "It sure is a surprise."

A familiar set of wide shoulders caught her eye in the crowd. Hannah did a double take as her breath stopped. Luke? Her pulse thudded through her ears and her smile no longer had to be forced. She took a step his way and looked back at Miles.

"Is that all right?" He stared at her for an answer.

Shoot. She hadn't even heard what the man

said. Some impression she was making. "I'm sorry, could you repeat that?"

"I was wondering if you could arrange for someone to show me the historical room that you mentioned in the application."

"Absolutely." Hannah held her breath and scanned the crowd. Who could she find to take him? She should do that, no doubt, but . . . Luke. She glanced back to where she'd seen him.

He hadn't moved much. Chet had stopped to greet him, and Luke hugged the older man before turning to introduce the woman next to him.

A beautiful blonde woman.

Hannah's stomach dropped as a stale taste settled in her mouth. Luke had returned and he'd brought a date. She might be sick.

She turned back to Miles. "I'll take you."

"You?" His face lit up with another smile. "Well, that will be great, but if you have responsibilities here then I understand—"

"No, I've been working on practicing delegation." Hannah strode over to where Thomas and Janie stood talking and flirting at the main table. She cleared her throat, bringing their attention to her. "This is Miles Cape from *Reader's Weekly*. I'm going to take him to see the historical room. I'll be back."

Janie's jaw dropped as she checked the time on her phone. "Now? But what about the auction?"

Hannah forced a smile to her face and cleared

her throat, refusing to look Janie in the eye. "Luke just showed up, so you might want to ask him if he's still planning on being in it. Other than that, I think you should be good."

"Wait, what?" Janie scanned the crowd before turning back to Hannah.

Tears pressed at the back of Hannah's eyes. She couldn't cry. Why had she never considered the possibility of Luke moving on this soon? She drew a breath and concentrated on her friend. "He's over toward the peanut stand introducing his *date* to Chet."

"Oh." Janie winced and shot a glare at Thomas. Why didn't either of them look as surprised as she'd expected them to? "Did you two know—"

"Is this not a good time?" Miles glanced between the two women.

Hannah shook the question away and smiled at Miles. "It's fine. Everything's fine. You guys have this. I trust you. And I need to . . . be somewhere else."

Janie's teeth tugged at her lip and she nodded.

Hannah turned to Miles. "Ready?" She had to get away before she started sobbing right in front of him.

The last thing she needed was to lose Luke and the contest all in one swoop.

twenty

He hadn't known what to expect when he returned, but he'd never have guessed this. Luke sidestepped a peanut vendor and grabbed Libby's elbow lest he lose her. His brothers had disappeared toward the concessions and his parents had wandered toward the crafts. He didn't want to lose Libby. He needed some backup if this didn't go as he hoped. He had only planned to bring his mom, but when the rest of the family heard, they vetoed that decision. Being in a family that cared and wanted to be part of everything was definitely a new experience.

The sweet scent of the waffle truck made his mouth water. He'd come back for some of that later, but first he had one mission. Find Hannah. He'd spotted her at the gazebo and he thought she'd seen him too, but she'd disappeared the minute he stopped to greet Chet. Either she hadn't seen him or—he didn't want to consider the "or." His heart tightened as he eyed the completed structure. Their gazebo. Maybe she hadn't missed him as much as Chet had hinted.

Luke scanned the crowd again. Nothing. Where could that girl have gone?

"Luke, glad you're here. I'm pulling for you."

Jack Hauser, his old boss at the lumberyard, patted him on his shoulder as he passed.

What in the world? If another person stopped and shook his hand and told him they were pulling for him, he might just scream. Pulling for what? Were they talking about the bachelor auction? Because that would be odd. It wasn't a competition.

Several had mentioned their signature, but that hadn't helped clarify. He should've asked more questions, but he just wanted to find Hannah.

"Luke!" Jimmy barreled into his side. "You're back." Then the boy pushed back and crossed his arms. "You left without even saying goodbye."

Luke squatted down to be eye to eye with him. "I know. I shouldn't have done that. I'm sorry."

"You back for good?"

"I hope so. But whatever happens, I won't leave again without talking to you. Deal?"

"Deal." Jimmy offered a fist bump. "I'm going to buy more popcorn. Wanna come?"

"I need to find Hannah. Have you seen her?"

"Nope. But her brother is over at that big booth with a banner." Jimmy waved a dollar in the air. "Bye."

Luke stood and scanned the area that Jimmy had pointed to. Thomas and Janie stood at a booth labeled "Information." Perfect. He led Libby that direction, dodging a couple kids carrying dripping ice cream cones.

Janie stood toe to toe with Thomas, whispering something that brought a low chuckle from Thomas.

Luke coughed to get their attention. "Go away for a few weeks and things can sure change."

Thomas turned to face him with a grin. "Luke! You're back. Just in time too." He reached under the table and handed him a large button with a number on it. "You're officially bachelor number one."

"And just in time." Janie pointed to the gazebo, where guys were starting to line up.

Luke took the button and flipped it over in his fingers. "Hannah will owe me big for this one. Where is she, anyway?" His voice sounded casual. Not nearly as desperate and anxious as he felt.

"Something came up." Janie's smile didn't quite reach her eyes. She glanced at Libby.

Right. Libby. How could he be so rude? He stepped back to make room for her. "Thomas and Janie, this is my sister, Libby."

"Sister?" Janie's voice raised a few decibels.

"I'm still getting used to it myself." Luke drew a deep breath and shrugged. "Actually, my whole family is here somewhere. Long story and I really want to tell you, but first I need to find Hannah."

"Sister?" Janie's mouth opened and shut a few times.

Thomas elbowed her and extended his hand to Libby. "It is so great to meet you."

"Oh no!" Janie covered her face with her hands, and all three stared at her. "No, I mean, you having a sister is great. You seem great, Libby. But Hannah saw you and her . . . and thought . . ."

Libby cringed. "Oh, Luke, I didn't mean to make things more difficult."

"I'll go find her." Luke scanned the crowd. "Which way did she go?"

Janie held up her hand. "No. The auction is starting. You have to go up."

"Hang the auction. I need to find Hannah." He dropped the button on the table.

"But people know you're here. If you back out now, the whole thing will fall apart." Thomas picked up the button and held it out to him, then pointed to the stage. "And if the auction fails, we won't have enough money. Come on, Luke, we'll find Hannah. It'll be all right."

"I'll call her." Janie pulled her phone from her pocket and tapped at the screen. "You get to the gazebo and line up."

"Ending up on a date with a stranger hadn't really been the plan here." Luke practically growled the words, grabbing the button and shifting his weight from one foot to the other.

"It's worse than you think." Janie bit her lip. "Cindy's here. I have a feeling she'll be bidding."

Luke bit back a few choice words and turned to Libby. "Do you have any cash?"

She dug in her wallet. "About eighty dollars."

Pulling three twenties from his own wallet, he added them to her cash. "Don't let Cindy buy me."

Libby's eyes popped wide. "How will I know who Cindy is?"

"If I look at you and blink, keep bidding."

Mayor Jameson stepped to the microphone and announced that the bachelor auction was about to begin.

Luke pointed a finger at Janie. "Get her here."

Janie's fingers tapped at her phone. "She didn't answer, but I'm texting her that she's needed at the auction ASAP."

Thomas shook his head. "Why not just say, 'The girl Luke is with is his sister and Luke is looking for you'?"

"Because '911 @ auction' was shorter."

"I think you're the slowest millennial texter ever." Thomas rolled his eyes.

Luke sighed and ran toward the stage. Nothing was going as planned.

He arrived at the gazebo just as they called his name. *Come on, Hannah.* He jogged up the three steps, turned to the crowd, and forced a smile. Still no Hannah.

"Don't worry, Johnson, I'm sure she'll show up in time to bid on me," Derek said from behind him where the rest of the bachelors stood, waiting their turn.

The guy was full of it. Whether Hannah wanted

him or not, she didn't want Derek. He continued to scan the crowd.

"Twenty dollars!" Cindy's familiar voice rang in the air.

Luke's gut tightened. This didn't look promising.

"Hang on, little lady, I haven't even told you about him yet." Mayor Jameson's belly shook as he chuckled and winked at the crowd.

"Forty dollars," Cindy yelled.

The crowd laughed as the mayor shook his head. "I guess the women are ready. Who am I to hold them back? We have forty dollars—do I have fifty?"

Luke scanned the crowd and found his sister, offering her a strong blink.

"Fifty," Libby yelled.

Good girl.

"Sixty." Drat. Cindy again.

Luke glanced back at Libby.

"Seventy."

Luke's heart stopped as his focus shifted from Libby to the woman twenty feet back. Hannah watched Libby and Cindy bid for him, and by the look on her face, she hadn't talked to Janie. All she saw was his "date" bidding for him. His gaze darted to the table. Janie watched the scene with wide eyes, jabbing at her phone. There was no way for her to make it to Hannah through the crowd and explain before the whole fiasco was over.

The bidding was up to a hundred dollars. Libby would soon be out of money.

Luke's heart dropped as Hannah glanced at her phone and turned away. *No. Think.*

Luke grabbed his phone from his pocket and jabbed at the screen. Where was it? There.

"Looks like our bachelor is phoning a friend, folks."

The crowd laughed but then fell silent as Luke held his phone above his head. A song blared from the tiny speaker on full volume. If this didn't work, it was all over.

Emergency at the auction? Whatever. Hannah had sprinted from the historical room only to see Luke's girlfriend and Cindy battling it out for Luke. *Lovely, Janie. Thanks.* Then Janie had the audacity for a follow-up text telling her to bid. Was she crazy?

Luke had chosen someone else. She didn't need to make a fool of herself by winning him—and then what? Spend the afternoon trying to convince him to stay and love her? If she hadn't been able to do that in twenty years, she wasn't going to succeed in an afternoon.

She needed to get away before she was sick. Not to mention that she'd left a very confused Miles Cape somewhere between here and Sharron Street. She'd probably just thrown their chances with *Reader's Weekly* in the trash.

The crowd laughed and then became quiet. A weird quiet. Hannah paused and glanced around. Everyone stood engrossed in something. Then she heard it. Faint at first but then over the sound system. "In Your Eyes" by Peter Gabriel.

Hannah whipped around to see where it was coming from. Luke stood with his phone above his head, looking like a goofball. And looking straight at her. The mayor's microphone was held up to the tiny speaker.

"Do I hear one fifty?" The mayor's voice broke the quiet.

"Three hundred dollars!" The words were out of Hannah's mouth before she could think twice.

The crowd let out a collective gasp as they turned toward her.

Luke smiled as he lowered the phone and slid it into his pocket.

"Wow, three hundred dollars, folks. That's a great bid. Going once—"

"Four hundred." Cindy's voice came back with a sharp edge.

Hannah shook her head. Three hundred was all her emergency cash. But even if Cindy won the date, Hannah had won his heart. She could tell that much.

She still really wanted this, though. Not to mention she didn't want Cindy going on a date with her man.

The petite blonde she'd seen Luke with earlier

dropped a hundred and fifty dollars in her hand. "Here."

"Four hundred dollars, going once!"

Hannah stared wide-eyed at her. Why was this woman helping her? Several other strangers surrounded her, all handing her cash. Hannah gazed from face to face but didn't recognize anyone except . . . She jumped. One of the guys looked like Luke. Just like Luke.

"Seven hundred thirty-three dollars and forty-five cents," the blonde whispered in her ear.

"What?" Hannah stared at her.

"Going twice!" the mayor said as he raised his gavel.

"Just say it!" the strangers yelled in unison.

She faced the stage. "Seven hundred thirty-three dollars and forty-five cents."

Cindy glared at her before marching away from the crowd.

"Going once! Twice! Sold to Hannah Thornton. Hannah, come up and claim your prize."

Hannah rushed toward the stage, but Luke met her halfway, his lips lifted in a half grin. He stopped a few feet back and shoved his hands in his pockets. "Hannah, Hannah, Hannah."

Her teeth tugged at her lip as warmth flowed through her. That night at his house seemed so long ago. But if he didn't get over here and kiss her soon, she might just find another spoon to throw at him.

He took a couple steps closer until they stood toe to toe. His breath brushed across her cheek as his fingers found her hand. "I've been in love with you since the tenth grade. I was a fool to walk away seven years ago, and I was a fool to walk away a month ago. You're God's gift to me, Hannah."

She'd always loved his voice, but he'd never sounded quite like this before. Like warmth and a little grit and . . . hunger?

She drew a slow, shaky breath. "I shouldn't have—"

His finger landed on her lips. "I should never have left. I'll never make that mistake again. Ever."

His fingers traced the edge of her face just before he lowered his lips to hers. He tasted of mint, but he smelled like . . . Luke. That musky scent she'd tried to forget was now hers. Hers forever.

He deepened the kiss and Hannah melted against him. Every nerve in her body came to life and muddled her thoughts. What she wouldn't give to already be married.

"Well, folks, I can't promise all the bids will get that type of reaction, but let's give it a try, shall we?"

Hannah looked up. Right, they weren't alone.

"My goodness, Miss Thornton." A winded Miles Cape appeared next to them. "You sure know how to stir things up."

Hannah cringed and turned to face him. "I'm so sorry. I understand if you have to give us a poor recommendation."

"Are you kidding?" He smiled and tapped his camera with his finger. "I caught the whole thing. You've done an amazing job in this town, and who doesn't love a happy ending? After I run this feature, Heritage will be a shoo-in for the finals."

"Wow. Thank you." Hannah squeezed Luke's hand tighter as Miles disappeared into the crowd. She glanced up at him. "I can't believe that just happened."

"You deserve it." He motioned to the whole square. "This is all amazing. I can't believe you did this."

"Not just me—everyone did it."

Luke entwined their fingers and pulled her toward the edge of the crowd, but Hannah pulled him to a stop. "I'm sorry I called Al behind your back."

Luke rested his forehead against hers. "And I'm sorry I never told you about the house, the photos, or any other number of things I didn't share over the years."

"No more secrets?"

"No more secrets." Luke kissed the top of her head and leaned back. "Let's start with this big secret. Libby is my sister. Turns out I have a whole family in Chicago." He motioned to the people who'd been offering her money.

"Everyone, this is Hannah. Hannah, I'd like you to meet my family."

Chicago. Hannah drew a deep breath. She could do that. She'd always dreamed of raising her family in Heritage, but when it came down to it, wherever Luke was, that's where she wanted to be. "It is so great to meet you. And thank you for the help. I'll pay you back."

"With ten percent interest, compounded daily." The one who looked like Luke spoke up.

The other young guy shoved him in the shoulder. "Well, since all you contributed was the forty-five cents, if she pays you tomorrow you'll have made a whole nickel."

"Hey, the corn dogs were good. I want another."

Hannah watched Luke as they all laughed. Something was different. A joy. A contentment. A place of belonging.

Hannah's photo vibrated with another text from Janie.

$10,247 raised from booths and bids. Auction still going.

She turned her phone so Luke could read the message. "We did it."

Luke wrapped his arm around her waist and tugged her closer. "I guess you breaking out your emergency cash inspired people. So does this mean winning me was life-and-death?"

Hannah struggled to keep a straight face as she nodded. "Pretty much."

He leaned in to steal another quick kiss.

"Luke Johnson." Bo Mackers's bass voice boomed toward them.

Luke extended his hand to the man. "Hey, Mr. Mackers. It's Luke Taylor now, actually, but what can I do for you?"

"Right. I saw that news clip. Quite something." He slapped Luke on the shoulder. "So glad you could make it today. It's not official yet, but I can't see it not passing. I mean, even Dale Kensington knows better than to fight the whole town."

Luke sent a questioning look at Hannah then at Bo Mackers. "With what passing?"

"The petition Hannah started to make the houses along Henderson Road and Richard Street that border the square a historic district. As you can guess, if Dale can't tear your house down, he'll drop his interest. So if you're at the next meeting to sign a few papers following the vote, we can write up another rent-to-own contract and—"

"No." Hannah pulled Luke to the side. "I can't pull you away from your family. You need to be with them. I've never seen you so happy. I can move to Chicago."

Luke eyed her. "You'd really leave Heritage and move to a new cookie-cutter, uninspired home in Chicago just for me?"

Hannah nodded. "No matter how much I love this town, I love you more."

Luke pulled her back to where everyone was waiting for an answer. "Bo, I'll be at the meeting ready to sign."

"Luke." Hannah pulled on his arm.

"Hannah, it has been life changing to find my family. But we can go visit, and my guess is they'll be visiting us too." He took her face in his hands and held her gaze. "I can't say I agree with my father or understand why he did what he did, but I'm glad God used it for good."

"For good?"

"Yes. It led me to you, and I think I'd like to start our life in an old house with a lot of history." His thumb trailed along her jaw.

She wrapped her arms around his neck. "So you finally figured it out?"

"What? That I belong in Heritage?"

"No, what I've known since the seventh grade." She reached up and planted a kiss on his dimple. "That you belong with me."

Hannah's mind flashed back to the glass starry sky. All the pieces had shifted into place by the Master's hand, and she'd never guessed it could be this amazing.

Epilogue

Hannah leaned toward her childhood bedroom window. Guests were claiming folding chairs around the gazebo, and there was just enough cloud cover to make the day comfortable for the guests and keep the flowers from wilting.

Burgundy roses adorned the aisle and every post of the gazebo. She hadn't wanted something fancy, just simple—traditional. Chet would stand with Luke, and Janie was her maid of honor. No flower girl. No big reception.

The pink lace of Janie's dress blocked her view. "He'll see you."

Hannah leaned back. "Oh, Janie, you look perfect."

They had found Janie's dress at a vintage shop in Chicago, but the long drive had been worth it. The pale pink dress straight out of the twenties, with its dropped waist and lace overlay, fit Janie as if it were made for her. And with her hair gathered in a mess of curls over one shoulder, she'd turn the head of any mob boss.

Hannah peeked out the window again. "I can't believe I actually pulled off a wedding in two months."

Janie held up the most recent edition of *Reader's Weekly*, which boasted a photo of Heritage on the cover. "Hannah, you transformed this town enough to win a major contest in just four months. I had no doubt you could make this happen. Now where's your veil?"

"Right here." Aunt Lucy stepped into the room with the long veil draped between both arms. "It took a little extra work, but I got the stain out. Now it will look as beautiful as the day your great-grandmother wore it back in 1927."

Hannah fingered the edge of the lace. The roses woven into the delicate fabric were almost a perfect match to the pattern in the lace that covered her dress from capped sleeve to modest train. Although modern, the dress had a definite twenties look, and the veil would complete it. "It's perfect."

Aunt Lucy lifted the headpiece, unshed tears clinging to her eyes. "May I do the honors?"

"Of course." Hannah sat on the edge of the bed as Aunt Lucy secured the veil with bobby pins.

Janie's hands flew to her face. "You make such a beautiful bride."

"You will too. Are you sure I can't talk you into a double wedding? I mean, you did buy your dress last week." Hannah wiggled her eyebrows at her friend.

"Double wedding? I'm in." Thomas burst through the door with a wide grin on his face. The men had opted for tan pants, a white button-down shirt, and no tie. It worked on Thomas, and she couldn't wait to see Luke.

"No." Janie laughed and swatted at Thomas. "We have a date and we're sticking to it."

"But it's six months away." Thomas's voice took on the whine of a child being told no candy before supper. "A wedding today sounds much better."

"You should have thought of that last summer." Janie rose on her toes, planted a kiss on his lips, then walked to the door. "Now walk your sister down the aisle, and I will see you at the reception."

"Yes, ma'am." Thomas saluted his fiancée.

"I must go find my seat as well." Aunt Lucy stepped back, giving Hannah a once-over. "Beautiful." She kissed Hannah on the cheek and walked out the door, leaving only Thomas and Hannah.

"Aunt Lucy is right. You look amazing." He blinked at her several times and then drew a deep breath. "And so much like Mom in her wedding photo."

Hannah gazed back at her reflection and smoothed her dress. Same dark hair, same hazel eyes, same pearl necklace. "I was thinking the same thing."

"Does that bother you?"

"Four months ago it would have. But now?" Hannah reached up and touched the pearls. "I've learned I can be like her and not make the same mistakes."

Music from the beginning of the processional

drifted through the window, and Thomas held out his arm. "So, bug, are you ready to become Mrs. Luke Taylor?"

Hannah slid her hand into the crook of his elbow and tugged him toward the door. "More than ready."

Discussion Questions

1. If you grew up in a small town, what did you love about it? If you didn't, what part of growing up in a town like Heritage appeals to you?

2. In the opening scene, Hannah describes Luke as her constant. Who is that person you can always count on to be there when life hits a bump?

3. In chapter 1, Luke questions what a home is. How do you see his definition of home evolve over the story? How would you define a home?

4. When Janie discovers that Thomas is engaged to Madison, she is frustrated by his crazy life choices but can't stop him. Have you ever had to watch someone you cared about make destructive life choices? How did you handle the situation? Looking back, would you have done something differently?

5. When Hannah learns that Luke might lose the house and how long he's known about it, she feels that it was "long enough that many replayed conversations in her head seemed a lot more like lies." At what point does a secret become a lie? Is there ever an appropriate time for a secret in a relationship? Why or why not?

6. Luke and Hannah have the opportunity to "redo" their senior prom. Is there any moment with a friend or significant other that you would like to redo if you could? If so, what would you do differently?

7. When Janie discovers the reason that Thomas broke things off, she says, "The only regret I have is trusting you with my heart in the first place. You obviously don't believe in me." Have you ever made a decision to protect someone, only to realize later you were really trying to protect yourself? What happened?

8. When Janie is talking to Nate, she says, "Have you ever been so sure you knew what God had planned for you, only to be completely wrong? I prayed about . . . something. And I believed I knew what His plan was, yet it all fell apart." Have you ever found yourself in this situation? What did you do next?

9. Thomas tells Hannah that it's time for them to stop living with their parents' mistakes hanging over their heads. Are there mistakes you or others have made that you allow to hang over your head unnecessarily? How might you change that?

10. Aunt Lucy tells Hannah that the broken pieces are only dangerous if they stay sharp, referring to both the broken glass and the broken pieces of the past. As Hannah changes the shape of the broken glass by

heating it in a kiln, how can we see her also reshaping the pieces of her past? How can we reshape some of the sharp, broken pieces of our past?

11. When Luke asks his mom how she is handling everything, she replies, "Some days my 'handling it' looks a lot like tears and yelling at God, but I'm confident He's big enough for that." Have you ever had a time when you yelled at God? What do you think of Ann's statement that God is big enough to handle our anger?

12. Aunt Lucy, Pastor Nate, and a few others provide a voice of truth to our characters. Who in your life provides a strong voice of truth for you?

Acknowledgments

It seems surreal to be able to write this page of the book. The saying goes, "It takes a village to raise a child." I would say, "It takes a village to get your debut novel published." There are so many people whom God dropped in my life at the right time to help me, guide me, and push me to the next step. So many I want to thank.

My Lord and Savior—Thank You for the gift of writing, for leading me on this grand adventure, and most of all, for opening my eyes in a slow, gentle way to this dream of writing. I would never have guessed that thirty years ago when I said yes to a life in ministry, You would lead me here. I am continually amazed at how big You are.

My parents, Dave and Joyce Thompson— Thank you for teaching me at a young age to follow wherever God leads, and for your faithful support of my dream. Seriously, I think you have put in more than twenty thousand miles on the road to care for my kids so I could attend retreats and conferences. Who does that? You do. Because you're awesome!

Scott Faris—Thank you for your support— emotionally, physically, financially—year after year as I have pursued this dream. And thank you for being not just my husband but my hero in every way. You make it easy for me to write swoon-worthy men. I love you.

Zachary, Danielle, and Joshua—Thank you for encouraging me to never give up. I have been pursuing this dream your entire lives, and I hope it helps you to remember to never give up even when things get hard. And never forget that God's plan is always the best plan.

Andrea Nell—You are the best craft partner ever and one of my dearest friends. Thank you for your friendship. Thank you for your encouragement. And thank you for telling me when my scene "needs more work." God truly blessed me with you.

My Book Therapy—This book would never have made publication without My Book Therapy, and that is not an exaggeration. The teaching, the books, the retreats—they made me the author I am.

Susan May Warren—You are my teacher, my mentor, and my friend, and I will never stop thanking God that I met you at that first ACFW. (It was the inciting incident of my writing journey.) You have taught me how to craft, write, and live a story worth telling. Thank you for always inspiring me to new heights.

Beth K. Vogt—God knew what He was doing when He paired us up. You have been His arms when I needed a hug and His foot when I needed a kick in the pants. I would never have made it here without your guidance, encouragement, and edits. Thank you!

The rest of the My Book Therapy staff—Rachel Hauck, you, my lady, are a force and an inspiration. Thank you for always encouraging me to look up. Lisa Jordan, you are a gift. Love working with you. Thank you for pushing me in my descriptions. Alena Tauriainen—thank you for always encouraging me in my writing and in my faith.

My agent, Wendy Lawton—Thank you for believing in me. And thank you for never giving up on this story even when I was ready to. You are a gift from God. And thank you to the entire Books & Such team—you are amazing.

My editor, Vicki Crumpton—Thank you for taking a chance on me and my story. I love how you have made my story stronger. I am so grateful!

The Revell team—Being part of this house is a dream come true. Each of you has been a joy to work with, and I'm thankful for how you have truly given to me and my story. I am so excited to be part of the family.

Wendy and Janette—From reading my rough drafts to delivering coffee when I was deep in editing, you are the best sisters in the world, and I am so thankful for all your encouragement and support from the very first story I wrote.

Libby, Hannah, Leah, Ellie, and Danielle—Thanks, girls, for lending your names to the series. It has been fun. And thank you, Hannah, for suggesting I use all your names. It was that suggestion that birthed the town of Heritage.

Jeanne Takenaka, Michelle Alkerson, Kariss Lynch, Tracy Joy Jones, Lindsay Harrel, Liz Johnson, Dawn Crandall, Kara Isaac, Kimberly Buckner, and so many more—Thank you for your encouragement, support, and friendship.

Kathy Cole, Gay Lorenz, 'Andra Lorenz, and Laurie Miller—Thank you for reading different versions of this and offering feedback. It truly made the story stronger.

Dan Runyon and his novel-writing class of 2010—Thank you for the time you spent editing my novel. This isn't the same story, but I learned so much through that experience and this book is better because of that semester.

Mrs. Short—Thank you for making me write the ten-page creative writing story my senior year of high school. That assignment sparked something in me that God fanned to a flame ten years later.

Tim Foley—Thank you for what you do every day to save people and for answering my endless questions about fire. Any mistakes are mine.

And thank you to everyone who has prayed for me and cheered me on every step of the way—Wade, Claudia, Angela, Michelle, Elaine,

Jeanie, Rufina, Evelyn, Janet, Rebekah, Amanda, Kristen, Cristi, Kerith, Dorene, Yvonne, the Faris family, and all the extended family of Thompsons and Kingsleys.

Like I said, it takes a village, and I am so thankful for each of you.

Tari Faris has been writing fiction for more than twelve years, and it has been an exciting journey for the math-loving dyslexic girl. She had read fewer than a handful of novels by the time she graduated from college, and she thought she would end up in the field of science or math. But God had other plans, and she wouldn't trade this journey for anything. As someone told her once, God's plans may not be easy and they may not always make sense, but they are never boring.

Tari has been married to her husband for seventeen wonderful years, and they have three sweet children. In her free time, she loves drinking coffee with friends, rockhounding with her husband and kids, and distracting herself from housework. Visit her at TariFaris.com to learn more about her upcoming books.

Center Point Large Print
600 Brooks Road / PO Box 1
Thorndike, ME 04986-0001 USA

(207) 568-3717

US & Canada:
1 800 929-9108
www.centerpointlargeprint.com